The Resort

International Intrigue on Idaho's Lake Coeur d'Alene

The Resort

International Intrigue on Idaho's Lake Coeur d'Alene

J.J. Hunter

Words Worth Press

Enterprise, Oregon

First Edition

ISBN 0-915214-39-3

Published by

Words Worth Press

P.O. Box 398
Enterprise, OR 97828 USA
(541) 426-6095

Printed and bound in The United States

J.J. Hunter is the penname the
author has selected for
The Resort

The Coeur d'Alene Resort was developed and is owned by Duane B. Hagadone and Jerald J. Jaeger who live in Coeur d'Alene. I thank them for allowing me to use their year-round 5 star destination facility as the setting for *The Resort.*

The characters and events of this book are purely fictional and bear no resemblance to the ownership, management, or the staff of The Coeur d'Alene. The story is presented solely for the enjoyment and entertainment of the reader.

The Resort, lake, and surroundings are truly beautiful and make a magnificent setting for a novel and a wonderful place to visit in real life.

—JJH

One

Mahomet Assad stopped his bone-white Chrysler well away from streetlights and used his pocket penlight instead of the overhead to check his map. The window glass in the Chrysler was darkened, standard equipment in Syria, but this was Spokane, Washington, coming into Labor Day weekend and the smoked glass cost Mahomet's boss something extra. This rental was a private agreement, requiring no ID and no questions, just a couple of Krugerrands in a purple Crown Royal pouch. The dark windows cost nothing in comparison.

Another piece of gold guaranteed the car was sanitized physically and electronically. The bleary eyed-Syrian plucked the coin from a fanny pack full of such coins, one more installment on a great investment that would burn the infidels in their beds. He pushed the precious pack safely under the leather driver's seat.

Mahomet Assad was not related to the president of his homeland, but he had discovered long ago that his name opened doors and, when pressed, he lied himself smoothly into the presidential family. He had not been so pressed on this trip and, besides, most Americans didn't know Syria from Shinola. Mahomet had traveled nearly non-stop for three days to complete all of the necessary arrangements for the car and his mission, and while picking up the Chrysler in Spokane he got to deliver his favorite line in English; "Money is no object." The expeditor in Spokane took him seriously and inflated his prices without a flinch. But the Syrian was amused, not angered. Some things were more valuable than gold and within hours Mahomet would be the conduit for such a thing. Besides, it wasn't his money. The prospect of using his favorite line again soon warmed him to smile. The digital clock on the dashboard displayed nine-fifteen.

Mahomet Assad allowed a leisurely hour before his rendezvous at The Coeur d'Alene Resort, thirty minutes away on a lakeshore in Idaho. After disembarking at the airport, he had spent an hour deliberately getting lost, then another getting lost again. This, he reasoned, would confound any snoop, government, or independent contractor. A device of his own, assembled in a Radio Shack parking lot, had swept the car for electronic treachery and detected nothing. He had observed no one following him in his meanderings throughout Spokane.

It is time, he thought, and took a deep, cleansing breath.

Crisp air tinged with the scent of fresh leather reminded him of long drives with his father across the plateau near his home. At his father's bidding, he had trained nearly thirty of his forty years for a job such as this. The next time the two of them drove the plateau would be in Mahomet's Mercedes, a generous personal bonus for a job well done.

But the job was yet to be completed. He shook the daydream from his head and smoothed his roadmap across his wrinkled slacks. The Syrian oriented himself quickly, then drove east on Sprague, well across town from the airport. Mahomet found the access to I-90 without difficulty and without any sign of pursuit.

Once caution, twice alive.

He patted the Glock 9mm under his left armpit out of reflex. This face-to-face rendezvous would be his most vulnerable moment and heavy body armor made his chest itch just thinking about it. Intelligence reassured him that his contact, Eric Cannon, never carried a weapon, but Mahomet knew that several serious competitors did. The Syrian had won the bid for a face to face, now all he had to do was keep it.

The Syrian had not showered nor slept in a bed for three exhausting days and he looked forward to enjoying both bed and bath by morning. Usually comfortable in America, he held dual citizenship through his American mother and he spoke nearly unaccented English. Still, completing this transaction in the heartland of Satan made him nervous.

Better some county sheriff in Idaho than the alternatives in Athens or Paris.

Such was his father's reasoning, but his father wasn't on the hot seat.

The Chrysler fishtailed on a patch of gravel and nearly slid into a pizza delivery van as it merged with Friday night traffic on I-90. The Syrian's pulse pounded against his tight collar and he stifled a curse. He was angry with himself for even a moment of weakness. By the time he reached the Idaho border, he had calmed himself nicely and was ready to do business.

The city parking lot near The Coeur d'Alene Resort Marina was nearly empty when he entered it more than ten minutes ahead of schedule. He drove slowly to the pre-selected vantage point overlooking the boardwalk's bridge. He sat for a few moments, enjoying the scent of the leather upholstery and listening to the *ping* of the engine as it cooled.

He was worried. The boat slips in the marina were covered, not open, as he had imagined. He had been required to call a number, memorize another number, and now deliver that number in person. That was all. He would carry away nothing of value, but he had learned long ago that paranoia could be a survival trait and that open spaces discouraged ambush.

Mahomet reminded himself to have faith; everything was playing out according to plan.

Good, he thought. *At least I'll be in the open up here. No one would kill a man in the open at a resort such as this.*

His was a false reassurance and he recognized it as such. "Whistling in the dark," the Americans called it. He had seen men killed in some elegant places and preferred not to think of that now.

He watched mist swirl up off the lake and into the halogen lights on the docks. Finally, it was time.

The Syrian hefted his heavy fanny pack and buckled it into place. The gold was a contingency, in case his contact required last minute expenses. He locked the Chrysler and walked to the bar at the entrance to the resort's boardwalk. He stood listening to his own breathing and the laughter of a young woman frolicking in the hotel's outdoor pool. He scanned the marina carefully. His observation post let him see most of the boats below.

Then, as agreed with the American, the soft flicker of a penlight winked three times from the deck of a boat just across the bridge. Mahomet waited a couple of seconds before sending his confirming signal to make sure he had fixed the location of the yacht in his mind.

Third boat south of the boardwalk bridge. Not under cover but out in the open. Good. Mahomet returned the signal but it was never received.

The boat owner was distracted by the "coo" of a seductive redbird. The mariner had admired this bird at the resort's outdoor pool earlier in the day and now, in her skimpy thong bikini, the luscious redhead captured his fancy for the second time. She paraded the dock line opposite his yacht and beckoned him to follow her as she teased him with her delicious derriere.

If I only had time for such a wonderful time, but my secret business is more important tonight than my private business. Thrill will have to wait, the captain thought.

He stared back toward the location where his blinks were to be acknowledged but the night was dark and blank with no return flash of light. He blinked his penlight three more times. Nothing.

Mahomet had already moved from his lookout to the entrance ramp of the boardwalk. He took one last look around before proceeding and noticed only a slightly tipsy couple in evening clothes making their way up the boardwalk.

Mahomet rubbed his tired face and put on the best appearance he could muster. He knew from experience that many Americans were put off by his appearance; bushy black eyebrows framed deep-set eyes above acne scarred cheeks. He looked rough and at times he had played the part well. His heavy beard required a shave twice a day and after three days' inattention it itched mercilessly. His thick mustache was neatly trimmed, however, and out of habit his thumb and index finger wiped across it as he walked the path toward the bridge.

The path was short, but flanked with pines and thick ornamental shrubs, so when he encountered the couple in evening clothes coming up the boardwalk there wasn't enough room for all three of them to pass. As the Syrian started to step aside, the woman, a tall blonde, tripped in her high heels and fell against him. Out of reflex, he reached to stop her fall.

A hairy arm and hand thrust forward from behind the woman and grabbed his wrist, jerked his left arm behind his back and cranked it upward, causing immediate and excruciating pain. The woman slipped Mahomet's Glock out of its holster smoother than he could have. He did not cry out when he slammed into the tree trunk face first and even though this Amazon blonde had his weapon he continued to fight with his feet. The only sound among the three of them was the scuff of pine needles and wet, heavy breathing.

Mahomet had not taken the customary combat drugs because this wasn't that kind of assignment. At least that was what he thought. The pain tearing through his elbow and shoulder socket rendered him helpless. He quivered on tiptoe against the tree and quit struggling.

The woman stuck a needle just behind Mahomet's left earlobe and he had only an instant to wonder who had betrayed him before he collapsed, unconscious, into the arms of the woman's partner.

If the marina's security guard saw the couple hurry their drunken friend to his car he would probably remember drinking cheap vodka as a teenager and approve of friends who didn't let their friends drive drunk.

The couple was careful to dust off the Syrian's face, his clothes and his low-cut Italian shoes before they belted him into the passenger's seat of the Chrysler. The woman slid in behind the wheel, checked her hair and the path behind them in the rearview mirror.

The Chrysler left the marina parking lot, followed by a black Lincoln Town Car, a rental from the airport in Spokane. The two cars wound their way slowly up to the freeway and returned to Spokane at exactly one mile per hour under the legal speed limit.

At twelve-fifteen both vehicles stopped in a gravel and

trash strewn lot near Riverfront Park that overlooked a noisy waterfall. A few dozen yards away, three teenagers stomped a wino for his bottle and his change.

The groggy Syrian was regaining awareness as the couple stripped him of his vest and fanny pack. The man replaced the Syrian's shirt and jacket, but left his tie on the passenger seat. Then the woman propped him up behind the steering wheel. Neither the man nor woman said a word.

Though she had worn white, elbow-length gloves the whole time, the tall blonde wiped down the steering wheel, light switches and shift knob, then picked up Mahomet's hands and pressed them onto the appropriate spots on console, dash, and door handle. He clung to the wheel like a robot just as she had left him and he could not will himself to do otherwise.

The woman closed the door, stood outside the car and knocked on the driver's side window. The Syrian slowly turned his eyes toward the noise.

Two 9mm rounds puffed through four inches of silencer, crashed through the window and exploded into his brain. A third slug was carefully aimed to explode behind his ear, destroying any evidence of the needle prick.

An anonymous phone call to the Spokane Police Department reported a beating and a shooting at Riverfront Park and several teenagers running from the scene.

The next morning's *Coeur d'Alene Press* reported a tourist murdered in nearby Spokane. This made three shootings and two deaths in the city in the past week, just the kind of life that Eric Cannon wanted no part of. But Cannon was missing a customer, a no-show the night before and he would be a fool, a penniless and dead fool, to ignore the possibilities.

Cannon nursed a booming sinus headache in his room

at The Coeur d'Alene Resort and ignored the rest of the morning paper. He protected his treasure, a photographic memory, by not permitting it to become cluttered. If an article piqued his interest, it was his forever, and he had grown tired of that nuisance long ago.

But Cannon was restless after the previous night's mix up and the paper gave him something to do with his hands besides rubbing his swollen eyelids. His allergies had hit critical mass at daybreak and he was sure it was his girlfriend's hairspray. His sinuses pounded mercilessly and he was uncomfortable and annoyed. But, the deal of a lifetime required patience, and Cannon practiced patience. He reminded himself that *he* was the one insisting on personal contact. And now there was a foreign dead guy in Spokane this morning.

Had he missed an acknowledgement of his penlight blinks? Sure, a young redhead in a string bikini who was strutting near his boat distracted him but it was only for a few seconds. And what about this foreigner in Spokane? Was it possible there was a connection?

Cannon rubbed his eyes and squirted antihistamine into each nostril. He thought about leaving a nasty message through their neutral e-mail connection on the Internet but changed his mind. He had what they wanted locked up in his head and he could wait. There were other interested parties. He would just have to up the ante for this frustration and inconvenience.

Eric Cannon patted the firm rear of the woman asleep in the bed beside him and thought of the pleasure she had provided. A man who didn't drink or do drugs needed a pastime and he enjoyed passing his time with women—preferably beautiful, naked women. He would enjoy the magnificent vistas of this resort, indoors and out. Once again, he had some time to kill. He vowed to make the most of it.

Two

Jack Bradley slipped the knot of his necktie tight, straightened it in the full-length bathroom mirror and triple slapped his solid belly.

Nearly forty, but who would know?

Jack's brown eyes inspected themselves in the mirror. He found a few flecks of gold around the inner rim of brown iris, but no wrinkles yet, no puffy baggage. If eyes were the windows to the soul, he saw nothing but his own reflection. He remembered a story from his Navy days, when he worked with a drug interdiction unit. His partner told him about a hippie who had gone hopelessly catatonic after dropping acid and staring at his own eyes in the mirror.

Guess I'm not that spiritual, he thought.

Jack patted a little after-shave on his cheeks and checked his twice-brushed teeth. He had worked out hard this morning and ended with a fast run over the pine-studded Tubbs Hill beside The Coeur d'Alene Resort, then a two-mile jog back to his house. Jack was between relationships and a hard daily workout kept him from thinking about the difference between alone and lonely. Between work and working out he didn't allow himself the opportunity to think about it much. He knew it was about time to face that issue. As manager of a five-star resort, Jack Bradley received the flattery and attentions of women, young and old, every day. But his company policy was no fraternizing with guests or employees. This had proven a difficult policy, a time or two, but he was glad that he'd always stuck to it.

Last night was the test, buddy, he told himself.

Jack had closed the evening with a few drinks and, as he made his nightly round of the resort, he had been sorely tempted by a voluptuous redhead in a string bikini prancing around the boardwalk. If he hadn't seen her coming on so strong to one of the hotel guests earlier, Jack might have loosened his personal code for the first time.

"Got to watch it," he said, and shook a finger at his image. "Without honor, we're nothing. Remember that."

Lately, he'd been thinking a lot about honor. Sometimes he thought he'd be better off in a society that put more of a premium on honor—like the Japanese. And now, indirectly, he might get his chance.

This morning Jack would greet the Japanese industrialist who, Jack had a hunch, wanted to buy The Coeur d'Alene Resort, even though it was not for sale. Tako Nakamura had marched a family fortune off the charts in Japan, and now he weighed in as one of the ten richest people in the world. Nakamura amassed a good deal of his fortune by buying properties that were not for sale.

Jack slipped into his jacket and walked out into another gorgeous northern Idaho morning. The early September air was unusually cool and crisp coming off Lake Coeur d'Alene and Jack kept his window open for the short drive to work.

As he approached the resort entrance, Jack squinted

against the bright spears of sunlight that pierced the wall of evergreens guarding the porte-cochere. He was in early today and the photocells had still not turned off the soft incandescent lights illuminating the hand-carved "Coeur d'Alene Resort" signs.

Two of Jack's young valets polished the chrome luggage carts, which were usually tucked out of sight at the resort's grand entrance.

"Good job, gents," he said when he pulled up.

The youngest, Rob, flashed him a wall-to-wall smile. "More shine, more tip," Rob said, and laughed.

Jack shook his head. "It's attitude, Rob. If you're really glad to have somebody visit your home, then *you* shine and it shows."

Jack turned his Porsche over to Tony and strolled towards the helipad, admiring the red splash of fifty thousand geraniums that lined the grounds. The Coeur d'Alene Resort was an outstanding property and he could understand why Nakamura, and others, would want it. Jack would like to own it himself, but that was a daydream way out of reach.

Ensconced among the pines beside the lake, the resort quickly acquired an international reputation as the gem of the mountains. The most restless guests quickly succumbed to hospitality and fresh air. Jack saw to it that they had nothing more pressing to wake them than the morning cries of hungry gulls. Visitors from all over the world came to Jack for elegance, relaxation and a secure wilderness adventure. Jack had known for years that this was the life for him—he loved making people happy and The Coeur d'Alene was an extension of Jack himself.

Jack looked back from the pad to the hotel and enjoyed the lived-in look that the hotel had with the hills. The resort blended the region's rustic heritage with absolute luxury. It did so with grace and a smile. Many guest rooms were suites and the restaurants, lounges, lobby and public spaces were carefully designed for comfort and discretion. Many a national or corporate policy had been wrought in the privacy of The Coeur d'Alene. If Jack couldn't own it himself, he at least intended to keep it in good hands.

The unmistakable mutter of a helicopter broke the quiet and Jack scanned the horizon.

He caught sight of the whirlybird while it was a small dot in the sky. Mr. Tako Nakamura of Japan was precious cargo, indeed. Jack knew something of Nakamura's wealth and power in his homeland, but little else. He had Bob, his chief of security, working on some background.

Jack's old friend, Aki Watanabe of Pacific International Hotels in Los Angeles, had made a special point to call Jack and ask him personally to provide the ultimate VIP treatment for Nakamura. Jack's hunch about him wanting to buy the resort was the result of "hints" Aki had made about the Japanese entrepreneur wanting to expand his holdings in America. Jack had always held a great fondness for Aki and wanted to make him look as good as possible in the eyes of Nakamura. He had learned the importance of ceremony, tradition and respect during several visits to Japan with Aki. His personal greeting of the Japanese tycoon would set the tone for a standard of service that would please the Emperor himself. Jack had even arranged for Japanese green tea and sweet cookies to be presented at the airport after Nakamura's long transpacific flight. Aki would be proud.

The American flag hung limp on its shiny pole in front of The Coeur d'Alene until the helicopter settled in for an all points landing on the grass and whipped the flag into a flutter. As the engine wound down and the big blades slowed, Jack approached the chopper. He waved at Marko Rivers, the wiry pilot who had operated the shuttle service for the past thirty years.

"Another perfect landing, Marko,"

The gray-haired pilot raised a thumb and smiled as he shut down the C-30 single-P jet engine. Marko kept his pride and joy, a brand new Bell Long Ranger III, in excellent condition. Jack was surprised to see two passengers in the aircraft. He had told Marko that this man was a super VIP, and he wanted him to have private, first-class transportation to Coeur d'Alene. Marko had even agreed to remove two of the seats from the six passenger aircraft and replace them with a small table to hold the tea and cookies.

Rivers extricated his lank frame from the pilot's seat and hopped down onto the skid. With his back to the passengers, Marko jerked his thumb toward the copter and silently mouthed, "He's got a girlfriend!"

Over Marko's shoulder Jack saw a very distinguished, silver-haired Japanese gentleman. A tall blonde, in her mid-to-late twenties, sipped a cup of tea across the table from him. She looked like she had just come off the cover of *Cosmopolitan*.

Both the woman and Nakamura set down their cups and then released the shoulder straps and seat belts. They removed the large headsets they had used to communicate with Marko. The pilot hurried to unlatch the door and set the steps.

Jack felt a moment of panic as he realized Nakamura's reservation was in the resort's finest suite but that it was one bedroom and the resort was not only full, but also badly overbooked. Aki had not warned him about a second person.

We're booked solid and how am I ever gonna come up with another room? I've already squeezed Nakamura in.

Nakamura got out of the aircraft as though he were a Japanese warlord viewing the spoils of some hard fought war. Jack approached with a smile and an outstretched hand.

As the two grasped a firm handshake, Jack said, "Welcome, Nakamura-san, I'm Jack Bradley. Our mutual friend Aki

Watanabe has asked me to take very good care of you. I am pleased to welcome you to Coeur d'Alene."

Jack spoke slowly and carefully mouthed his words. Aki had told him that Nakamura spoke English, but he hadn't elaborated on how well he spoke it. Jack opted for a discreet caution.

"Thank you Jack," Nakamura replied in perfect English. "Aki has told me many fine things about you and your resort. I'm very much looking forward to my visit this weekend and appreciate you personally meeting me so early in the morning. Let me introduce you to my associate, Lindsey Redding."

"Ms. Redding," Jack said, and took the hand she offered. Her handshake was firm, confident, and warm. She was nearly as tall as Jack and her perfect figure rippled athletically under the attractive cling of her blue knit dress. Her blue-eyed gaze fastened onto his own and he was pleasantly surprised at the twinkle of intelligence and sophistication displayed there.

This is no air-head, he thought. Then he turned to Nakamura to address their immediate problem. "Mr. Nakamura, we have our finest suite set aside for you but . . .ah . . .Aki indicated there would be only one person. . ."

Miss Redding smiled and said, "Aki did not know I would be coming with Tako. I take care of public relations for him here in the states and agreed to join him at the last minute."

She smoothed a few loose blonde strands behind her ear and added, "Don't worry about accommodations. We'll be sharing your hospitality and I'm sure we'll find your suite perfectly comfortable."

Jack realized his relief was probably visible as he said, "Very good. Please, let me know whatever I can do to ensure your comfort." Jack was impressed—Lindsey Redding had quickly resolved a potentially embarrassing situation with her straightforward manner, and she had done so without giving away any details about her relationship with Nakamura. In Jack's experience, straightforward was not in the vocabulary of most PR people.

The threesome strolled the fragrant grassy lawn from the helicopter to the front entrance of the resort, soaking in fresh air and the sun. Jack couldn't help but wonder just exactly what kind of "public relations" Lindsey handled for Nakamura. But what the hell, it was none of his business, and after all, this is the modern world, even in Japan.

"You speak excellent English," Jack said. "I wasn't sure whether we might have a language problem or not."

Tako Nakamura smiled and said, "It always sounds like a script from a World War II movie when I explain. My father sent me to his alma mater, UCLA, and I lived in the United States for six years after graduation. Then my father died and I returned to Japan to take over his business and real estate holdings."

Tony had already unloaded their luggage from the Bell Long Ranger and followed close behind with his shiny cart. There were three pieces of matching Louis Vuitton luggage, very expensive, and one unmatching hard-covered Samsonite piece that had qualified for mileage-plus many times over.

Jack guessed the Louis Vuitton was Lindsey's and that Nakamura, even with his fortunes, still used the same type of luggage preferred by many of his countrymen; huge, indestructible and wheeled for easy maneuverability through crowded airports.

This was a daybreak arrival, but Aki was an important enough friend that Jack had held Nakamura's suite vacant the night before so it would be ready immediately. Jack had already picked up Nakamura's pre-registration packet the night before, including his room keycard and guest privilege charge card. "Your keycard and guest card," Jack said, as he handed the packet to Nakamura. "We will have duplicates for Miss Redding in a few minutes."

Lindsey Redding's blue eyes flashed. "I would appreciate that, Mr. Bradley, but I'll pick them up at the desk later on."

As they talked and walked to the suite, Jack learned that Lindsey lived in Portland and had connected with Nakamura when she met his plane at Spokane International Airport. She originally met Nakamura in Japan, five years ago. She had lived on Honshu and worked with the Nippon Fashion Modeling Company. Now she handled Nakamura's American investments. The line between PR and paramour was unclear to Jack.

When they reached the double doors leading into the Bavarian Suite, Tony graciously took the key packet from Nakamura and swung the door open for his General Manager and guests.

"Welcome to your new home," Tony said, with a slight bow and sweep of the hand. "May I present our Bavarian Suite, the finest accommodations of The Coeur d'Alene.

The Bavarian Suite was named for the birthplace of the German munitions industrialist, Max Von Bueller, who had built the resort. Jack always thought the room was magnificent no matter how often he saw it. Three thousand square feet made it three times larger than the average Japanese home. Even Nakamura, who had several residences around the world, appeared awed by its luxuriousness.

"Very nice," he said, nodding approval. "Very fine, indeed."

The Bavarian Suite took full advantage of the pristine view with a panorama of lake and mountains from its huge bay windows and balconies. The private courtyard included a sun deck, soaking pool, and gardens. It featured two wet bars, private dining room, and a spectacular master bedroom. In Jack's opinion, it was one of the finest suites in the country. *In this country or any other*, he thought.

"This is the room that Max Von Bueller built for himself, correct?" Nakamura asked.

"Yes," Jack said, a little surprised. "Do you know Mr. Von Bueller?"

"Our families have entertained certain business arrangements over the past three generations," Nakamura said. "Max and I have cooperated on several projects that rewarded both parties."

Like the chemical weapons in Iraq, Jack thought, but he kept the little he knew of Von Bueller Industries to himself.

Lindsey Redding stood at the bay window, her body framed in sunlight, and her magnificent thighs silhouetted clearly in her dress. Nakamura did his best to remain unemotional in the Japanese tradition, but Jack could tell from his eyes as he scanned the room that, even as a man of substantial means, Nakamura was very pleased. Jack glanced again at Lindsey Redding's legs as she moved from the window to inspect the horn of plenty fruit basket on the table.

"Tako," she said, "your favorite." Tako discovered the bottle of Chivas Regal Scotch, and Lindsey began carving a green apple with the paring knife from the place setting. Nakamura inspected the bottle and rubbed his hands together in anticipation. Jack watched Lindsey's sure, quick hands turn the apple into a peacock in a matter of seconds. She set the peacock and the knife into the fruit basket with a smile at Jack and then turned back to the windows.

She is certainly talented with that knife, Jack thought admiringly.

"You have done your homework, Jack," Tako said. "Chivas is my favorite, as Aki must have told you. I am very, very pleased." He bowed slightly. "Thank you so much."

Jack returned the bow.

"I'll let Tony settle you in," he said, "and I'll leave now

so you can relax after your flight. I've made arrangements for a special dinner this evening at eight to welcome you properly to Coeur d'Alene. Will that be all right?"

"Fine, yes," Nakamura said. Then with a one-sided grin, "Miss Redding is welcome too, I trust?"

Jack felt his cheeks flush. When Lindsey Redding turned from the window she had that same one-sided grin, but she was blushing too. Jack spoke to Lindsey instead of Nakamura. "You're most welcome, Miss Redding," he said, and he meant it. "I'll see you both this evening then, Mr. Nakamura."

Tako Nakamura did not offer his hand, so Jack made a slight bow, which Nakamura returned. With a final glance at Lindsey Redding, whose expression was unreadable, Jack pulled the door closed. He walked back to the lobby, sure that Aki would be satisfied with the treatment Tako Nakamura had received so far. Jack had a good feeling about making his old friend Aki look good. But he had a bad feeling about Tako Nakamura.

Jack intercepted Bob Perkins, his chief of security, outside the gift shop. "Bob, come over to the office, would you? I've got one of those projects you're always saying you want."

"Tracking down Elvis?"

"That's it. Tickets to Graceland, right here." He patted his jacket pocket, then led the way into his office.

Bob closed the door and asked, "So, what's up?"

"Our new guest, Tako Nakamura, has been in business with Max Von Bueller. Did you know that?"

"I just found that out, Jack, as a matter of fact."

"What kind of business?"

"Von Bueller Chemical, Nakamura Electronics, Von Naka Properties which specializes in huge acreages of raw land in remote places—Honduras, Yemen, Indonesia."

Jack poured them each a coffee and handed one to Perkins. "Von Bueller sold chemical weapons to the wrong side in Desert Storm," Jack said. "We learned that much from the newspapers. The Coeur d'Alene is making money but Von Bueller claims he's going broke from the weapons backlash. How do he and Nakamura fit together?"

"It seems that Nakamura and Von Bueller formed a joint venture recently," Bob said. "Von Naka Properties. The paperwork states basically that they're nature lovers and they're buying up wetlands worldwide to protect it."

"And that was the news about Nakamura we were waiting on?"

"The hard news," Bob said. "But it's the scuttlebutt that interests me."

"What scuttlebutt?"

Bob sipped his coffee and settled himself into a leather chair. "Von Bueller Chemical produces chemical warheads and propellants. Nakamura Electronics has a small division in Portland that builds specialty timers and guidance systems for missiles. Von Naka Properties gives them room for training ground troops and testing long-distance ordnance."

Jack felt the pit of his stomach flip and he set his coffee aside. "So," he reasoned, "if either of these gentlemen owns the resort, we're still working for a glorified gun-runner."

"Gunrunning from way back," Bob said. "The Nakamuras and Von Buellers supplied Russia and Japan with weapons in their 1905 war. They've been at it ever since, under a dozen different companies and every continent but Antarctica."

"How'd they manage so well after World War Two?"

"Not everything was devastated in Germany and Japan," Bob said, "particularly 'old boy' networks. Diversification, a Yankee game, came along after the bomb. Von Bueller invested in neutral countries during the first half of the war. He knew Adolph Hitler personally, which didn't hurt him at home."

"Why didn't he invest in Germany?" Jack asked. "Didn't investing in neutral countries look like a lack of faith in the fatherland?"

"It was a lack of faith. He never believed in Hitler's ability to govern after . . . well, after there was nobody left to hate. Von Bueller Industries was a favorite of the Fuhrer because they had a track record in weapons development and production. The chemical division interested him because he had this 'Jewish' problem."

"You mean Von Bueller supplied the gas for the gas chambers?"

"He didn't flinch a bit when he told me," Bob said. "He said it was 'regrettable.' Shooting was impractical, though Von Bueller manufactured the cartridges and would profit either way. Both Degesch, a subsidiary of I.G. Farben, and Von Bueller were ordered to produce Zyklon-B in the form of chalky pellets stored in airtight canisters. Von Bueller claims he had no idea what Hitler truly had in mind."

"I suppose if you're a gunrunner, you check your conscience at the door," Jack said.

"Yeah. Well, Von Bueller learned the truth. He joined the underground movement to assassinate Hitler. They failed but he was not found out. After the war his role in the assassination attempt, building the timer/detonator, came out and the allies let him and what was left of his organization off without a slap."

"Now things aren't going so well," Jack said. "It's relatively peaceful, at least, there are no two-sided high-tech wars except the continuing battle against terrorism. 'Liquify' has been the watchword for assets this year."

"Yeah, they've unloaded a lot of their portfolio, a fleet of floating casinos, travel agencies and a computer company."

"And holding on to the very weapons divisions that are

losing them money," Jack said. "I don't get it. Why not sell *them* instead of *us*?"

"Because nobody wants to touch munitions suppliers who sold to the wrong side of Desert Storm," Bob explained. "And it's my guess that Max Von Bueller knows there's another hot one coming, and he's pretty sure he'll get the deal of a lifetime if he can just hang on long enough."

"The deal of a lifetime, and with Tako Nakamura. Now, what do you suppose they're up to?"

"I wish I knew," Bob said, "and I wish I had some money to invest. These guys are out to make something happen." Bob pushed his coffee cup aside and stood to go. "I just hope we're still around when they do."

"We'll be here, Bob," Jack reassured him. "They can't find any two people who belong here more than we do." *As the door closed Jack hoped he was right.*

Three

Tako Nakamura stood on the balcony of the Bavarian Suite and stretched out the airline kinks that twitched his calves and lower back. He had been exhausted when he arrived at the resort, but the pleasant walk up the geranium-lined lawn, the mountain view, and pine-scented air all conspired to reinvigorate him. This was a setting fit for an emperor and Nakamura considered himself on a par with any emperor. His domain spurned the notion of national borders and boundaries and his private support of several space exploration projects pushed his empire beyond the confines of the globe.

In spite of his wealth and aerospace investments, Nakamura-san traveled by commercial jet, coach class. Conversations with previously unknown seatmates gave an anonymous Nakamura many personal and professional insights, which had proven to be valuable. Unlike other entrepreneurs or industrialists, he did not have to hire people to be in touch with reality. Nakamura did not use his money as a barrier to the world, but as a bridge, across which as much commerce as possible might flow.

Lindsey Redding and the bellman, Tony, went through the ritual of the luggage, hanging clothes in closets, fetching fresh ice. As instructed, they had left his suitcase untouched. Tako Nakamura preferred to pack and unpack his own things in his own time. Lindsey joined him on the balcony.

"There is so much land here in America," he said. "I don't think the people who live here realize how truly lucky they are."

"Japan is half the size of California, but with half the population of the United States," she remarked. "With Japanese ingenuity, the possibilities here are staggering."

"Possibilities, yes," he agreed. "Our people are well-fed, well-clothed. Their living situation is crowded, but luxurious by the standards of most of your countrymen. That is why we buy land throughout the Americas, reserving it for generations to come."

"Buying the world instead of conquering it?"

"It is a civilized notion," he said.

The bellman had finished his duties and Tako heard his steps in the doorway behind them. He had been a most courteous, helpful young man. In most cases, Japanese considered tipping inappropriate and many visitors to America were confused by the custom. Nakamura knew America better than most Americans and he was impressed with Tony's dedication and attention to detail. He turned from the rail and noticed with amusement that the young man glanced at his closed right fist in anticipation.

"Is there anything else I can do for you, Mr. Nakamura?"

"Thank you, Tony," he said as he handed him the tip. "You've done an exceptional job."

Tony accepted the money without looking at it and bowed graciously. "Thank you, Mr. Nakamura. If you need anything at all, please dial 22 and ask for Tony." He bowed again.

"Have a pleasant stay here at The Coeur d'Alene."

Tony closed the door quietly behind him, and Tako imagined the warm feeling that a mere twenty dollars would give the young man.

If all business efforts were rewarded this immediately, how much more pleasant would the world be?

Now that they were alone, Lindsey put her arms around his neck, hugged him and kissed his cheek.

"Tak, you've shown me the world," she whispered. "But this is the absolute best." In her heels, Lindsey stood taller than Tako. He found tall women very stimulating.

"Yes," he agreed. "Aki has redeemed himself nicely after the Fiji disaster." The soft ring of the two-line telephone interrupted their first passionate kiss of the day. It was Ogura, his assistant in Tokyo. "Ogura-san, what are you doing up so late? It is the middle of the night in Tokyo, is it not?"

"Yes, but I wanted to make sure you arrived safely. I have reports and figures prepared on the hotel peripherals, as you requested. If your machine is prepared, I will transmit them for you now."

Tako saw that Lindsey had plugged his laptop into the other line and set it to receive. "You are very efficient, my friend," he told Ogura. "Please follow encryption protocols and then get a good night's sleep. I will speak with you soon."

Tako Nakamura was a dedicated wheeler and dealer who had spent the better part of the past twenty-four hours on business, by plane, fax, and face to face. Now it was time to play, something that his stature in Japan offered him less and less these days.

Lindsey spoke as if on cue. "Tak, you must be exhausted. I know you can't sleep on planes. Let me give your tired muscles a good massage before you take a nap." She loosened his silk tie and unbuttoned his starched white shirt.

"I think that I can stay awake for a few more minutes,"

he said.

Lindsey poured both of them a glass of freshly squeezed orange juice from the refrigerator and walked Nakamura to the suite's private Jacuzzi. He shucked the rest of his clothes and slipped into the hot bubbles as Lindsey kicked off her red high heels, slipped out of her dress and peeled her red lace underwear off with a seductive flair. As she stepped into the water she unfastened her lace bra from the front and let it fall to the tile floor. Nakamura rolled onto his tight, flat stomach and she massaged his aching back and legs with her long, perfect fingers. He could only sigh his pleasure and grunt, occasionally, when she worked out a knotted muscle.

Lindsey lived near the mouth of the Columbia River in a condominium he had purchased for her two years ago. She drove a new red Porsche Carrera and her "expense account" was generous. Her position, on paper, was "Public Relations Executive," and her skills returned his investment in her tenfold. Her professional skills were not in PR, but in corporate intelligence and security and her willingness to share her body with him was icing on the cake.

Lindsey was a valuable resource for Nakamura outside of Japan, but inside his native country she could not be as effective because so many of his countrymen did not value good advice if it came from a woman. That was one reason why he consistently outstripped his countrymen. Yet, times were changing. Even the Crown Prince had married a commoner, albeit a Harvard graduate and career woman from Japan's diplomatic service. However, the role of a Caucasian woman in the land of the shogun demanded invisibility. Lindsey Redding had many talents, but being invisible was not one of them.

"Tak," she whispered, shaking his shoulder. "You're falling asleep on me. Come out of the Jacuzzi so you don't drown." She wrapped him in one of the resort's soft white bathrobes and led him into the master bedroom, where she tucked him in and kissed his forehead as though he were her son instead of her lover. She closed the drapes against the brightness of the midmorning sun and slipped naked under the sheets next to him.

Momentarily, the world was confused for Nakamura and he had to remind himself, *America, Idaho, Coeur d'Alene Resort.*

Lindsey's gentle fingers explored his body under the satin sheets and he found himself, and his body, reawakening. She played Tako like a baby grand and she moaned her own operetta to the background *slap slap slap* of sweaty bodies resounding to an age old score.

Tako breathed deeply for a few moments afterwards, briefly napped, then rose from his bed like a sumo wrestler and lumbered into the marbled, walk-in shower of the master bath. In a few more moments, he was refreshed and ready for business. He toweled and dressed casually in slacks and an open-collared shirt.

"Lindsey," he called out, "please order us some room service. I'm going to walk the property and will return by the time it arrives."

"All right, Tak," she called back, but the door had already closed behind him.

Four

First thing on Saturday morning, a dark-skinned man entered the Syrian delicatessen on Lafayette Street, not far from the Grand Wayne Center in Fort Wayne, Indiana, a city filled with churches, humanity and humidity. The Khadduri family deli used to be part of an alley, so it was a long, narrow shop with high shelves that bowed under their loads of bottles, bags and boxes of Middle-Eastern foods. The dark-eyed stranger stood at the front of the store, careful not to lean his gray silk suit against a cold case displaying meats and cheeses. A tiny, old-fashioned cash register sat atop the case, its "No Sale" flag rung up.

Mustafa Khadduri bent over a butcher block behind the counter and finished cutting fresh lamb chops with a sharp cleaver. He was careful to weigh and price each ounce. Mustafa worked alone, as usual, and there were no other customers in the store.

"Good morning," the customer said.

Mustafa thought of his father when he heard the man's

distinctive accent, but of course his father was now three years dead so he did not look up from his work. "Hello," he replied, and continued chopping. "I'll be with you in a moment."

"I am interested in purchasing goat cheese from the Palmyra region in Syria."

Mustafa set down his cleaver and turned to the customer in surprise. "I am sorry," he said. "I do not have any goat cheese from Palmyra. But that you should ask for cheese from that area is quite a coincidence. I was born there, as was my father."

The stranger smiled and Mustafa could not help notice the gold lining his straight, white teeth. "I know that, Mustafa," said the man. "I am here to give you special instructions."

Mustafa felt a chill wash over him in spite of the humidity. "Who are you?" asked Mustafa. A colder chill swiped his spine as he wiped the grease and lamb's blood from his hands onto his well-stained apron. The man did not offer his hand.

"No name is necessary. Surely your father told you this. Please listen carefully."

"Are you with the council," whispered Mustafa. He leaned as close as the counter allowed.

"Shhhhhhhh," chided the man. He pressed his finger to his lips. "You must certainly know I could never answer such a question. I mean no disrespect."

Mustafa's father had spoken often of respect and honor. He wanted to honor his father's memory now, but he was quickly becoming afraid. Mustafa whispered, "I understand. What do you wish from me?"

The man reached into the inside pocket of his suit and pulled out a large, leather wallet. He opened the wallet to display a man's photo. The man had a cruel squint in his blue eyes. "Do not write anything down," the stranger said. "Simply remember what I am telling you. This man is Eric Cannon.

He has information that is very important to us."

Mustafa had already guessed the Baathist Islamic Sovereignty Council was the "us." His father had been a founder of the organization and he'd told Mustafa many times that the day would come for his son to play an important part in their plans. That was well and good when he was younger, but Mustafa was married now, with two children and a good business. He liked his life in Fort Wayne very much. Still, he squirmed at the thought of disappointing his father, who had made all of this possible. "I see him," Mustafa said.

"He waits at this resort in Idaho," the stranger said and handed Mustafa a colorful brochure of The Coeur d'Alene Resort. "He waits there for contact from us. If you do not contact him within three days he will sell this very important information to someone else."

Mustafa did not want to know who the opposing bidder might be, nor did he want to know the information. Mustafa suddenly found himself without curiosity about any of this. The stranger awaited a response. "Why do you come to me?" asked Mustafa.

"Because your father promised you would help us at the proper time. This is that time."

"But my business, my family . . . "

"Neither your business nor your family exists except through the blood and the grace of your people," the stranger said. His dark face darkened further and his black gaze slid like a blade into Mustafa's soul. "Your family and your business will continue to survive only with the blessings of the blood and the grace of your people."

Mustafa fought off the icy fist that gripped his heart. "My wife," he said, "I should call her."

"Of course," the stranger said, and nodded towards the telephone behind the counter.

She answered on the first ring. "Hello."

Her voice, usually vibrant and on the verge of song, was flat, frightened, and dead.

"Are you all right?"

"Mustafa, there is a man here. He says he is a cousin of your father's, but he gives no name."

"I love you," Mustafa said. "All will be well. Praise Allah." He hung up, and then turned to the dark stranger at his counter. "Do not harm my family."

The stranger ignored the comment and spoke as though he recited the bus schedule. "Here is your airplane ticket. If your man prefers to do business in Damascus, tickets await at the airport in Spokane and you will accompany him. Your passport is in order. I took the liberty of bringing it from your home." Mustafa, feeling an unpleasant numbness wash over him, accepted the tickets and his own passport from the stranger.

"The message we seek will be passed electronically, not in your presence, at this resort, and this is the telephone number that you will call to initiate the transfer. Memorize it now and do not write it down when I leave." The stranger paused, obviously waiting for Mustafa to memorize the number. It contained a country and city code unfamiliar to him but was a simple combination that was almost all nines and ones.

"I have it," Mustafa said.

"Cannon will be paid electronically," the stranger went on. "Nothing more will be required of you unless he demands a meeting in Damascus. There is a link in this chain that he may insist on passing face-to-face. Our people in Damascus will take Mr. Cannon off your hands immediately after arrival in Syria if that trip becomes necessary and you will be able to return to your home. Mr. Cannon is of extreme importance, so you will follow his wishes to the letter, whether you understand them or not. "Once you have made contact with him and his message is passed, do not contact him again unless instructed by me. Do you understand everything I have told you?"

"Yes," Mustafa said and swallowed hard. "How will I know him?"

"You have seen his picture, you know his name, and you know where he's staying." The stranger's voice dripped undisguised scorn. "What more could you require?"

Mustafa did not answer.

"Here is some money for your traveling expenses. Cannon may require a hard currency advance. That will be provided after you register at the resort."

Mustafa picked up the sealed, plain brown envelope. It was thicker than he would have imagined. "How will I contact you in case I have questions?"

"You will not. Follow through with these instructions exactly as I have given them to you and all will be well. Good luck, Mustafa. Praise be to Allah." With that, the man slipped out the door and disappeared into the heavy foot traffic on Lafayette. Mustafa watched as the man disappeared heading toward the Maumee River.

Mustafa remembered many talks with his father. He remembered especially well the promise that he had made to his dying father to support the cause he had been taught, since birth, to fight for. He prayed it had been an empty deathbed promise but now the devil himself had come to his store to collect.

Mustafa Khadduri had been born in Palmyra, Syria, in 1964 and had moved to this country with his parents when he was just two years old. He had lived a very normal life and his father saw to it that he received a good education. Thanks to his father, he was set up in a modest but respectable and legitimate delicatessen business, which he liked and did not want to lose. Mustafa pulled back the flap of the manila envelope and saw that it was filled with hundred-dollar bills.

He wanted to call his wife again, but he put the "closed" sign in the window instead. Though it seemed it was too late for thinking, Mustafa had to think for just a moment.

They may contact me at the resort, he thought. *That means I'll probably be watched.*

The task seemed simple enough and, after all, he was not being asked to kill for the council. The threat to his family was real enough, so this task was worth their lives, at least, and his own.

Khadduri's father had told him often how the generations before him had all been scarred by the violent and tumultuous history of his birthplace. Turks had killed his grandfather in 1915 when the Syrians, along with other Arabs, had revolted against the Turks and allied with Great Britain to fight the Ottoman Empire. Their promised independence was stolen from them when the League of Nations divided greater Syria into the four states of Syria, Lebanon, Palestine and Transjordon. His father's brother, Ahmed, was killed when Syria invaded the United Nations insult called Israel in 1948. His father had been inconsolable, even to his death.

Just before Mustafa was born, Syria's Baath Party rose to power. In 1963, in neighboring Iraq, Abdul Salam Araif and Ahamed Hasan al-Bakr, who were members of the Nation's Baath Party, overthrew and assassinated General Abdul Karim Qasim, the nation's premiere. Mustafa's father, Adbul Khadduri, had worked closely with both Baath parties and was personally the instrument who set up a super-secret organization linking the common threads of both nations. The Baathist Islamic Sovereignty Council was his child as much as Mustafa was. Its secret headquarters squatted like a Bedouin camp in the Syrian desert at the border of the two nations south of the Syrian city of Abu Kamal.

Mustafa's father cried easily and often for too many loved ones lost in the region's many wars. When Mustafa was born, his father feared he, too, would become a casualty. It seemed a natural consequence of his blood. To continue to be a patriot and also to be able to protect his son, Abdul convinced leadership of the BISC that they would need intelligence information from within the United States. In this way he was able to move his family to relative safety while still playing a role for the Baathist cause from the shores of America.

All throughout his developing years, Mustafa heard BISC propaganda preached nightly by this father. He was no coward, and for his father's sake, he voiced strong belief in the protection of the Baath principles. Mustafa had thus become a deeply planted but unenthusiastic mole in America, totally unknown to the U.S. intelligence community. Before he died, his father had warned him that at some time he would be contacted by BISC to perform a great service for his people. Now Mustafa had to wonder just who those people were who would threaten his wife and his children to force a man to carry a mysterious message. Mustafa had been well indoctrinated, but when he was called upon, he found himself very reluctant to serve.

The politics of Syria and Iraq were closely intertwined. Their sovereign flags shared identical backgrounds of blue, white and red and their coats of arms are both eagles. When placed side by side on a map, the Iraqi eagle faces Syria, and the Syrian eagle faces Iraq. BISC funding originally came from both nations and resources were plentiful. Only the highest levels of the Baath's party of both nations had knowledge of the shadowy organization. However, during the Desert Storm war against Iraq, a schism appeared.

Because Syria's government supported the UN sanctions and the war, BISC activities now were run out of Iraq, even though most of its members were Syrian nationals.

Mustafa was aware of Syria's stance during Desert Storm, but he was unaware of Syria's fluctuating role with regard to the council. However, it probably wouldn't have mattered. Mustafa's father was of the old school. Mustafa was not. He merely held the safety of his family to be paramount, and set about making sure he did nothing to endanger them more than they were.

Khadduri peeled off his apron and sat at the counter, eyeballing his plane ticket to Chicago, then Seattle and finally Spokane. He tried to feel pleased that he now would be able to help strike a blow for the cause that his father believed in so strongly. He did not feel pleased. All he could muster was fear, for himself and for his family.

Mustafa had no memory of either Syria or Iraq, since he left as a baby and certainly had never been to the secret desert headquarters of the BISC. He realized now that his father kept him as far away from the region as possible, so that when his services were needed, he would be under no suspicion of any kind by the American authorities. Mustafa's father clearly had kept the Arab council well informed as to his son's progress and had assured them of his complete loyalty prior to his death. Mustafa moved his goods from the cooler to the freezer as quickly as he could, then locked up the deli and caught a cab to the airport. Two hours later he stood at an airline counter in Chicago, behind the most obnoxious woman he had ever seen.

"Don't you dare tell me you don't have three first-class tickets," boomed Veronica Whitcomb. The overworked United ticket agent, who was under attack, stiffened noticeably, but her face maintained a neutral expression. "I'll have your job and you'll be selling pretzels on the street corner!"

Mustafa knew the young woman's name because it was embossed on her luggage, all seven pieces. He could not imagine accepting such insult from a woman so calmly as this agent did.

Without comment, the agent rechecked the Apollo computer to verify reservations. They obviously remained unchanged. "Excuse me," she said, "I'll get my supervisor." The seasoned agent was fully equipped and experienced to handle this situation, but today she was on her fourth hour of overtime and didn't have the patience to handle even one spoiled princess with the world's biggest chip on her shoulder.

"That's a good idea," the rich girl shouted right in the woman's face. "It will be a relief to talk with someone around here that knows what in the hell they're doing." The agent absorbed the final barb by turning abruptly and walking away. Veronica Whitcomb stood her ground at the counter as the supervisor manufactured a smile and approached with a lively step.

"Mrs. Whitcomb, I am Mr. Davis, supervisor for United here at O'Hare."

"Of course you are. Now prove that you are not a skycap in disguise and solve my problem."

"Mrs. Whitcomb, according to our computer, when your travel agent made your reservation, we explained that we did not have three first-class seats available all the way to Seattle."

"Well, Mr. Davis, first-class is a matter of money and I have money. Name your price for three first-class seats."

"Didn't your travel agent inform you?" inquired the supervisor.

"Don't be impertinent." She tapped her right index finger on the counter top with each word to emphasize her command. "Look, Mr. Stephen Wells is a personal friend of mine. Do you want me to call him to settle this silly misunderstanding?" Whitcomb had met the United Airlines Chairman of the Board briefly at a charity reception for the homeless at the Plaza Hotel in New York City. It was one of those events where rich people put on their finest clothes, drank the best champagne, mingled with each other's egos and wrote off the cost of the festivities against their taxes on behalf of the homeless, about whom few of them really gave a damn. That momentary encounter now allowed Whitcomb to drop the airline chairman's name as though they were intimates.

"Ms. Whitcomb, as I said, we have you confirmed first-class to Seattle. While you are boarding, I will do everything possible to try and clear two more first-class seats."

"That's more like it," she snapped. "I don't sit with the little people in the back and I certainly don't expect members of my personal staff to suffer that indignity either." She turned to two large young men behind her. "Check the luggage," she ordered, and waved her index finger, signaling them to move the luggage forward.

Mustafa was relieved that he would not be flying first-class with Ms. Whitcomb. He felt himself unlucky enough to be on the same airplane. Mustafa stepped up to the counter and presented his tickets.

"One first-class ticket to Seattle," the new agent recited. "Your seat selection is confirmed. Do you have baggage to check?"

"First-class?"

"Yes sir," the agent said, brightening. "Didn't you know you had a first-class ticket?"

Mustafa hesitated. "No," he said. "It was a gift . . . I assumed . . . "

"Well, Mr. Khadduri, perhaps you overheard the misunderstanding with the previous passenger?"

"Yes, I. . ."

"We could offer you a generous cash rebate on your first-class ticket if you would be willing to fly coach. I could put you in the bulkhead seat, right behind first-class, and instruct the cabin attendant to give you our first-class treatment."

Mustafa had flown only once before, when his parents brought him to the United States, and all he remembered was that his ears hurt him terribly. He appreciated their problem with the obnoxious woman and he was sure she would continue to be obnoxious throughout the flight. For these reasons, he was tempted to cash in the ticket, though the money meant nothing.

But the Council knows which seat I'm in, he thought. *If I were being watched, they would expect me to be in that seat.*

Mustafa decided that, with his wife and children at stake, he had better go through with this scenario exactly as it was laid out for him.

"Sir?"

"I'm sorry," Mustafa said. "I'd prefer to keep the first-class seat."

The agent's smile cooled and gave the slightest expression of exasperation. "Very well. Baggage?"

"No. No bags."

The agent lifted an eyebrow, handed back the tickets and sighed. "Then you may precede directly to your gate, B-11. First concourse to your left. Enjoy your flight."

"Thank you," Mustafa said.

He felt as though he should joke about the obnoxious woman, or apologize for something, but the supervisor was already asking, "May I help the next person, please?"

With nearly an hour before boarding, Mustafa had time to shop for a few essentials. He bought a shaving kit, toothbrush and toothpaste. While on his way to the gate, he saw a sign advertising the "Northwest Shop." He looked down at his faded khaki pants and his frayed white shirt, and he realized why the agent was so willing to offer him a cash deal on his ticket.

He glanced through an issue of *Pacific Northwest* magazine for ideas and then bought two pairs of Dockers pants, one gray and one black, and two long-sleeved shirts in teal and purple. He added a leather carry-on bag to his selections. After making the purchase he went to the Men's room to change. He chose the purple shirt and gray pants for the trip, buffed his faded black shoes with the leg of his khaki pants then dropped his old clothes into the wastebasket.

The obnoxious Whitcomb woman was arguing with the attendant at the gate, still trying to bully her way into two more first-class seats. Mustafa hung back, cocooning himself in thoughts of his safe return to his unharmed family. He was thankful for his window seat in 4A, but disappointed he would be cornered for hours so close to Veronica Whitcomb who, with much flourish, settled herself into 4D. Her two young musclemen secured her carry-on bags into the overhead storage compartments and buckled into their seats just behind the bulkhead.

A cabin attendant pulled the purple first-class curtain closed and the blond muscleman reopened it slightly so he could still see Veronica Whitcomb. When the attendant came to close it again, the young man motioned her to him and whispered something in her ear. She left the edge of the curtain open.

Because of their uneasiness, and Whitcomb's, Mustafa realized the two men must be bodyguards, accustomed to doing an excellent job. She was young, perhaps late twenties, but they were younger, and fit and eager.

And handsome, he realized.

The plane hadn't been pushed out of the gate yet and the loud-mouthed woman was already regaling her seatmate with her woes. "I'm calling the Chairman of this airline the minute we land in Seattle. This kind of treatment is inexcusable!" Her seatmate in 4C was a well-dressed but disheveled middle-aged man who looked as though he had traveled all night. He sipped a drink he'd hoarded from the last leg of his flight and nodded agreeably as she spoke.

At 31,000 feet the captain announced a heavy, unseasonable fog over Sea-Tac airport but he was confident that it would clear before their arrival. Whitcomb was already on her second Beefeater martini by the time Mustafa was served a glass of orange juice. He was grateful to receive it because his mouth had been dry since the stranger first spoke to him in his shop.

The passenger in 4C was ordering two drinks at a time and he downed them rapid fire. Mustafa had tried alcohol a couple of times while he was in high school. Things like this happened in America, but he had never developed a taste for it and had adhered strictly to Muslim law ever since. The man in 4C had switched from a colorless alcohol to a whiskey, and he beckoned the stewardess often to freshen his drink. The middle-aged man was clearly warming to the attractive woman next to him. He was unsubtle in his attention to her low-cut blouse and she obviously enjoyed leading him on. Actually, she was unabashedly flirtatious to the point of being an outright tease, not something Mustafa would have expected of her after seeing her unseemly display at the ticket counter.

He had the time now to notice details he'd missed before. Her make-up perfectly accentuated her dark, glittering eyes. Every time 4C glanced at her drink, Whitcomb's sensual fingers caressed the stem of her martini glass, her nails perfectly manicured and lacquered with a light red polish. Her teeth were perfect and her smile seductive. She crossed her long shapely legs and her crème-colored St. John knit rode high up on her thighs. She recrossed and the knit rode higher. That was when 4C made a terrible mistake. A mistake that Mustafa had seen coming; one that, had he not seen her at the counter and had he not been happily married, he might have made himself. 4C reached a hand high up on her thigh.

Veronica Whitcomb gasped an over dramatic gasp and slapped 4C smartly across the face, spilling his drinks into the aisle.

The slap and the gasp alerted the blond bodyguard, who leaped through the curtain, snatched the bewildered drunk by the shirtfront and smashed a well-educated fist into his face. The cabin attendant shrieked.

"He's my bodyguard!" the Whitcomb woman snapped. "He was doing his job. This is the creep who should be arrested. He tried to . . . to molest me!"

Given a cold compress for his bloody nose, 4C agreed to switch seats with the bodyguard. Of course, Veronica Whitcomb had to gloat for everyone's benefit, "If they'd permitted my people to fly first-class in the first place, none of this would have happened."

Mustafa studied the brochure for The Coeur d'Alene Resort, hoping his mission there would be swift, smooth, and that he would leave there with some of the serenity that he detected in the superb color photos. This day had been the longest of his life. He had not been able to enjoy the luxury of the first-class accommodation in flight, thanks to Veronica Whitcomb, and he hoped for a glimpse of the good life at the resort. He had convinced himself that, as long as things went as planned, the Baathists would treat his family as richly as they were treating him.

"I see you have excellent taste in resorts."

It was a moment before Mustafa realized that the honeyed voice of the passenger from hell was speaking to him. He risked a glance at the woman, who leaned across her bodyguard until it seemed her pale breasts would spill from her blouse right into Mustafa's hands. The bodyguard stared straight ahead, scowling. "Yes," Mustafa mumbled, "I'll be there for a few days on business. An opportunity. . ."

"My favorite hotel," she interrupted. "I'm there so often that some of the people think I own the place. Perhaps I will. I'm going on business, too." When Mustafa didn't respond, she continued, her voice pitched for maximal eavesdropping. After spending tonight in Seattle, I'll be going to Coeur d'Alene tomorrow to meet Clint Diamond there," she said. "You know, the movie star? I'll be producing his next film."

By the slight raise of the bodyguard's eyebrow, Mustafa presumed this to be speculation, wishful thinking or an outright lie. None of that mattered to Mustafa. He wondered whether this abrasive woman would ever be out of his life. Fortunately, she simply ordered another drink and prepared for their landing in Seattle. He had to change planes for the short flight to Spokane. Mustafa was eternally grateful that Veronica Whitcomb would not be on it. He prayed his mission would be over in time to avoid any possibility of being around her at the resort or anywhere else in the entire world, ever. He distracted himself by watching an older couple in 3D and 3C who seemed oblivious to the disturbance behind them as they enjoyed their tiny New York steaks and champagne. Mustafa recognized them from the picture and story in the *Chicago Tribune* which be bought at O'Hare. It chronicled their recent huge lottery win. He noticed several flight attendants congratulating them on their good fortune and obviously enjoying being close to so much "new money." The couple talked quietly, heads together and held hands throughout the flight. They seemed happy and very much in love, like Mustafa and his wife Jasmine. His thoughts were of his beautiful wife and wonderful children back in Fort Wayne.

Mustafa survived the rest of his journey by imagining his wife at his side, her hand on his arm, their future as bright as the sun above the iron gray of the clouds.

Five

Eric Cannon lay comfortably beside the hotel pool and half listened to his friend, Bob Kent, banter with Julie and Rory, the young women who shared their suite. Sweat prickled his close-cropped hair but he resisted the urge to scratch and instead visualized the rivulet that ended behind his left ear and dripped to the deck. A lifetime of petty allergies lent him a great tolerance for minor physical discomfort and for now the antihistamines held the pollens at bay. He had lied about his allergies when he applied to the Naval Academy and by the time the Navy caught up with him, he had proven himself a prize worth keeping.

A prize worth a helluva lot more than they were willing to pay, he thought.

Cannon kept his eyes closed and sipped lemonade through a long straw as the others gulped their pina coladas. Rory, the blond-haired woman, spoke about him as though he wasn't there. "So, how long have you known Eric?" she asked.

"Almost fifteen years," Kent said. "We were in the same class at the Naval Academy."

"I'll bet you two were the 'girl in every port' type, too." Kent laughed. Cannon had always liked Bob Kent's laugh because it was deep and free, a liberated laugh completely unlike his own that he knew to be a strained and disconcerting cackle.

"*Two* girls in every port," Julie interjected.

The purr of Julie's husky voice reminded him of her dark hair swirling on his belly after he and Kent had switched women for the night. He shifted his position on the recliner to take the strain off the swelling that began in his shorts.

"Two girls, but no port," Kent said. "Neither of us ever saw sea duty after training, except for renting ski boats on the Potomac."

"Oh, Washington, D.C.," Julie said. "The Pentagon, secret stuff. . ."

The alarm on Cannon's watch interrupted her and it was just as well. Eric didn't care much for the turn the conversation was taking. He shut off the alarm, sat up and mopped his face with a towel. "I'm going to the boat," he said. "Back in a little bit."

"When do *we* get to play on your boat?" Rory asked. "We've been good little bad girls, haven't we?"

Eric's gaze took in her black string bikini that didn't quite cover all it was supposed to. Rory saw the direction of his gaze and teased him with a playful shimmy that would have scored on the Richter scale.

"Business first," he said, "then pleasure. We'll take her out for a midnight swim when I close this deal, how's that?"

Rory faked a pout with her full lips, then bounced up from poolside and kissed him, exploring his mouth with her teasing tongue. "Won't forget me?" She asked when she came up for air.

"I'll hold that thought," he promised and headed down the boardwalk to his boat. The 42-foot *Bewitched* was Cannon's pride and joy. It had set him back a pretty penny, but his careful manipulation of certain assets on the information superhighway took up the slack. Still, he had gone out on a long and brittle financial limb, mustering every nickel of credit to buy and outfit the boat.

But what do I care? He thought. *I'll pay it off in cash and have a lot more left over.*

The deal was for ten million U.S. dollars up front and a million a month for two more years. If he had to travel to the Middle East, the price doubled. Within three days, half of the deposit would be wired to the secret account he had opened in the Grand Caymans. He would verify the transfer from his communications center aboard *Bewitched,* before he encrypted the first of a series of formulae to be transmitted to the secret location of the BISC headquarters. The balance would be paid as a legitimate consulting fee for engineering services rendered in the development of a series of hydroelectric dams on the Euphrates River. Sure, he'd have to pay Uncle Sam taxes on the consultations, but that was well worth it. He would have the ten million upfront money free and clear. There would be no suspicion then about his newfound wealth and that was well worth the tax bite on the twenty-four million balance. He was being downright patriotic, ponying up his taxes like a good citizen.

Cannon suspected that the BISC hatred for America and Israel was so strong, and their desire for revenge after Desert Storm so acute, they would have paid more, perhaps much more. But Cannon feared a double-cross and worried that, after he gave them the formula, he could be toast. That's why he structured a reasonable deal, with a reasonable down payment—verifiable in advance. This would be an honorable deal among thieves. Besides, they needed him to help implement the program over the next couple of years. The hydro scheme would be a perfect cover for future trips to the famous cradle of civilization.

He boarded the 42-foot Carver and paused to rub some seagull dung from the teak rail with his handkerchief. *Bewitched* had been specially trailered west from Polasky, Wisconsin, where it was built. The bow contained the master bedroom suite with a king-sized vibrating bed, low lights and a sensual sound system. The teak afterdeck was spacious, warm and it shone with the luster of the daily rubdown that Cannon ritually performed.

The living area amid ship featured a professional galley, bar, dining room and a second set of controls to match those on the flying bridge. Twin Cummins diesels rated at 400 horsepower each rested below decks.

When *Bewitched* was unplugged from shore power, her Onan generator operated all of her electrical equipment with power to spare, including the refrigerator, stove, air conditioning, microwave oven and hot water tank. More important to Cannon was the guarantee of uninterrupted power to his communications equipment, which took up its own cabin. This was his lifeline to the outside world. This was what made *Bewitched* possible.

With his Navy background, Cannon made sure the boat was outfitted with hydraulic steering and electronic shifter and throttle controls. *Bewitched* was a $400,000 office and operations center disguised as a playboy's toy.

As captain of his own vessel, Cannon fulfilled a career fantasy that had been with him since his days in the Navy. When he stood at the controls, he felt the freedom of the breeze and the power of commanding his own vessel. He had polished her from bow to stern and his pride of ownership overflowed to the gunnels. Christopher Columbus must have had a similar feeling when he took command of the *Nina,* the

Pinta, and the *Santa Maria.* Cannon had never left port during his Navy career. His time had been spent in naval scientific laboratories, and that time served him well now. But he had always dreamed of his own captaincy. He inspected the craft now as he did daily, as though she shipped a crew of hundreds, standing by, ready to jump at his command. From the engine room to the galley, the Carver was polished, shipshape and ready to launch. Captain Eric Cannon took the helm of his flagship and imagined himself the commander of an impeccable fleet.

Cannon was a handsome man with a playboy look. Most people who have eidetic imagery are stereotyped as a little bit sloppy and absent-minded, but this was far from the case with Eric Cannon. He was a sharp dresser who kept his condo and his Mercedes safari wagon neat as the proverbial pin.

He entered the communications cabin and locked the hatch behind him. This cabin was double-sealed against moisture and contained an air purifier to defeat the ambient humidity of the boat. He opened the teak door to a large cabinet and several telltale lights winked at him with their red and green eyes. Two of the lights represented cellular phone lines, one for voice and one for fax/data transfer. It was the fax/data line that interested him now.

Cannon switched on his high-density monitor and watched a cluster of nonsense characters coalesce at the corner of the large, color screen. He spoke to the screen, enunciating clearly. "Eric Cannon here. Screen my Lucy."

His decryption program went to work immediately and the nonsense letters on his screen blanked out. They were replaced with the simple message: "Data alert."

"Screen my Dolly," he said. Cannon's machine blanked its screen while assembling his data. The Pentium based machine was no longer the fastest on the market, but it was the last of a line to be manufactured without the government's "clipper chip." The clipper made the installation of an encryption/decryption chip fruitless and was required on all boards manufactured for sale in the United States. Possession of a board with encryption chip intact was now a felony, and the federal charge was "possession of an illegal weapon." He might as well be holding a rocket propelled grenade or a cruise missile. When he thought about it, he had to smile. The secret Eric held was infinitely more deadly than a cruise missile.

A message, decrypted and stripped of its various network tags, scrolled onto his monitor. "Representative enroute your hotel. Accounts verified. NOTE: Previous representative robbed and killed in Spokane. Apparently unrelated our situation, but strictest caution advised. Cash deposit will be wired to representative upon check-in. End."

Cannon performed a full erasure, shut off the screen and sat back in his bleached oak and leather chair.

"Previous representative robbed and killed in Spokane!"

That could have been the result of a careless man's flash of cash. However, Eric *had* injected a certain amount of competition into this process, just in case one bidder fell through. Cannon exhaled the breath he'd been holding and rubbed his hands in anticipation. These squabbles were someone else's worries. Life was good. Cash was on the way.

Six

Jack Bradley poked at his keyboard on the credenza of his rosewood desk and waded through the resort's monthly financial statement. In spite of the large screen, his eyes were beginning to strain and his neck felt stiff.

Halfway there, he reminded himself. *Hang in there and it'll be out of your way*.

"Jack," the intercom interrupted, "Mr. Dan Stricklin called from his room and wants to see you right away. I think he's on his way down right now."

Damn, thought Jack, *I'm never going to get through this thing*. "Thanks, Christine," he said.

Jack entered his code word into the resort computer, then he punched up the guest registration directory and typed the letters S-T-R-I-C-K-L-I-N. The new computer system included interactive telecommunications and it could track a roll of toilet paper by the square, but after a frustrating first month it was just becoming a serious asset.

The screen blinked out *Stricklin, Dan, room #112*. He

had checked in the day before, and on a government rate!

Why are we handing out a government rate on a full weekend? Jack wondered.

After a soft knock on his door, Christine ushered Stricklin into Jack's office. "Mr. Bradley, this is Mr. Stricklin."

"Thanks, Christine, come in, Mr. Stricklin. What can I do for you?"

The guest said nothing by way of introduction and made sure that the door shut tightly as Christine left the room. Stricklin set a black sub notebook computer on the credenza and, without a handshake or small talk, reached into the inside pocket of his suit coat and pulled out a leather wallet, which he quickly opened to expose a badge and photo identification.

The picture matched the man, who was middle-aged with a short, military cut to his brown hair. A few grays were starting to show through at the temples and the thinner hair on top was made less noticeable by a good tan. Stricklin wore a proper J.C. Penney dark brown suit and wide wing tips, with thick soles. His socks were black.

Definitely a cop, Jack thought.

"Mr. Bradley, my name is Dan Stricklin and I'm with Gem State Investigations. We believe that one of your guests, Mr. Eric Cannon, has defrauded several individuals and organizations of hundreds of thousands of dollars. We would like to catch him at it and I'm asking for your help."

Jack reached for Stricklin's ID and the man gave it up, reluctantly.

"Have a seat, Mr. Stricklin," Jack said. "I'll want you to talk with our chief of security."

Stricklin stopped himself in mid-protest as Jack buzzed Christine.

"Ask Bob Perkins to join us, please."

Jack studied the man's new leather wallet. The picture

on the ID was Stricklin's all right, but Jack hadn't heard of any "Gem State Investigations," and the ID badge could come from any major copy service. Jack had been out of uniform for eight years now, but his alarms were still set. Stricklin set off a lot of them.

He wants something, but he doesn't shake hands, Jack thought. *He thinks he's in charge, here, and this is just a formality. And since when does "Gem State Investigations" get a government rate?*

Jack and the resort were on excellent terms with local law enforcement, but he didn't want to make the mistake of cooperating with this rent-a-cop to carry out some ex-wife's personal vendetta.

"Mr. Stricklin, I appreciate your openness. But you must realize that, without the proper paperwork, I must respect the privacy of my guests. Unless, of course, he's an immediate danger to himself or others. Is he?"

Stricklin opened the tiny computer on Jack's desk, pressed a button and turned the screen towards Jack as a picture and dossier on Cannon formed on the color screen. This computer was faster, and the image clearer, than the top-of-the line brand new desktop unit that Jack was breaking in. And it was almost small enough to fit into a suit-coat pocket.

"He's ruining innocent people financially," Stricklin said and tapped the top of the screen for emphasis. "He's doing it with a computer from one of *your* rooms, using *your* phone lines. We would like to keep this quiet."

"Yes. I can see why you would."

Pictures of Cannon's associates formed and dissolved on the screen.

How does some two-bit private investigator afford a little beauty like this? Jack wondered.

Bob Perkins knocked and entered at that moment and Jack took the opportunity to beat Stricklin's bush a little.

"Mr. Stricklin, do you carry a weapon?" Jack asked.

Bob froze near the door, quickly assessing the situation between the two men.

Stricklin flushed, caught by the quick switch and by Jack's hard gaze. His lip twitched in a near-smile and he pointed towards the ID on Jack's desk. "In the pocket behind the badge," Stricklin said. "My Idaho concealed weapons permit."

Jack unfolded the permit with the tips of his fingers, found that it was only four days old, and returned it.

"Mr. Stricklin, this is Bob Perkins, our chief of security," Jack said.

Stricklin stood and shook Bob's hand.

"Bob, Mr. Stricklin is a private investigator looking into one of our guests. Now, Mr. Stricklin, you still didn't answer my question."

"No," Stricklin said, patting his left underarm, "I checked it at the door. It's in one of your lock-boxes."

Jack smiled. "Very good politics, Mr. Stricklin, but unless that's a splint around your left ankle, I'd say you're lying to me. That's not very polite at all."

Stricklin looked down to see that static clung his cheap slacks against wool socks, and clearly outlined his backup piece in the ankle holster. He sighed deeply, and in that sigh aged another ten years. "I've just got myself off on the wrong foot here," Stricklin said. "I have a personal reference from somebody you know—Patrick Douglas from Georgia. In fact, here's his number."

Jack accepted the slip of paper and felt a little vertigo as the tables turned. Patrick Douglas was one of those names from his past he had hoped he'd never hear again. After the Naval Academy, Jack had volunteered for CGI, Naval Intelligence. CGI spook school was in Glenville, Georgia, and Patrick B. Douglas had been on loan there from the Training

Office of the CIA. Six years later, when Jack left the Navy, Douglas was there to offer him a job with the Company.

"Bob," Jack said, "I'll set up an appointment for Mr. Stricklin to talk with you about his project. Right now I'd like to speak with him alone. Sorry I brought you up here for nothing."

"That's okay, Jack. Always a pleasure . . . Mr. Stricklin." Bob Perkins closed the door quietly behind him.

"So," Jack said, "quit dicking around. Do you tell me what's going on, or do I call Douglas?"

Stricklin shrugged, bland faced and returned to his chair. He shut off his little electronic wonder, closed it and set it beside him on the floor. Jack punched out the phone number on his keyboard. It didn't surprise him that the area code was for Virginia. While waiting for the connection, he mumbled, "This better be good."

Stricklin stared straight ahead with all the personality of a mannequin. Just a couple of clicks later a familiar, nasal voice answered, simply, "Gem State Investigations."

Routed direct, Jack thought. *He was waiting for this call. He expected me to bust Stricklin.*

Jack pressed the "memo" feature on his keyboard, to record their conversation. He didn't think for a minute that Gem State Investigations had a Langley, Virginia prefix and he didn't like the wash of helplessness that came with knowing it.

"Jack Bradley, Mr. Douglas. You have a message for me?"

There was hesitation on the line, the sound of a muffled sneeze. "Stricklin has a message for you," Douglas said. "I hope you busted him without blowing his cover altogether."

"I did. It doesn't make me feel good about you, Stricklin or the message."

"I don't give a rat's ass how you feel," Douglas said.

"Listen to Stricklin and stay out of his way."

"I've gone private," Jack said, "you know that. Why. . .?"

"National security that's why," Douglas snapped.

"What about my hotel? My people?"

"Safe," Douglas reassured him. "The target never carries a weapon."

"Wish I could say the same about Stricklin." The line went dead. Jack was sure that, should he call it again, he'd get a recording saying that number was no longer in service. "Well, Mr. Stricklin," Jack said. "Let's take a little stroll around the grounds while you tell me what the hell's going on here."

Jack checked out with Christine, then he walked Dan Stricklin outside and across the boat launch area to Tubbs Hill Park. A hiking trail wound its way up the hillside, through the trees, and Jack had a favorite lookout that was perfect for sunsets. Neither man had spoken, except for Jack's greeting of several employees, since leaving his office.

"Isn't it illegal for you guys to operate inside the country, against a citizen?"

"Rules change," Stricklin said. "Things come up that are bigger than rules."

"Like some computer hot shot who's skimming bank accounts?" Jack asked. "Doesn't sound like a national security threat to me. Bob Perkins could pop that guy in twenty-four hours."

"This is an NFIP problem," Stricklin said.

National Foreign Intelligence Program, Jack thought. *The CIA stepping on the FBI's toes.*

Jack didn't know much about NFIP, but he knew it was ultra secret. He didn't expect to find out much from Stricklin, but Jack would soon have the perfect connection right here in the hotel and he intended to educate himself ASAP. He and Stricklin had climbed only about a hundred feet and the man was sweating already. *The NFIP must be focusing a 'little' attention on China after their hot shot fighter pilot wrong way Wang Wei rammed into one of our EP-3P spy planes and forced it down on the Chinese island of Hainan. Plus a 'whole lot more' attention on worldwide terrorism after the horrific attacks in New York at the World Trade Center and Washington D.C. at the Pentagon,* thought Jack. *Now they're here in Idaho. Something big must be in the works.*

"Well, Mr. Stricklin, how can I help you?"

"We've got a real problem, as you must imagine," Stricklin said.

His voice was firmer now, more confident and commanding. Jack guessed that the bumbling private investigator was just another role for an experienced actor.

"The short version is this," Stricklin said. "You've got a guest by the name of Eric Cannon. He owns that big Carver out there on the far pier. With him are three other people; Julie Adams, Bob Kent and Rory Finley. They've got rooms #362 and #364, which I believe you refer to as parlor suites."

"Actually, the two rooms together form a parlor suite," Jack corrected, absently. "They have a large connecting wall between them that opens wide."

Stricklin grunted.

Jack was impressed. Stricklin had done a little footwork after all. Jack always emphasized guest security. The staff wasn't allowed to give out room numbers either over the phone or in person. He did not permit a guest's room number to be spoken aloud, even at check-in, and required his staff to write it out for the guest alone to see. The Coeur d'Alene Resort had very few security problems. Jack ordered security to walk any guest to his or her room if they lost a keycard or locked one inside and that, only after they showed a picture ID.

Jack believed that Stricklin's homework was correct.

"Well, I believe we have them listed as Mr. & Mrs. Cannon and Mr. & Mrs. Kent, so you know more about them than we do."

Stricklin leaned back against a tree trunk and folded his arms across his chest. He grinned an all knowing, taunting grin that Jack remembered seeing on Patrick Douglas more than once.

"Mr. Bradley . . . Jack, there is virtually nothing in this country, nor very little in the world, that the NFIP *doesn't* know. Some of that is good old-fashioned surveillance."

"And some of it requires access to their rooms and the boat. And I could make that easy for you, right?"

Stricklin bristled. "*We're* the good guys, remember?" Jesus! All right, here it is. Cannon's not quite a genius, but he's got something that even a genius envies."

Jack didn't want to listen to Stricklin, much less drag the story out of him a piece at a time to feed his need for attention. "What's that?"

"Eidetic imagery," Stricklin whispered. "Photographic memory. He can remember every word of every page he's ever read. No, he sees the page, and reads it over again. Better than that, he can glance at a page—words, equations, schematics—for only a second or two and then he has it. He can reproduce that page anytime, anyplace, from memory."

Jack was beginning to see what had happened, why the FBI wasn't handling this guy.

Cannon was one of theirs, Jack realized. *And they didn't know about his memory. And now he's dirty.*

Jack was not amused that they'd run their target to ground in his hotel. "Who did he work for?"

"After the naval academy he went into Naval Intelligence/Weapons. He was assigned to a category Sigma team working on a better nuclear power source for Navy vessels." Again, Stricklin paused for effect. Except Jack could see that Stricklin was looking past him towards the marina.

"And he memorized some plans to make some cash," Jack said. "Hundreds of people have done the same thing. What makes him so special?"

"He memorized everything that NIS/Weapons had under CNWDI."

"CNWDI?" Jack asked. One thing he didn't miss about the military was it's infinite combinations of letters and numbers. "What's that?"

"Critical Nuclear Weapon Design Information. One device in particular concerns us. It's beyond top secret and has a clearance of its own. Jack, I'm no nuclear physicist, but this is what I understand. The trigger for a hydrogen bomb is one or more atomic bombs surrounding the hydrogen. The atomic explosions cause the extreme compression and heat, which creates the hydrogen fusion. We've been able to keep a handle on who has these doomsday weapons by carefully auditing the materials required to construct such devices. You know plutonium, uranium and all that kind of stuff."

Some kind of 'stuff,' Jack thought.

Stricklin lectured, "The Navy was working on a medical imaging problem and called in their best computer and nuclear brains to assist. By accident they stumbled onto a big chunk of the Grand Unification Theory of Physics."

"What the hell is that," quizzed Jack.

"It's the one theory that describes how everything in the universe works," the agent responded.

"How'd they do it," Jack asked as he leaned closer to hear every detail.

"The problem they were working on required research into the effects on Navy Seals exposed to ionized gases. They fine-tuned their imaging equipment to the point where they could actually read and track, with the use of high-speed computers, the density of a gas down to the individual atom. The team learned hydrogen atoms aren't uniformly distributed but cluster into mini-galaxies. The big break came when they discovered the Strong Force, the force that holds the nucleus together, has a resonance to it like a tiny radio transmitter...and here's the scary part!"

"What's that," gasped Jack.

"Once they figured out how to track the nuclei of a clustered bunch of atoms, they learned the frequency required to oscillate each nucleus. They could cause it to explosively tear itself apart! Voila, a poor man's hydrogen bomb."

Oh my God, thought Jack as he squeezed his eyes shut tight trying to comprehend what he had just heard.

"I'll be damned," sighed Jack, "they split an atom the same way an opera singer shatters a crystal goblet. What's the triggering device?"

"Ironically enough, the perfect machinery for that job would be a plain ole' Model T magneto that was modified slightly to focus energy directly onto a cluster. The most exotic part of the bomb would be as simple as a laptop you can buy at any Radio Shack to track the atoms you're about to split," Stricklin said.

"You've got the nuclear equivalent of the Oklahoma City bomb that was made from common farm supplies," reasoned Jack.

"That's about right. Nobody knows what light, electricity, or gravity really are but we've learned how to manipulate 'em. We don't know what the Strong Force is yet but the formula shows how to manipulate it, and Cannon's got the cluster and oscillation formulas locked in this treasonous head!"

"I see your problem," Jack said. "Why don't you just give him the measles? If he dies, there's no problem."

Stricklin snorted. "Other opportunities."

Jack could guess at a few and they didn't make him any

happier.

"He's on the market," Jack said, "and you want his customers."

"I want his customers and his communications network," Stricklin said. "Then I want him. He carries nothing with him. We can only get him if we can document the transfer of that information. Meanwhile, we'll take all the peripherals we can get."

"I see."

"The formula is extremely complicated. Typed, it would fill three to five pages. That's what that asshole's got stored in his brain, and as long as it stays in his brain it's not evidence."

"So, I take it he's marketing here at the hotel?"

"Correct."

"Shit," Jack said. Then, reluctantly, "What do you need?"

"He's trying to sell this information to at least three organizations. Current top bid is from the Middle East. Eidetic imagery rarely survives adolescence, so Cannon knows he's been on borrowed time for awhile now." Stricklin cleared his throat. "I'd like to go through all of your guest accounts, as well as review your expected arrivals for today and tomorrow."

Jack sucked in a quick breath.

"Mr. Bradley," Stricklin added, "I can subpoena all this information and force everything out in the open. But my problem with that is time. This thing could go down at any minute."

"No," Jack sighed, "a subpoena won't be necessary, Mr. Stricklin. I told you we certainly want to cooperate. Let's head back down and I'll personally help you get whatever information you want."

Stricklin started reciting his wish list as they scuffed down the trail. "I want to look at Cannon and Kent's room charge folios to see if there is anything unusual on them or if they made any long distance telephone calls and to whom.

"I'd also like to see your registration records and any information you have on the occupant of room #306."

"Do you have a name?"

"No, not yet," admitted Stricklin.

So, Jack thought, with some satisfaction, *they don't have all the information in the world.*

Back in his office, Jack punched up 306. "His name is Mustafa Khadduri of Fort Wayne, Indiana. I'll get you his registration card, credit information and folio."

"Thanks, Jack," Stricklin said, offering his hand.

Jack shook it, and found it sweaty.

"You're welcome. Good luck."

"Sorry about that first impression." Stricklin said, from the doorway. "Douglas warned me that you were good. I just had to see for myself."

Then Stricklin was finally gone. Jack was left to his accounts and to his unwelcome ghosts from the past.

Seven

Richard Portman had been assistant manager of The Coeur d'Alene Resort for over twenty years. Richard knew every inch of the resort and was a master at remembering names and pampering guests. Even though the front desk staff was highly qualified and trained, Richard enjoyed the personal contact of check-in and check-out. He filled in gaps before they became gaps—behind the front desk, answering the phones, facilitating special needs. He prided himself in being a real roll-up-your-sleeves kind of manager; he worked himself up from valet and was well liked by staff and guests alike.

In all his sixty years, Portman had never won anything. Not a raffle, not a drawing, and certainly not a major state lottery. He had just checked in Earl and Betty Hanson, a Midwest couple who had won 140 million dollars in the Illinois State Lottery.

"We read about your resort in *Sunset Magazine* last summer," Betty said. "Who would have thought we'd be here today?"

Richard instantly liked the couple. They seemed like a hardworking, unpretentious pair who would go about enjoying their money sensibly, with a treat like The Coeur d'Alene thrown in for the tickle.

Neither of them had been to the Pacific Northwest and their home near Chicago's O'Hare International Airport, on a busy street, was everything but quiet and relaxing. Since the news of their new millionaire status went public, the Hanson's spent a day and a night answering the phone. Inevitably it was a real estate agent, a car salesman, an investment counselor or some relative who hadn't bothered to call them before. The second day they called the travel agency and shut off their phone.

"What were the instant millionaires like?" Rosemary asked. She was his assistant and liked working the front desk. The Hanson's had been the end of a flurry of check-ins, and this was Richard's first break in nearly an hour.

"Well, they were sure pleasant," Richard said. "Mr. Hanson claims he's keeping his job at Windy City Packing and Betty wants to see the world after thirty years of marriage and raising four kids. What do you want to bet that Windy City Packing's seen the last of Earl Hanson?"

Bellman John passed by the front desk after rooming the Hanson's in the resort's honeymoon suite. He flashed a crisp one hundred-dollar bill that confirmed that Earl and Betty were here to have a great time and money was no object.

Richard gave him a thumb's up congratulations, then focused on the white super stretch Lincoln limousine under the porte cochere. His joy turned into terror when he recognized the woman getting out of the limo. She brushed away the hand of the uniformed driver who was trying to help her and instead handed him the leashes of her two snarling, perfectly matched and coiffeured toy white poodles. Her new bodyguards, as usual, looked like winners of the Mr. Olympic Body Building Competition. They helped the bell staff unload what seemed like an endless number of matching French luggage, hat holders, toiletry cases and hanging bags. Two bell carts had already been completely filled and John was on his way with a third.

"Veronica Whitcomb," he whispered.

"God," Rosemary answered. Then, her reluctance apparent, she said, "I'll take her if you want a break."

"Too late," he whispered. "She's seen me now."

Richard knew Veronica Whitcomb all too well. He had known her parents, who built a fortune out of nothing. For all of their excellence in business, they were complete failures as parents. Veronica Whitcomb was testimony to their failure.

She made her grand entrance into the resort and Richard flurried "WHITCOMB" over the reservations computer keyboard. Nothing appeared. He cleared the CRT unit and simply typed in the word W in case a careless clerk had misspelled Veronica Whitcomb's last name. The computer flashed "working" on its screen for what seemed to Richard a very long time. Finally, a long list of W's printed out alphabetically on the screen from Watkins through Wurt, but no Whitcomb was in the system. As she sashayed dangerously closer to the front desk Richard tried next day arrivals. Nothing. He smiled.

"Ms. Whitcomb, it is a great honor to have you with us again," said Richard. "I would have greeted you myself, but I didn't realize you were arriving today."

Stressed, Richard felt his fingers push hard against the unforgiving granite of the desktop.

"Of course you didn't Richard. It's a surprise. Fog in Seattle forced us to circle for an hour and then we were rerouted to Spokane. It's certainly your lucky day, but I am exhausted. Be a dear and show me to my suite, please."

Veronica Whitcomb, the striking femme fatale, daughter and sole heir of the recently deceased financier Lawrence Whitcomb, was used to getting whatever she wanted whenever she wanted. She considered the Bavarian suite her personal quarters and Richard knew she would fully expect to have it available even though she arrived with no reservations or notice. Richard's calm exterior betrayed the Richard inside, who now raced through the computer's "Rooms clean and vacant" screen.

Of course, he knew Mr. Nakamura was in the Bavarian Suite, and as Jack Bradley's special guest, there was certainly no chance of moving him. Richard made the decision to offer Ms. Whitcomb the resort's second finest suite even though it had a prior reservation, which, frankly, was an upgrade at a rate lower than the suite's normal rack rate. As pushy and bossy as Ms. Whitcomb was, she always paid top dollar and never quibbled about price.

Brag, yes, Richard thought. *Quibble, never*.

"Ms. Whitcomb, had we known you were coming, we would have held the Bavarian suite open for you. Unfortunately, it's already occupied. However, I've made some adjustments and I'm pleased to offer you the Juniper Suite which, as you know, is a magnificent room as well."

Richard's fingers pressed harder against the granite until the ends under the nails were white and his shoulders cramped.

"Damn," she huffed. "I guess that will have to do, but I'm certainly going to miss staying in *my own* suite."

Richard smiled wider and, without letting his relief show he checked Veronica Whitcomb into the Juniper Suite personally, at the rack rate of $2,400 per night. This was a significant improvement over the upgraded guest who would have paid $850.

Richard handed her registration packet and key to the bellman and reserved the connecting room for the bookend bodyguards, even though this overbooked the resort even further, taking the room count down to a minus seven.

Richard knew this was a large arrival day and he was counting on several no-shows. He glanced up to see that Veronica Whitcomb remained at his counter and when she spoke he got a sharp whiff of alcohol.

"Are you absolutely sure that my personal suite can't be made available?"

"I'm sorry. We already have a guest . . ."

"I realize that, Richard, but that's not the point. Can't you move whoever is in that room to the Juniper suite so that I can stay in the Whitcomb suite?" This wasn't the first time that the pushy heiress had changed the name of the Bavarian suite to her own. Now she affected a pout and her finger traced non-existent designs onto the granite countertop. "After all, Richard, I'm Veronica Whitcomb, and you've told me many times that I am the most important guest here at The Coeur d'Alene."

"Ms. Whitcomb, you certainly are and we are very pleased to have you with us. But, unfortunately, we cannot move a person who has already checked into the suite. I hope that you can understand that."

She sniffed. "Actually, I cannot. Tell whoever it is that I will pay for his accommodations, as well as my own, if he will only get the hell out of my suite."

Richard knew that he was in a lose-lose situation. There was absolutely no way he would even consider asking Mr. Nakamura to vacate the suite and he also knew Veronica Whitcomb would not take no for an answer. He would have to be what her parent's weren't—firm. He was sure she wouldn't like it.

"I'm sorry, it's just not possible, Ms. Whitcomb. You truly

are our most important guest and had we only known that you'd be arriving today, we would certainly have held . . . "

"Don't try to placate me, Richard. Mr. Jack Bradley and I will speak about this later."

Before Richard could reply, Veronica Whitcomb snapped her fingers at her bodyguards and haughtily led her entourage toward the Juniper suite.

"She's a pretty tough cookie, isn't she?" Rosemary said.

"She's . . . well yes, Richard responded. "She's a little mixed up with lots of attitude to go along with it." His description was the nicest way possible to say that Veronica Whitcomb was a real bitch.

As Richard retracted his hands, the sweaty imprint of his fingers was clearly visible on the desk. He interlocked his fingers, squeezed them tightly together to return circulation and breathed a sigh of relief. Tomorrow was his day off. Jack Bradley was welcome to her.

Eight

Jack Bradley knelt just inside the main entrance to the lobby, side by side with Rann Love, the resort's interior designer. Both men, on hands and knees, inspected the lamb's-wool carpeting.

"It's going much faster than we expected," Jack said. "I thought we'd get a lot more wear for the price we paid."

"I thought so too, Jack, but your business has nearly doubled since we put this in. Twice the shoe leather, twice the wear."

"Jack, how the hell are you?" A booming voice interrupted. "It is good to see you doing honest work and it's damned good to be home." Jack turned to see an entourage behind him and in the middle of it was his long-time friend United States Senator Carl Wilder. Jack snapped to his feet, brushed off his pants and stuck out his hand.

"Senator, welcome back to The Coeur d'Alene." The two shook hands vigorously. "You're looking great," Jack said. "How in the heck do you survive that madhouse in D.C.?"

The two embraced and patted each other on the back. Senator Carl Wilder was easily the most popular politician in the state. Wilder, like many major politicians, was an extremely likable individual. People on both sides of the aisle admired the Senator and enjoyed his earthy wit and countrified sense of humor.

Wilder had his detractors, all politicians did, but even many of these would admit in private that the good Senator had done a great deal for his home state and for his country.

"Let's get you checked in so you can relax and let your hair down a little," Jack said.

"What hair I've got left." Wilder said, patting a bald spot that shone through the gray.

Jack escorted Senator Wilder to the front desk.

"Rosemary, you know Senator Wilder. He's back with us again, licking his wounds from those wolves in Washington. If you'll give me his key packet, I'll see him safely to his room."

"Absolutely, Mr. Bradley."

Rosemary smiled a warm welcome to the Senator as she handed Jack the packet.

"Senator, it's nice to have you back with us again," she said. "Enjoy your three-day visit."

"Rosemary," Jack said, "We'll also need a keycard for Ron Larson's room."

Jack was always careful to acknowledge the Senator's travel staff. Larson appreciated the recognition, because so many times staffers were totally lost in the shadow of the Senator, or the Governor, or the elected official for whom they worked. Jack knew that most of a politician's work is done by staff. A good relationship with the staff made for excellent relations with the dignitary. Though Senator Wilder was a personal friend, Jack insisted on his usual attentiveness to the staff.

Over the years, in the Senator's numerous elections, Jack and The Coeur d'Alene Resort had been big supporters, both in terms of cash contributions and in-kind favors. Whenever the Senator had a fund-raiser, the resort would write off large portions of the bill. When he wanted a complimentary room, it was provided.

Senator Wilder steered a number of high-level federal meetings to Jack's hotel and was a good friend of Idaho's hospitality industry. Jack knew he could call Senator Wilder and that his point of view would be heard. A machine did not sign letters to Jack. But he knew also that Carl Wilder's vote could never be bullied or bought. The lawmaker voted his conscience, and a sound old conscience it was.

Jack needed to remain politically neutral in public, because both Republicans and Democrats utilized the resort. But Senator Wilder was an exception and Jack supported him whole-heartedly.

Senator Wilder slapped Jack's back as they walked toward his room.

"How about some early-morning golf?" the Senator asked. "My jet lag will give me a three-hour morning edge for the next day or two and I want to take advantage of it."

"I'll find somebody up to your challenge," Jack promised. "Just leave them enough to pay their bill, that's all I ask."

The Senator loved the attention and the special treatment the resort afforded him. Jack knew that ego was a big motivator, especially of successful people and those constantly in the limelight. They arrived at the room, and Senator Wilder wanted to talk a little more.

"Jack, come in and let me buy you a drink. I'm so glad to see you and get away from that school of piranhas back

East. Don't head back to work quite yet. Sit down. Let your assistants do their stuff."

As usual, Jack's gift of a bottle of Black Jack Daniel's bourbon awaited them in the Senator's suite. Jack mixed a pair of drinks as Wilder loosened his tie, slipped off his shoes and sat back on the couch in the living area of his room. He was a grandfatherly type with pure white hair.

Distinguished, Jack thought.

His age was beginning to show in a slight stoop in his back and the Senator's belly bulged a little against his bright red suspenders. He took a big slug of his favorite whiskey.

"You know those dumb asses in Washington don't have a clue how to live like we do out West," Wilder announced.

It was his usual introduction and required no response.

Jack simply nodded his agreement.

"It's unbelievable the crap you have to go through to live in that godforsaken place. It's an hour or more to drive each way to work and it costs a fortune for everything you do. I can't tell you how good it is to be back home."

Senator Wilder had his share of perks and a legion of lobbyists helped to soften the blow of the cost and inconvenience of living in the District of Columbia. Jack clearly understood what a rat race it was to livc away from "God's Country." On the other hand, he also knew that his friend, Carl, like other politicians, was driven by the dichotomy of serving his fellow citizens and, at the same time, feeding his substantial ego. Nevertheless, Carl Wilder was a good friend and claimed Jack's loyalty and admiration.

"Senator, I know you want to relax, but do you mind if I pick your brain for just a minute?"

"You know I don't have much to pick, but anything I can do for you would be a pleasure . . . go right ahead."

"Tell me, what in the hell is the NFIP?"

The Senator set his drink down on the coffee table and

sat up straight.

"Jack, why in the world would you ask me that?"

"I had an unusual thing happen today. A fellow came into the resort, flashed a badge and PI identification, but turns out to be with NFIP. I'm sure he's on the up and up and I was totally cooperative, but I thought that maybe you could enlighten me as to who this guy really represents."

"Are you in any kind of trouble? I mean, is there anything you want to tell me?"

"Oh, no, I'm just trying to figure out who this guy really works for and whether it's a problem for the hotel."

Wilder tugged on his earlobe and tightened one side of his cheek in thought.

"Well, because of my seniority, I'm on the Senate Foreign Relations Committee and a member of the Armed Services Committee. The NFIP is one of the most super-secret organizations of the intelligence community. It answers only to the Director of the Central Intelligence Agency."

Wilder was up, walking to the wet bar that had been stocked in his room. Jack's glass was yet untouched but Wilder had already drained his and reloaded with the pride of Lynchburg. Five plump ice cubes and a generous pour of whiskey with just a splash of water. He stood in the middle of the room as if addressing Congress.

"These guys are no-nonsense and virtually immune from Congress. I mean, I'm the third ranking majority Senator in the United States today and I have yet to see their budget. They seem to be the one pocket of government that's untouchable by either party or by any President. The manual says they're responsible for national security in communications and foreign intelligence. Jack, they're just not people you screw around with. Are you sure you're not in trouble now?"

"No. No. We've got a guest in the hotel . . . seems like a

good guy . . . it's probably nothing. I just worry about spooks, is all. You understand why."

"That thing that happened to you in the service, Jack, that was a bad bunch." the Senator said. "And don't forget, you put them away for a long, long time. Not everyone in intelligence is like them. You weren't. These guys probably aren't."

Jack didn't say anything as Wilder stirred his drink with his index finger.

"I wish I could tell you more, and there is a little more I do know that I can't tell you. But frankly, there's a heck of a lot I don't know. NFIP has a helluva lot of power. I'll see what I can find out. If I can tell you, I will. Just be careful and don't get crossways with them."

"I won't, Senator." Jack stood to leave. "Listen, you have a great visit. If there's anything at all we can do, you let me know. Thanks for all you do for tourism and for our state. Relax tonight and get a good night's sleep. I'll talk with you over some golf in the morning. It's got to be tough to go across three time zones, particularly with your hectic schedule."

"Hell, when I was twenty years younger, three time zones didn't mean a tinker's dam, but today it's catching up with me a little bit."

The Senator reclined on the comfortable davenport, closed his eyes and was nearly asleep before Jack left the room. Quick sleep where you can catch it was another survival skill of a successful politician.

Jack walked back to his office and reflected on his relationship with the Senator. He had fond memories of Wilder's many visits over the past eight years. Just last year the Senator had held a fundraiser at The Coeur d'Alene. Jack never failed to be amazed at how an elderly Senator from such a sparsely populated state could attract bigwigs from the East to come to a little dinner he was putting on. The Senator's seniority placed him on a number of powerful committees, which made him the constant target of lobbyists, power brokers, and the moneyed elite.

Jack had attended the thousand-dollar-a-plate fundraiser at the resort as the Senator's guest. Several large companies had shared in the cost of cocktails, dinner and entertainment so the entire ticket price went directly into Wilder's campaign coffers. The Senator was in rare form. Even though he'd had a copious quantity of Jack Daniel's under his belt, he was still able to fluently rail against big government spending and the sprawling bureaucracy in Washington D.C. Though he had been a part of that power base for nearly thirty years, he still blamed the nation's problems on those nameless villains that he mud-wrestled daily in the District of Columbia. The Senator always put on a good show.

Jack reached his office and smiled at the surprise he had ahead for the Senator. He had two guests in mind for a perfect round of early-morning golf—movie star Clint Diamond and Tako Nakamura.

So, it was with a double helping of pleasure that he opened his office door and saw Lindsey Redding speaking with Christine.

"Mr. Bradley," Christine said, "You've met Ms. Redding."

"Yes," he nodded, and offered his hand, "a pleasure to see you again. Is there a problem?"

Lindsey Redding shook his hand firmly, held it for a heartbeat or two while staring into his soul, and then released him back to reality.

"Not really, I was explaining my dilemma to Christine. My guest card charges my purchases to Mr. Nakamura's account. The money itself means nothing to him, but I would rather be responsible for my own purchases. I would appreciate you putting my phone calls and incidentals on a separate bill for me. You understand, don't you?"

When that blue-eyed gaze held his, Jack felt as though he understood everything—and nothing. He felt fifteen years old again, and his body came alive with a new breath and vigor. At the same time, a small voice in the back of his mind screamed, *Danger! Danger!*

"Of course," Jack heard himself say. "Christine, would you take care of this for Miss Redding? And have the desk bring her keycard and packet over here."

Christine was already on the phone to the front desk.

"I was about to have tea and salad sent over," he told Lindsey. "Would you care to join me?"

She glanced at her watch and smiled. "Why, yes," she said, "I would like that."

Christine sent Jack's usual late lunch over for two and they ate in the undisturbed quiet of his inner office overlooking the marina, the lake, and the mountains beyond. The conversation was mostly small talk other than confirmation of his dinner appointment with Nakamura and his invitation for Nakamura to join him and the Senator for golf in the morning. He didn't mention Clint Diamond.

"I'm sure Tako would enjoy a round of golf with you and the Senator," Lindsey said. "It sounds suspiciously like I'm uninvited. Is this supposed to be a man thing?"

Jack laughed.

"Yes," he said, "I guess it is. I thought the Senator and Mr. Nakamura. . ."

"Believe me," Lindsey interrupted, raising a hand, "I understand. I can't say I'm used to it—I'll never be used to it—but it's the way of business in Japan. Besides," she sipped her tea and set the cup aside, "I'm a scratch golfer, myself. It's not considered polite to beat the boss or your host so I'll try to find some knitting to pass the time!"

At this they both laughed. Jack's attraction to Lindsey was growing by the minute. Her request for her own guest card encouraged Jack to think that she did separate business and pleasure, after all. And if she was all business with Nakamura, perhaps . . ..

His intercom toned for his attention.

"It's Bob Perkins to see you, Mr. Bradley. He says it's urgent."

"Thanks, Christine I'll be with him in a moment."

Jack and Lindsey Redding stood and looked into each other's eyes for a moment.

"Bob's my security chief, if he says it's urgent."

"Yes, I understand. Well, maybe you'll save some time for a golf game, just the two of us? I warn you, I don't pull any punches to let the man win."

"We'll do that," Jack said, and once again shook a warm, strong hand that lingered in his. "I'll see you this evening at dinner."

Jack showed her out the privacy door, and then buzzed Bob Perkins in.

Bob didn't waste time on pleasantries, "We have a couple of problems."

Jack interpreted Bob's unusual gruffness to being left out of the loop in the conversation with Stricklin. *I'll have to find a way to bring him in on that one*, he thought.

Jack pushed back his frustration at the day's interruptions. It wouldn't be right to take it out on Perkins. Besides, Bob had been an LAPD cop for twenty years and if Bob said something was urgent, Jack knew he'd damned well better interrupt whatever he was doing to listen. Bob wore his crisp beige uniform as though expecting an inspection by the toughest drill sergeant in the marine boot camp he had survived twenty-five years earlier.

"Jack, Richard Portman alerted me that we have a cash-only guest, under the last name of Smith, checked into room #523. There is something fishy with this one!"

"Why?"

"During last night's security check of Beverly's dining room, Peter Harding mentioned that Smith had ordered every meal through room service and was paying cash with crisp twenty-dollar bills each time. Peter checked them out and they weren't counterfeits—but it still seemed strange."

"What worries you about that?"

"Drugs," Bob said. "All this cash might mean he's a dealer."

Jack thought, *there goes cowboy Bob again . . . always looking for the bad guys.* But he decided to be safe rather than sorry and asked "Do you think he's dealing in the hotel?"

Bob shrugged. "Nobody's been seen entering or leaving his or her room. Not even them. I just have a feeling . . ."

Here we go again. Another feeling. "Not much we can do, Bob. The law says that they've bought their privacy while they're here."

"I could take a look," Bob said. "How about if I put on a room service uniform and deliver their breakfast in the morning? That's not illegal, is it?"

Jack tapped his teeth with his pencil.

"If you're an employee there on business and you see something illegal out in the open, you can report it. But you can't search and I want you to handle it yourself."

Bob brightened considerably.

"Good enough," he said. "I'll call you as soon as I know anything more."

Bob headed for the door, then turned to add something more. "By the way, Nakamura just opened an account here in Coeur d'Alene; two million dollars for starters. Does that sound like a man whose just sightseeing for a few days?"

Nine

Beverly's, the resort's signature dining room, was fully booked for the evening. Food and beverage manager Peter Harding usually held back a couple of tables for unexpected VIP's or an occasional reservation mix-up, but not this evening, and there was no room for error.

General Manager Jack Bradley's special table would require very careful attention. Bradley had asked Peter personally to make sure the service was outstanding, as he wanted to honor his guest, Mr. Tako Nakamura. At Bradley's instruction, Peter had reserved this special table for three to include Mr. Nakamura's associate.

As if a full house weren't pressure enough, Richard Portman had called from the desk to warn Peter that Veronica Whitcomb had pulled one of her surprise visits and he should expect her to demand a table for three on short notice. While Ms. Whitcomb was very difficult to handle, she generally did call ahead for her dinner reservations. She craved the perfect table in the center of things, where she could cultivate the attention of her fellow guests. She loved the spotlight.

The resort was laid out in such a manner that Beverly's also provided room service. Beverly's had the largest of the resort's three kitchens and was convenient to the guestrooms.

Peter Harding began his career at The Coeur d'Alene as a waiter. He took to the food and beverage business with flair and quickly moved up the management ladder to become the manager of Beverly's, as well as the resort's room service program. Many hotels treat room service as a necessary evil, but Peter Harding worked very hard to make it first class and profitable.

Tonight was no different than usual in that most guests preferred to dine between 7:30 and 8:00 PM. Room guests were primary customers in Beverly's due to the isolation of the resort and the lack of suitable competition. But the resort's award-winning restaurant also had a good following by the locals. Many of them chose Beverly's for special occasions and tonight it seemed as though they were hosting every birthday and anniversary in the county.

Peter set up the dining room by assigning stations to his team of servers and assistants. He knew very well that, while Jack Bradley was likable and very well thought of by the entire staff, he was a stickler for quality service. Peter knew his own life would be much more pleasant *if* service on Bradley's table was flawless and attentive. In honor of his Japanese visitor, Jack had ordered some special sushi appetizers. He also asked the executive chef to prepare a special dinner of Shabu-Shabu, a fondue-type Japanese dinner featuring a boiling hot caldron of beef broth in the middle of the table. Large platters of very thinly sliced, lean, prime cuts of New York strip beef were then brought for the guests to cook in the boiling caldron and to dip into their choice of a ponzu sauce, a soy & rice wine, or sesame sauce with Japanese mustard.

In Japan the finer restaurants use Kobe Beef for this delicacy, but the chef special ordered a cut of prime beef that would work nicely. A large platter of vegetables including tofu, mushrooms, carrot stars and broccoli follows the beef. Finally, thoroughly seasoned by the beef and vegetables, the remaining broth is made into aromatic noodle soup. At least that's the way the dinner was drawn up and Peter knew it better damned well go that way.

Bradley's table was all set for him complete with large bottles of chilled Sapporo beer to be followed by hot sake and Chivas Regal Scotch whiskey.

Lottery winners Earl and Betty Hanson were used to eating early and their biological clocks were still on Midwest time. They were the first patrons that evening, but from what Peter had heard of their celebration so far, they might well be among the last to leave. He planned on no table turn for the Hanson party that evening. The resort's wine sommelier had already invited the Hanson's for a special private tour of the resort's award-winning wine cellar.

Peter noted from the reservations list that the notorious Cannon party of four was coming back into Beverly's at the same time that Jack Bradley was bringing in his special guest. They had been in every night for a week and every night they got a little louder and more uninhibited. Peter definitely wanted to keep their table as far away from Bradley's as possible. Last night the two couples had enjoyed themselves to the tune of a thousand dollar dinner tab. No one seemed to be sure what they were celebrating, but there was no question that the four of them were liberated couples of the new millenium. There were no holds barred during their escape to The Coeur d'Alene Resort.

The Cannon table alone might help Beverly's set a liquor sales record, Peter thought, *even though Cannon himself stuck to tonic and lime.*

He assigned them a table as far as possible from Jack Bradley's party.

Murphy's law of "What can go wrong will go wrong" seemed to be holding true to form this evening. Room service, which was dreadfully understaffed, was busier than usual. With that, on top of the heavy bookings in Beverly's, the kitchen staff was hustling to keep up.

Jack Bradley entered the restaurant as Earl and Betty Hanson returned from their tour of the wine cellar. The sommelier carefully carried their selections to their table as Peter introduced Bradley to the lucky couple. Jack graciously congratulated them on their lottery win and thanked them for choosing The Coeur d'Alene for their special celebration.

"This wine cellar is unbelievable," Earl said. "The wine steward said you have more than 14,000 bottles of wine dozing down there."

"Over half a million dollars worth," Bradley said. "You enjoyed the Vintage Krug, I trust?"

Peter himself had delivered a complimentary bottle of 1964 Krug Vintage Champagne to their room prior to their arrival. It was a favorite of Jack's.

"Very nice," Betty said. "One glass and *poof* no more jet lag, no more worries."

"It was thoughtful of you," Earl said, with a slight bow. "Thank you."

"I see you selected a pair of wines for dinner," Jack said. "If you don't mind my asking, which did you choose?"

"Well," Earl said, hitching up his pants, "we're having the lobster cocktail, so I thought a bottle of 1985 Montrachet Louis Latour would do the trick there."

Jack smiled and nodded his agreement. Peter admired Mr. Hanson's flair. He was amazed what a quick study Hanson was. Lots of new money and a little knowledge from the sommelier made him an instant connoisseur. *That's $575 a* *bottle, just for the appetizer*, he thought. "And for your entree?" Jack continued.

"It's got to be the prime rib for me," Betty said. "I'm still a Midwest girl at heart."

"And a double cut New York for me," Earl said. "And the perfect wine for that combo has to be your 1928 Chateau Latour Bordeaux."

For the first time, Peter saw Jack surprised beyond words. The resort had only two bottles of 1928 Chateau Latour, and they listed at $2,200 a piece. There was no question that the Hanson's lottery wine was the best the resort had to offer. Peter had never tasted such a wine and suspected that Jack had never had the pleasure, either.

"I'm stunned," Jack admitted. "I guess I expected the Latour and I to grow old here together. Please give us a review of its performance.'

"With pleasure," Betty said. "By the way, we'd like to give all of the couples here one of those disposable cameras that you have in the gift shop *and* the developing. We'd like everyone to remember this wonderful night."

Peter walked them to their table and on his return Jack took him aside and spoke in a low voice.

"Bob Perkins wants to deliver the morning room service to the Smith party," he told Peter. "Coach him a little, will you?"

"Sure, Jack," he said. "You think they're really up to something in there?"

Jack shrugged and said, "Could be. They're not going anywhere, so I don't want to rush into anything we'll be sorry for later. He just wants a look at them. Ah, here's Mr. Nakamura now."

Jack returned to the entrance to greet Tako Nakamura and Lindsey Redding. Peter took the opportunity to hurry back into the kitchen to check with the chef on the progress of Bradley's Shabu-Shabu dinner. He stepped aside as a room service waiter pushed his fully loaded cart toward the guest room corridor.

"Just a moment," Peter said. "Let me have a look." Peter double-checked the cart to see if everything was complete. One of the toughest challenges of room service was to anticipate the guest's needs. Peter knew it was generally the little things like salt and pepper, steak sauce, cream for the coffee or a soupspoon that made the difference between a great room service presentation and a frustrating one. He noted the order was going to the Smith room, selected a disposable camera from the supply cabinet and placed it on the cart.

"Tell them the Hanson's, the couple who won the lottery, gave cameras and processing to all couples in the hotel. Everything here looks good," Peter said, waving the waiter on. "Don't forget to smile."

The Smith family had been checked into the resort for several days and every meal—breakfast, lunch and dinner—had been served through room service. Peter noticed that, in spite of the excellent weather and magnificent surroundings, none of them had left their room. Smith had checked in on a cash-only basis and because he left no credit card, did not have charging privileges. He paid cash for each room service order and tipped exactly fifteen percent.

Peter thought it was strange, but he was glad for the extra business in room service because part of his monthly bonus was based on achieving sales goals. *Even the camera counts*, he thought, and continued on to help out where he could in the kitchen.

By the time Peter broke free to assist in the dining room, Beverly's was packed and room service was backed up for over an hour. This was not a situation acceptable to Coeur d'Alene's management, but a glance at Jack Bradley's table showed that management was too intent on his guests to worry about anything else. The room service phone was so busy that calls had been diverted to Beverly's hostess station, and as Peter grabbed it for yet another time, he instantly recognized the chilling voice of Veronica Whitcomb herself.

"I've decided to dine in my suite this evening with my two bodyguards," she said.

Peter was relieved. If there was to be a display of drama, he would much rather she perform in her room.

"Very well, Ms. Whitcomb," Peter said. "What will you have?"

"Tell the chef I would like an appetizer of breast of quail wrapped in pancetta sent to my room immediately with a bottle of 1988 Chateau Laville Haut Brion."

Her speech was much slower than usual and thick.

Drunk, Peter thought. *Pity the waiter.*

"Twenty minutes later," she continued, "deliver your hearts of palm salad with raspberry yogurt. For the entree, I'll have Coquille St. Jacques. Also, send a bottle of 1983 Corton-Charlemagne from your cellar. Do you understrand?"

The extra "r" she added to "understand" confirmed for Peter that, in addition to a tough day in an airplane, the "rich witch" had lavishly sampled the full bar set-up he had placed in her suite. There was no mistaking the usual asperity of her voice, but the slurs added an interesting twist. Veronica Whitcomb was really letting her hair down.

Peter noted her order, then asked about the bodyguards.

"What would the gentlemen like to eat?"

"They can eat the same thing that I do and make sure that it's not late," she snapped.

The line went dead as she abruptly hung up.

The one-hour room service wait had now grown by one more order, because there was no way that Peter could let Veronica Whitcomb wait. The thought of her drunk and storming into the dining room gave him the shudders. He personally reviewed the order with the chef and within minutes, a room service waiter was on his way to the Juniper Suite with three appetizers and the dry white French Bordeaux. Peter Harding felt only slightly guilty about not warning the waiter about the harsh peculiarities of Miss Veronica Whitcomb.

Ten

Nakamura loved the special touch of Sapporo Beer and the sushi that was served immediately after the trio had been seated.

"Compi," said Nakamura to Jack as they toasted the beginning of the evening.

"Compi," Jack replied.

The next toast was to their mutual friend, Aki, upon whose suggestion Nakamura had visited Coeur d'Alene. Of course, generous toasts continued throughout the evening as the men, and Lindsey Redding, got better acquainted.

When the boiling Shabu-Shabu broth was brought to the table, Nakamura's practiced neutrality of expression gave way to a broad, satisfied smile. Aki had tipped Jack that, even though Nakamura had traveled the world over many times, he was always homesick for his native Japanese foods. As the evening's toasts moved from beer to sake, Lindsey's knee bumped Jack's all too often and twice her hand brushed his thigh when she reached for her napkin.

Jack did not reciprocate and though he found her increasingly attractive, he thought she risked too much for so little. It would not do to embarrass a warlord in public.

By now, Bradley and Nakamura were dipping the Shabu-Shabu vegetables into the sauces and closing in on the Chivas Regal Scotch and the soup-slurping phase of the dinner. Nakamura commented between bites that the sesame sauce was almost as good as home.

The resort's sommelier approached the table with a bottle of wine.

"Mr. Bradley," he announced, "Mr. and Mrs. Hanson would like you and your party to enjoy this last bottle of 1928 Chateau Latour. It should go well with your Shabu-Shabu, don't you think?"

Jack could scarcely believe his ears. The wine cellar had a stock of just two bottles of this great wine and the Hanson's had purchased both of them tonight. In all his years, Jack had never tasted such a wine. Even though he was successful in his own right, to spend $2,200 for a bottle of wine seemed a bit much.

"This . . . this is very generous," Jack stammered.

"They absolutely insist, Mr. Bradley," said the wine sommelier. "They really want you and your guests to have this." He smiled broadly and added, "And they requested that Peter and I taste it as well."

"This is a rare honor," Jack said.

He tipped his cup of sake toward Earl and Betty and the smiles on their faces and the return tip of their wineglasses convinced Jack that he should accept their generosity. He could see that it made the couple feel very good to share their good fortune with their newfound friends in Coeur d'Alene.

Jack had never tasted a finer wine. It was served perfectly. The sommelier let it breathe in the bottle and then poured the ruby liquid through cheesecloth into a decanter to separate the wine from any sediment in the bottom. Nothing would limit the experience of drinking this magnificent vintage.

Jack gave the honor of tasting to his imperial guest who gratefully accepted. Nakamura studied the cork, which showed no signs of a broken seal, and sniffed it with great delight. The sommelier poured a small amount into Nakamura's glass and the tycoon, handling it by the stem, admired the wine as though it was liquid gold. He carefully examined the rich color and magnificent aroma. After twirling the glass and observing the translucent sheets left on the sides, Nakamura took a proper taste of the Latour. He let it swirl in his mouth for a moment and swallowed with great satisfaction. With his approval, the wine was then poured into Lindsey's glass, then Jack's and finally the honored taster's. Jack and Lindsey repeated the tasting ritual and the trio unanimously agreed that it was the finest wine they had ever tasted.

The three of them stood as Earl and Betty Hanson began to leave the room to return to their suite. Jack introduced his two guests and thanked the Hanson's profusely for their thoughtful gift.

"Now, be sure to save a taste for those two young men," Betty said. "They've both been very good to us here."

"I'll see to it personally, " Jack assured them. "Please let me know if there is anything that I or my staff can do to make your stay more enjoyable."

"I don't see how that would be possible, Mr. Bradley," Betty said. "I'm having the time of my life."

The Hanson's left and as Jack returned to his seat a shrieking voice caught his attention. A party of four, quite late for their reservation, was being seated across the room from him and an attractive blonde was acting as social coordinator.

"Shall we sit boy, girl, boy, girl or girl, boy, girl boy?"

she asked.

She could be the poster child for Airheads of America, Jack thought.

Even though Jack's table was fairly well isolated from the notorious Cannon party, the General Manager could still hear their laughter and boisterous talk across the room. Normally, such noise wouldn't bother him. The sound of people who were having fun was his company's *raison d'être.* Although, in this case Stricklin's information weighed heavily on Jack's mind. He was just a few paces away from a traitor. One who may very well get away with betraying his country in Jack's own hotel, and Jack didn't like it.

Julie Adams, Bob Kent, Eric Cannon and Rory Finley lived it up, but Jack wondered what it would cost the country tomorrow. Both women wore evening dresses cut low and high and both could have graced the pages of many a man's magazine. It appeared to Jack even across the room, that both couples shared not only their food and drink but probably each other, as well. All four had become *very* close personal friends and they didn't care who knew it.

"Mr. Bradley," Lindsey said, her hand on his arm, "is something wrong?"

"No," Jack said, realizing that he'd ignored his guests. "No, nothing's wrong. I was concerned about the noise from that table, but it seems to be harmless fun."

"Here's to harmless fun," Tako said, raising yet another glass.

Lindsey removed her hand to join the toast, but the tingle of her touch remained.

Oh shit, Jack thought, as he sipped the magnificent wine, *I hope I don't do anything stupid.*

Eleven

Mustafa Khadduri lay on his bed and stared at the ceiling, trying not to worry about his family. Propped up as he was, with his arms behind his wiry black hair, Mustafa had a sultan's view across the blue placid lake.

Such a beautiful setting for such treachery, he thought.

Mustafa had always wondered whether something like this would really happen. He'd loved his father and listened to his political tales, not as indoctrination, but entertainment. Mustafa had no interest in politics beyond the local chatter that governed his deli business and his home. But he had promised his father to help if called upon and Mustafa never violated a promise.

When he was a teenager, he'd looked forward to the romance of a call to arms, but now that it was here he felt only depression, anxiety and gut wrenching fear. His stomach was tied in knots and he trembled as he thought of the danger he'd put his family in.

My father did this to us, Mustafa thought.

But the momentary bitterness passed, he didn't have the energy for it. He simply wanted to accomplish his mission and return to his wife and children in Indiana as soon as possible. He hadn't even been able to tell them where he was going or what he was doing, but his wife trusted him and that was all that counted for Mustafa. He could not shake the image of a strange man in his house with his wife and children. Against better judgment, he decided to call.

If I just hear her voice. . .

Jasmine answered on the first ring, as though expecting him. Mustafa heard the click of the extension phone.

"I wanted to hear your voice, "he said.

"I'm so glad," she said. "We are well. The cousin stays in the guestroom and apologizes for his intrusion. You?"

"Homesick," he admitted. "But the business goes well and I'll be home soon. The children?"

"They miss their father. They are in bed already. The cousin plays video games with them and they ask why you left without saying goodbye."

"What do you tell them?"

"That you were doing the will of Allah and so should we by not asking questions."

In spite of his anguish, Mustafa chuckled at this.

"It's true," he said. "Now, I have to go. I love you and I will see you soon."

"I love you, too, Mustafa," she whispered. "Praise Allah."

Then she hung up and the extension hung up. Mustafa was back in his luxury room, more alone than ever. His stomach rumbled.

As long as somebody else is paying, I might as well have a good meal, he thought. *Perhaps Cannon will be in the restaurant and I can get this done quickly.*

He phoned in a reservation, shaved and showered. Then he tried on some new clothes, and headed down to Beverly's.

Tammi, the hostess, greeted him with a warm smile. She had the same dark-eyed impishness that he associated with Jasmine.

"Good evening," Tammi said. "Are you the gentleman who just called for a table for one?"

"Yes," he said, "Mustafa Khadduri."

"Your luck is with you, Mr. Khadduri," she said. "We've been overflowing all evening but we do have a very nice table ready for you."

Mustafa was accustomed to having dinner much earlier, but he would gladly forego food for the prospect of connecting with Eric Cannon. He scanned the room and was surprised that he quickly located Cannon and his party. Like other couples in the dining room, they were photographing each other with one of those cardboard cameras.

"Excuse me, Miss," he said. "Would you point out my table for me?"

"Of course, Mr. Khadduri," she said, and nodded discreetly towards the windows. "It's the nice table by the window, an excellent view."

"That will be perfect, thank you."

Tammi walked him past the Cannon party and pulled out the chair to seat her guest. He hesitated, checking the exits in case of emergency and figuring the best position for monitoring Cannon.

"Mr. Khadduri," Tammi prompted, "this seat will give you an excellent view of the lake and the mountains."

"If you don't mind, I would prefer to sit at the other side of the table. I enjoy watching people."

"Oh, of course, sir. That will be no problem."

Tammi quickly moved the silverware, napkins, water glass and wineglasses to the opposite side of the table.

"Enjoy your dinner."

"Thank you," he said.

Mustafa enjoyed an excellent view of Eric Cannon and

his friends, who were far too involved in their drink and flirtations to notice him. Past the Cannon table, on the other side of the room, sat the only other single diner of the evening. He reminded Mustafa of a detective from Fort Wayne, a faithful customer, who was overwhelmed by middle age, bachelorhood and his career. Mustafa got the feeling that this man was watching Cannon so he decided not to approach Cannon any time this man was around.

Mustafa was pretty sure Cannon did not know him, but the efficiency of the Baathists already had surprised him more than once. Perhaps it was his imagination that Cannon's gaze occasionally flicked toward him. Cannon was expecting contact soon. In spite of his call to Jasmine, and his urgency to get back to his family, Mustafa would be extremely cautious. He resolved to use this evening and the next day to observe Cannon and the stranger carefully. He would gain a better understanding of Cannon's habits before approaching him.

Mustafa remembered the instructions perfectly along with other instructions that had awaited him with his registration packet. He knew Cannon and his three friends were in #364. He took a deep breath and told himself he was poised to serve the cause.

Mustafa ordered rack of lamb and a soothing herb tea and watched the two women at Cannon's table flounce, bounce and jiggle their way through the evening. They aroused him, yes, but he could not see how a man could be seen in public with such women. Jasmine was more beautiful than either of these cheap women. What aroused him about Jasmine was that he was the only one who knew her beauty, cloaked in privacy, for him alone.

He was getting to know Cannon much better by observing him in action. It was surprising to him that a man who seemed so irresponsible could carry top secrets so important to the country. No matter, because the best interests of BISC were now Mustafa's best interests and Eric Cannon's degeneration didn't concern him a bit.

By the time Mustafa ordered his raspberry torte, Cannon was rising again for a trip to the men's room. On an impulse, Mustafa decided to use the moment for a possible contact with the Judas. The other single diner entered the men's room behind them as the two stood side by side at the urinals. Cannon and Mustafa even exchanged greetings. Cannon glanced at Mustafa several times, obviously expecting some sort of introduction, but the mystery man from the dining room was seated in one of the stalls. Mustafa decided to let the close encounter remain just that. He would contact Cannon tomorrow. There was no point in taking a foolish risk on such an important mission. The safety of his family was at stake.

Twelve

Lori was one of Beverly's most experienced servers. She had mastered techniques of service that pleased the guests and sales techniques that pleased the management. She knew that when it was time to sell another round of drinks, all she had to do was make good eye contact with the person most apt to want another drink. That person would, nine times out of ten, say, "You bet!" He'd twirl his index finger in a counterclockwise motion and, in that instant, decide for the entire table. Lori would increase the guest check and her tip. She did not need to employ that technique tonight.

At the Cannon table, several fingers twirled every time she looked up—except for Cannon, who stuck to tonic and lime. Knowing there was a designated driver who would probably only be piloting the elevator, she served the table two or three rounds more than she might have otherwise.

Lori saw the hotel manager, Jack Bradley, looking her way several times. The two couples were getting louder and even more indiscreet, so it was time to drop their check and let them get on with their evening in the privacy of their own rooms.

The bill was just under nine hundred dollars and only Cannon reached for it.

"I forgot my guest card," he said. "Do you trust me?"

"I trust you, Mr. Cannon, but I have to have the number to close this out in the computer. We can't do it by room number alone."

"Don't sweat it, Lori, our charge number is 31496F6311. Punch that into your computer, and it'll show Eric Cannon, room #364." He took a confident swig of his tonic.

Lori didn't get the whole number the first time and Cannon repeated it. To her amazement, the computer clearly displayed the name Eric Cannon, room #364 and the other pertinent data. When she reported the results to the table, the young women were equally surprised.

"How in the world did you remember that number, Eric?" Rory asked. "I have trouble with my social security number."

Cannon tilted his head to the side and raised a partially open hand in what he must have thought was a sophisticated gesture.

Bob Kent answered for him.

"It's something Eric's been able to do since he was little. Once he sees a series of numbers, he never forgets them."

"It's the only way I got through nuclear physics and all that crap. Hell, most of those guys in the academy were a lot smarter than me, but I was able to remember all those tricky formulas perfectly. I couldn't miss!"

"Is that why you don't drink?" Julie asked. "I thought maybe it's the allergies."

"They say it's something you lose as you get older," Cannon said. "I don't intend to hurry it along any."

"A photographic memory," Rory said, "You've got a

photographic memory? That's incredible."

The four celebrants stumbled out of Beverly's to their connecting rooms to continue what Lori suspected would become a continuing orgasmic event for all.

Thirteen

Peter Harding checked the ticket and realized it was time for Veronica Whitcomb's entree to be sent to her room. It had been seventeen minutes since the appetizers had left the kitchen. The coquille was just coming out of the oven and would be ready to be served within seconds. Not a room service waiter was in sight because they were all busy making other deliveries. Peter grabbed the cart that had been previously set up by the room service dispatcher for the Juniper Suite, checked for details and placed the three hot entrees under cover in the lower heated portion of the cart. It certainly was not above him, as the resort's food and beverage manager, to make a room service delivery himself. After all, outstanding personal service is what the resort was known for. He remembered the Hansons' offer and added a disposable camera to the tray.

Peter knocked on the door to the Juniper suite and glanced at his watch. He was pleased he was within one minute of the delivery gauntlet that had been laid down by

Ms. Whitcomb.

"Come in."

Peter opened the door that had been left wedged ajar to allow admittance.

"You're two minutes late. Serve it here in the bedroom," Whitcomb's voice commanded.

Peter dutifully rolled the cart through the spacious living area into the suite's master bedroom. As he entered, he suddenly stopped, took a step backward and in shock, stared at the canopied king-size master bed. Sandwiched between the two muscular bodyguards, barely under the sheets, Veronica Whitcomb flashed him a devilishly seductive smile and a full helping of curves in black lace. This was a scene totally at odds with the chic socialite image she tried so hard to portray. She was now the queen surrounded by her yoked Knights of the Round Table. Her black hair flowed back toward the pillows. Her warm eyes sparkled with mischievousness. Peter saw the outline of her shapely legs under the sheets as she spread them and rubbed their muscular legs with her toes. The perfectly constricting strings of lace accentuated the cleavage of her rounded breasts. Both of her hands disappeared under the satin sheets and Peter could only imagine their intended targets.

Rumors had abounded in the hotel for years, since the death of her wealthy father, that Ms. Whitcomb's assortment of bodyguards provided far more than just protection, but the scene was still a jolt for Peter. The resort had experienced its share of room service stories over the years—a server walking in on naked guests or those engaged in intimate activities—but this was the story of stories.

Ms. Whitcomb, obviously tipsy, was not one bit embarrassed. Her speech, however, required some concentration on her part.

"My escorts and I will partake over here," she said.

Peter placed the cart to the side of the bed and the muscleman closest to him rolled his eyes as if to say, "it's a living."

Talk about the ultimate gigolos, Peter thought.

He picked up the half-finished appetizer plates from the nightstands and poured the Corton-Charlemagne for each to enjoy. He concentrated on his task and on not staring.

"Sign my name and add a 25% tip," Ms. Whitcomb said. "Don't worry about dessert, I've brought my own!"

She laughed and made a two-handed grab under the sheets. The two hulks jerked upward in surprise.

Thank you, God; I've seen it all, Peter thought.

"Yes, Ma'am," was all he said as he hurried back to Beverly's. He cracked a smile as his mind recreated the scene that he had just witnessed. Then his thoughts returned to work.

"I hope they've served Bradley the Shabu-Shabu noodle soup," he mumbled to himself.

He was relieved to find that the Hanson's generosity had totally changed the timetable for Bradley's special dinner. As Peter re-entered Beverly's, he noticed Eric Cannon and a haggard-looking Middle-Eastern man coming out of the men's room. Peter watched as Cannon rejoined his table and the Middle-Eastern man walked quietly to his table alone. He remarked to himself on the tremendous difference between the solo man enjoying such a pleasant, quiet dinner and the raucous, uninhibited display of Cannon's party.

It's the only world we've got, he reminded himself, *and it takes all kinds*.

Louis, one of the room service waiters, silently prepared another cart. His downcast silence was a marked change from his usual cheerful demeanor. Louis was usually the kitchen clown, keeping everyone else up and on the go.

"What's up, Louis?" he asked.

Louis reached into his jacket pocket and, without explanation, handed Peter one of the disposable cameras. It was twisted in half.

"What happened?"

"The Smith party," Louis said. "They seemed fine, watching a movie. The baby was asleep on the bed beside them, so when I finished setting up their dinner, I showed them the camera and offered to take a family portrait. Mr. Smith jumped up, grabbed the camera, broke it and threw it at me. Said if he wanted his picture taken, he could damned well afford to have it done right."

"I'm sorry to hear that, Louis. How did you handle it?"

"I don't remember exactly what I said, I was so flustered. But I did apologize and just tried to get out of there as fast as I could. Mrs. Smith followed me to the door to pay me. She gave me an extra twenty and started to apologize. He pulled her back into the room, yelling that nobody had to apologize for him. I was just glad to get out of there."

"Well, I'm sorry you had to go through that, Louis. You did the right thing. Before you leave tonight, report what happened to security. Do you still have that twenty?"

"Yeah," he said, "right here."

Louis fished the bill out of his tip pocket. Peter exchanged it for one in his own wallet.

"I'll call over to security now and see whether Bob Perkins stuck around tonight. This is something he would want to hear."

Louis finished the preparations on his cart and Peter checked it over. He saw that Louis had placed a camera on the tray.

"Getting right back on that horse?" he asked.

"Yes, sir," Louis said. "That's my job."

"Then don't forget to smile."

"I won't forget as long as I stay out of the line of fire."

Peter wrote down the serial number and denomination of the bill and then set it aside in his wallet.

I should have done this when I checked for counterfeit, he thought. *I'll have the staff save any bills he gives us from now until this is cleared up.*

Peter called security, but Bob Perkins had gone home. When he returned to the dining room, he found that Bradley's party had retired, too.

Oh, well, he thought. *It'll keep.*

Fourteen

Jack woke to the pulse of his alarm and the insistent throb of a hangover that would measure a six on the Richter scale. The first hint of light crested the mountaintop outside his window through which he could look out across at the resort. He was thankful that his daybreak appointment was for golf and not racquetball. He lurched into the bathroom, downed two aspirin and two antihistamines, then propped himself up in the shower and let the magic steam do its stuff.

What must Nakamura feel like? He wondered. *He downed at least twice as many as I did.*

He had less than a half-hour to make it back to the resort before Clint Diamond touched down at the clubhouse in Marco's chopper.

With Diamond, the Senator, and Nakamura, this would be a very special game of golf. Jack had always loved the sport but wasn't addicted to it like some. It was great fun and an excellent way to build business relations at the same time. Jack wasn't sure whether Nakamura would feel like golfing, but he knew the Senator wouldn't miss it no matter how much he'd put away the night before.

Jack's medication started to kick in and by the time he'd shaved and dressed, he was feeling pretty good. The pine air invigorated him, and he drove to the resort's award winning golf course with his window open so that he could listen to the birds. His car phone beeped him out of nature and into business. He punched the hands free speaker.

"It's Perkins," his security chief announced.

"Yes, Bob."

"I checked with my buddies over at the sheriff's department about the Smith couple who pay cash. They think we've got a possible 10-85 suspect here. Two, counting the wife."

"What the hell's a 10-85, Bob?" Jack asked, with a sigh. He didn't know the police call codes Bob and his staff used and he wished they would just speak English.

"It's a robbery suspect, Jack. Last week the Bank of Montana was hit at St. Regis. Two days later, the First National Bank of the West in Colby was hit. Three days ago, First National at Kellogg was nailed. The security camera at St. Regis got a so-so picture of the guy and FBI is faxing one here to the sheriff's office. Richard Portman checked Smith in two days ago and his description of Smith fits the FBI description of the suspect."

"What now?" Jack asked. "We don't want any disturbance in the hotel . . . "

"That's why I called. Smith called in their breakfast order last night to room service, for 11AM. I'd like to go ahead with our plan and serve him. That'll get me a good look and by then the sheriff should have the picture to me for comparison."

Jack hated having the resort involved in these types of hassles. Legal problems were few, and usually petty. But Jack knew busting bad guys was what Perkins and his staff lived for. From his Naval Intelligence days, he even remembered something akin to what Perkins was now feeling. Like the Canadian Mounted Police, Bob wanted to get his man, but Jack's concern was operating a quiet, first-class, five-star resort. He rubbed the bridge of his nose as he drove, trying to think his way past the muddle of Nakamura, Stricklin, Cannon, and now this.

"Okay," Jack said, "but let's keep this thing low key. I don't want a damned firefight erupting in the resort. Make sure you keep your cool, Bob, and keep me informed. The sheriff is with you on this?"

"Absolutely. I'll keep you posted. They don't list a car on their registration so one of our people is double-checking license plates in the garage and nearby lots with the sheriff, just in case."

"I'll be out on the course," Jack said. "Be careful and be legal."

"Will do, boss."

Jack pulled up to the clubhouse as the chopper was settling onto the pad. Between the hangover and Perkins' call, he felt pretty tense. A brisk round of golf in the early morning mountain air would take care of that.

Jack saw the *Eagle,* one of the resort's pair of speedboats, pull into the slip with Senator Wilder and Tako Nakamura on board. The Coeur d'Alene featured *Eagle* and *Double Eagle,* the matched pair of Honduran mahogany shuttlecraft, to get golfers quickly from the resort to the course. Sometimes after an intense people day, Jack took one of the boats out for a moonlight spin on the lake.

Wilder was a dedicated public servant whose life had been spent in serving others. But he had the same basic instincts of all politicians, self-preservation and re-election. This golf game would introduce him to two powerful men and Jack was very curious to see how this game would play out.

Jack drove his blue custom golf cart to meet the lanky movie star as he stepped out of the chopper.

"Good to have you back, Mr. Diamond. I hope this time you can stay awhile."

"Hello, Jack."

Diamond's handshake, like his voice and his gaze, was firm.

"Actually, I have a meeting at the hotel with the producer of my next film. But I have to fly out this afternoon. I have to make some money, Jack. You got me so excited about this hotel business that I'm buying my own resort. Maybe you could give me a little advice if I promise not to take your money today."

"Advice is cheap," Jack said, "but this game's going to cost you. Our partners are just getting in on the *Eagle.*"

Diamond wore a blue Ashworth golf sweater along with Oakley sunglasses and a broad-brimmed hat to mask his identity from autograph hounds. No matter how early, late or surreptitiously Clint Diamond arrived, word always got out and the fans followed. Fortunately, he had never been accosted while golfing with Jack. This good fortune made him comfortable enough to keep coming back, even if he had to fly round-trip from California just for the game. Diamond's flight time was never wasted. His cellular phone and a pile of scripts kept him plenty busy. He swung himself into the cart and they met the others at the slip.

"Mr. Diamond, let me present our guest from Japan, Mr. Tako Nakamura."

Tako looked none the worse for wear and he shook the star's hand with the enthusiasm of a teenager.

"Very pleased to meet you, sir," Nakamura said, and bowed. "I have seen all of your pictures. They bring us much pleasure in Japan."

"Thank you," Diamond said, returning the bow. "I'm

happy to hear that."

Jack turned to the Senator.

"And our state's great United States Senator, Carl Wilder. Mr. Clint Diamond."

Diamond and Senator Wilder shook hands. Wilder, too, seemed dazzled to be in the presence of such a popular figure.

"Mr. Diamond, if you're as successful on the course as you are at the box office, we're in for a heap of trouble this morning."

"Senator, I have heard great things about you and not just from our friend Jack. So, let's start this friendship by you calling me Clint and not Mr. Diamond."

"Fair enough. I'm Carl, this is Tako and time's a wasting."

Jack envied the Senator's ability to make everybody comfortable. He'd only met Tako on the boat ride over from the hotel and already they were old friends.

The skipper of *Eagle* delivered the visitors' golf clubs to the bag room as the foursome changed from street shoes to soft spikes.

Diamond explained further how his visit had come about.

"You met my associate, Dick Roberts, on my last trip, Jack. We're so excited about The Coeur d'Alene that we're buying a resort together on the California coast."

Jack noticed that Nakamura hung on every word.

"I hope it doesn't mean we won't be seeing you any more after it goes through," Jack said.

Diamond laughed.

"Well, we both figured if you can be as successful as you are up here in the wilderness, we'd better damn well get up here and find out some of your secrets. Of course, it'll wind up being one more project for me to get away from."

"Well, I am complimented," Jack admitted. "But the

real secret is simple—you have to treat it like it's your own home and you have to love company. Maybe next time I pry myself away from here I'll get to take your money on your own course."

"Fat chance," Diamond said. "But you're welcome anytime you want to try."

"I don't know about Tako, here," Jack said, "but Senator Wilder and I are not quite in your league, golf wise. You know, we can only golf up here about half the year and down south, you get to play year round."

"Uh oh, Tako, I can feel a wager coming on," cautioned the movie star.

Nakamura smiled. It was a very confident smile.

"All right," the Senator said. "Let's get down to it."

"What's your true handicap, Clint?"

"I'm an eighteen."

"Tako?"

"Twelve."

"All right. That's perfect," Wilder said. "Jack and I will take you on with no strokes, since we're both around fifteen."

"Perfect," Clint said.

"Tako, I've got two carts or four caddies on standby," Jack said. "Would you prefer to ride or walk?"

"Walk."

"Definitely walk," Clint agreed. "I've already done a half-day's work on the plane and my legs need stretching."

"Great, I'll set it up. The Senator will ride because of his tender hip and the three of us will walk. What are the stakes, gentlemen?"

After the obligatory 4 or 5 minutes of posturing and sandbagging they agreed on the wager and the match was ready to begin.

As they walked outside, Senator Wilder started one of

his famous stories for the star's benefit.

"You know, I was playing that famous water hole awhile back with this old fellow—you know, hitting the cup on a green that's floating out in the lake is pretty damned tricky, you'll see."

Jack chuckled to himself. Carl was seventy-three and Jack wondered what his definition of an "old fellow" might be.

"Oh, yeah?" Diamond said, graciously playing the straight man, "What happened?"

"Well, the old man teed off with a brand new ball and put it in the water to the left of the green. He took another brand new ball and put it in the water to the right of the green. He took another brand new ball and was short, another brand new ball and was long . . . all of them smack into the water. Finally, after watchin' all this, I asked the old geezer, 'Why in the heck don't you just use an old ball?'"

The Senator paused for effect.

"Hell," the old-timer said, "I've never had one!" The foursome laughed and relaxed as the good-natured badgering and story telling continued with the game. The morning was picture perfect. A slight breeze off the lake kept them cool in the mountain sunshine. A few puffy white clouds dotted the clear blue sky and the air was fresh and clean. Jack's hangover remained at bay and Tako's game seemed unaffected by the previous evening's celebrations.

Diamond hit his ball into an enormous trap on the thirteenth hole.

"What club do you think I ought to use, Senator?" he asked.

"I don't know what club you should use," quipped the Senator, "but take along plenty of food and water!"

During the game, both Diamond and Nakamura quizzed Jack about the hotel business.

Jack's responses were easy for him because of his philosophy that finding, motivating, and retaining great people who wanted to buy into the resort's philosophy of creating "Great Guest Moments."

Nakamura nodded his approval.

"That's a great philosophy," complimented Diamond.

Without looking up, the movie star swung mightily and badly sliced his shot into the woods. He swore, but didn't miss a beat of the conversation.

"How ya hitting 'em boys?"

The resort's popular director of golf called to them from the golf marshal's cart. Michael D. Short had headed up The Coeur d'Alene's golf program since the course had opened over ten years ago. Jack had never seen him without a smile and his greeting was always the same.

"Mike, I would like you to meet Tako Nakamura, of course you know our good friends, Senator Wilder and Clint Diamond."

"You bet I do. Mr. Nakamura, it's great to have you out here. Mr. Diamond, Senator, welcome back."

Short had the look of a professional athlete. Tall, good-looking and well tanned, he was one of the most likeable people in a resort filled with likeable people.

"Anything we can do to help?" offered Mike. "Are you remembering to turn your left hand over on the club, boss?"

"I'm trying," Jack said. "Actually, Mike, my short game is really good today.'

"Oh, yeah?"

"Yeah, but unfortunately, it's off the tee."

Nakamura laughed a beat behind the others, and louder. Jack realized that Nakamura thought it polite to acknowledge Jack's humor in front of Mike, Jack's employee. In that moment, Jack understood that Tako Nakamura did not joke with his staff.

"Who lives in the big house, Mike?" asked Clint.

He sighted down a five iron towards a massive wood and glass home overlooking the lake and the course. A long grass pathway wound its way from the front entry staircase through the beach to a long dock and boat slips.

"It's owned by a Mr. Von Bueller, Max Von Bueller. He owns The Coeur d'Alene Resort, among many other interests."

"I've never met the man," Wilder said, "and I've been coming here since you opened."

"He's very private," Jack said. "He stays completely secluded."

"Perhaps he has your philosophy, Jack," Nakamura said.

"Which one is that, Tako?"

"Choose the best people for your needs, and stay out of their way. I find that works for me, as well."

"How old is Von Bueller?" Clint asked.

"Mid-eighties," Jack said. "And he's very mysterious. Take the deal he's made with Mike, for example. Mike?"

Mike scratched his head. "Well he said, it's sure made him popular here at the clubhouse. Whenever Mr. Von Bueller plays, which is seldom, one hole ahead of him and one hole behind him is kept open. He books twelve tee times so he can have his privacy. He never golfs with anybody else, just two bodyguards and occasionally me or one of our instructors. He never speaks except for questions about the game. He doesn't allow suggestions unless he specifically asks for them."

"Boy, he really wants to be left alone," said Clint. " What an eccentric way to play golf and what a way to live life to its emptiest."

"Yep," Mike said. "He's made a deal with his favorite caddy. He pays Scott two hundred dollars a day—every day of the year, whether he plays or not—just so Scott's always available. I've never seen him inside the resort. Mostly he shuttles back and forth to the airport. He uses three identical black limousines with smoked glass. That way nobody can tell which one he's in."

"What is he, some sort of Mafioso or something?" Clint joked.

Jack caught a glimpse of something dark that washed over Tako's face, swallowed just as quickly by his neutral mask, and quickly changed the subject, "Well, gentlemen, one more hole? Let's seal our fates and then enjoy some lunch."

Their wager came down to the final green, where each was playing bogey. Tako's putt slipped the rim of the cup and his opponents magnanimously gave him the final stroke. Jack sank a five-footer to push the Senator and himself into the lead. Clint matched the challenge, so everything rode on the putter of the senior Senator. Two decades of lobbyist hospitality showed in the shake of the good Senator's hands as they gripped his putter. The air was so still that Jack heard the wheeze in the old man's nostrils as he breathed.

Three erratic putts later, the industrialist and the movie star pocketed Jack's money.

"Jack, damn it, I'm sorry," Wilder said. "I blew this one for us."

The two of them walked slowly to the cart and a pale, huffing Senator climbed into the seat.

"Are you kidding?" Jack said. "Your strategy was perfect. Clint Diamond leaves our golf course a winner. He'll talk us up even more. Missing that putt on purpose was brilliant."

The Senator grinned and held out his hand. "Hell, since you put it that way, I guess it was."

Jack shook the Senator's hand vigorously.

"If you ever need PR work, young man, look me up."

Jack laughed at the Senator's obvious compliment.

"You know why they call it 'golf,' don't you, Senator?"

"Why is that?"

"Because when it came time to name such a frustrating sport, all the other four-letter words were taken."

"You're absolutely right. This doggoned golf is such an aggravating, frustrating game. I sure am glad I don't have to play it again until tomorrow!"

Jack joined the others aboard *Eagle* for the trip back to the resort and lunch. As they approached the marina, the skipper handed him the cellular phone with Bob Perkins on the line.

"Jack, we've got us a situation," Perkins said. "Get Marco Rivers and his chopper up here as quick as you can."

Jack felt an old sickness squeeze his belly.

"What is it?"

"It's Mr. Smith," Perkins said. "He's invited me and the Hansons for a little sightseeing flight."

Jack moved as far away from the others as he could on such a small boat, then cupped his hand around the mouthpiece and whispered into the phone.

"Bob, if you're in danger, tell me what time it is."

"Eleven-twenty seven," Bob said his voice tight. "And we're already late."

Fifteen

Bob Perkins swallowed hard and tried to control the quiver in his voice. He was scared, the nine-millimeter muzzle that tapped the back of his head made sure of that. From the balcony of Smith's room, Perkins watched *Eagle* nuzzle up to the pier. Smith's cellular phone was sweaty in his grip, so Bob carefully, slowly switched hands.

"Marco's gone for the day," Bradley told him. "He's flying somebody up to Canada."

Bob repeated the message to Smith, who didn't hesitate for a blink.

"Then I want that boat," Smith said. "And the manager, I want him, too. Have him put the boat someplace where we can get to it without a lot of attention. Keep the phone line open; I want to hear everything he says."

Bob relayed the message to Bradley, who sent his passengers and the skipper up to lunch without him. Bob couldn't exactly relax with a gun to his head, but he breathed a little easier knowing the Senator, the industrialist and the actor would not add to Smith's hostage supply.

If Smith only knew what was slipping through his fingers right now, Bob thought.

Then he tried to unthink it so they wouldn't be jinxed.

Bob pretended to cover the phone's mouthpiece and leaned over to Smith.

"That boat's not big enough for everybody," Bob said, trying to stall.

"Then I'll just have to shoot somebody, won't I?" Smith answered. "Don't jerk me around, stupid, I got eyes."

Jack Bradley came back on the line. His voice was flat, serious and focused.

"Don't challenge him. Agree to anything he wants. I'll come around to the eastside and pull into the cruise boat slips. You can come right out the back door and down the handicap ramp to the boardwalk."

"Tell him to take it slow and stay on the phone," Smith said. "We have some packing to do."

Bob and Smith stood at the doorway to the balcony, where Smith could watch Bradley's progress in *Eagle.* Mrs. Smith and the Hansons packed more money than Bob had ever seen in one place into their pillowcases, two backpacks and four suitcases. Smith had them hide the pillowcases and backpacks under a tablecloth on the room service cart. Mrs. Smith emptied the baby's diaper bag and stuffed it with packs of twenties and hundreds. She carried the bag and baby and made the Hansons carry the suitcases.

"Okay," Smith said, "tell your man to start counting so I know he's on the line. If he stops counting before we see him outside, you're dead."

Bob relayed the message and Smith laid the phone down on top of the tablecloth, where they all could hear Bradley counting over the grumble of *Eagle's* engine. Smith walked beside Bob as he pushed the cart down the hallway and into the elevator.

When they reached the lobby they took the back hallway, which led to the recreation center and spa.

Bob had been so confident of his role that he had not arranged for backup. He'd expected to simply shove a cart into the room, get paid for the meal and leave after getting a good look around. He had not seen Peter's report from the night before about the smashed camera. Nor was he aware the room service waiter had explained the camera was a gift from the Hansons who had just won the Illinois State Lottery.

Smith seemed to smell opportunity. He had called the Hansons to thank them for the camera. He invited the Hansons to their room for a champagne breakfast, on the pretext that the baby was fussy and they didn't want to disturb anyone in the restaurant. Smith told them he wanted pictures of the baby with them for good luck.

When Bob knocked on the door and entered with the room service cart Smith recognized him. He had seen him in his security uniform when they checked into the resort and Smith never forgot the face of a cop. The bank robber was already jittery and agitated and the sight of a security man in a room service uniform spooked him. He knew he needed to get out of the Resort and he didn't care how, just how fast. With no bird available, the boat was the next best thing.

The trip from the room to the ramp had taken less than three minutes. Smith kept his weapon aimed at Perkins and the Hansons but concealed it with the baby's blanket.

"You," Smith told Bob, "toss that stuff from your cart into the boat. You," he nodded at Mr. Hanson, "you catch them. Becky, honey, you get where you can cover everybody and stay there. You," Smith nodded at Jack Bradley, "step back from the controls and do only what I tell you."

It took Bob less than a minute to toss the stuff to Mr. Hanson and, at Smith's command, to get aboard. Smith pushed them off and scrambled in.

"South into open water, Mr. Big-Shot," Smith ordered. "And don't attract attention."

Without a word, Jack eased the boat away from the dock, the big engines sounding like impatient horses wanting to run. They were only a few hundred yards from shore when Smith handed Mr. Hanson one of the cellular phones. That was when the baby started crying.

"Call your bank," Smith said, "and punch up a transfer for one million dollars to our account. Becky, give him the account number and *shut that baby up!*"

Mr. Hanson stared at the phone in his palm like it was a dead rat.

"I can't do it," he said. "The money's not there."

Smith shoved the pistol into Earl Hanson's face and Bob almost made his move but was stopped by the nearly imperceptible shake of Bradley's head. Then he realized that Mrs. Smith had anticipated his move, covering him with his back-up pistol even as she juggled the baby, trying to shush it.

"You're going to have to watch everybody while I dig out a deposit slip," Becky told her husband.

The baby's crying escalated into screams and Smith got even more agitated.

"Shut her up, or I'll do it for you," Smith snarled.

"She's scared," Becky snapped. "Let her cry, she's not hurting anything. Damn! Here it is."

She handed Earl Hanson their deposit slip and it was becoming obvious to Bob that none of them were going to survive this cruise.

"Now, what do you mean, the money's not there?"

"We don't keep a million dollars in checking, or even savings," Earl said. He shrugged. "It's a waste of money."

"How much *do* you have in there?"

"Maybe twenty-five thousand, tops," Earl said. "Anything else, we both have to go in and sign for it."

"Get it," Smith ordered and thrust the cell phone toward Earl.

The baby had screamed herself nearly rigid and Becky could barely hold onto the struggling form. She dropped the diaper bag and covered the baby's mouth with her free hand while keeping the pistol pointed at Bob's chest.

Then Smith turned his attention and pistol on his wife. "You shut that brat up or I'll shut her up for good!"

While the two were arguing, Jack eased the boat around so the sun was in Smith's eyes.

"Shut up, yourself!" Becky snapped. "You're crazy! You haven't slept for four days and you're plain nuts. The baby's not hurting anyone, so just back off."

Smith cracked. His color went from red to pasty white and he gritted his teeth so hard that Bob could hear them grind. Smith's breathing came faster, shallower, and his sunken eyes squinted.

"You dumb bitch, you've been pissin' me off from the start."

The baby caught her breath and screamed again, arching her back, kicking and flailing her arms at her mother. Mrs. Smith shifted the pistol to her other hand and was trying to shift the baby to her other arm when her pistol accidentally went off, barely missing Smith.

"You dirty little bitch," Smith said, "you tried to kill me!"

"No," she said, "I . . .

But that's as far as she got. Smith shot her point-blank, dead center of her forehead, spattering blood and brains all over the cockpit of *Eagle*.

Sixteen

As Becky's instantly dead body fell, Mrs. Hanson instinctively reached to cushion the baby's fall. As if directed by a higher force, the child fell straight into her protective arms.

"Throw her overboard, " Smith said.

"No," Betty Hanson said. "I won't do that."

Smith took a step toward her and slipped on the gory mess spreading on the deck. Jack yanked the flare pistol out of his belt and fired point blank into Smith's chest. The flare knocked the crook off balance and stuck, burning, to his shirt and skin.

That was when something overcame Jack. Something big and dark that he hadn't felt in years. Jack screamed, snatched Smith's pistol out of his hand and stuck it to Smith's neck as both men fell to the deck. Jack screamed again, his face right up to Smith's nose and this time he slammed the pistol through a couple of teeth and into Smith's mouth. The flare still burned between them and the air was filled with the stench of burned flesh.

The red smoke cut visibility to zero and Jack began to choke, but he held tight as Smith continued to struggle underneath him, not to get away but to tear the burning flare out of his chest. Jack stuck his head up for air, then knelt on Smith's throat and smashed the pistol against his nose, flattening it against his cheek. Smith slowed his struggle, his eyes bulging and unseeing, and at Bob's urging Jack started to come back to reality. Bob Perkins had control of Mrs. Smith's gun and a fire extinguisher, which he sprayed on Smith's chest and on the chunk of flare that still burned on the deck.

"Back off, Jack," he was saying. "He's not going anywhere, boss, back off." Bob looked at Jack with more fear than he'd looked at Smith. Jack staggered backwards to the rail and leaned there, wavering, while he covered Smith with his own gun.

"Bring up some line from the anchor well," Jack whispered. He didn't blink, or twitch. Smith stared cockeyed at the gun muzzle and gagged trying to catch his breath. Bob came up with the line.

"Secure this prisoner," Jack whispered, "before I break down and shoot him. You've never seen me break down, have you, Bob?"

Jack felt out of time, out of emotion. He had forgotten this feeling which he had experienced only twice in his life. It was a feeling both frightening and liberating. He held a steady stern look at Smith's eyes and the gun muzzle to Smith's bloody face. Jack's own voice sounded to him as emotionless as a shell casing.

Bob rolled Smith onto his side and wrapped him up. Mr. Hanson already had the 9-1-1 dispatch on the cell phone. Betty Hanson rocked the baby in her arms while she searched the diaper bag.

"This little one's just hungry," she muttered.

Betty pulled handfuls of bills, packs of twenties and hundreds, out of the bag, but she didn't find a bottle for the baby. Suddenly, with a guttural cry of anger and frustration that surprised everyone, she grabbed the strap of the diaper bag and flung it, money and all into the lake. The baby laughed.

And when the baby laughed, Jack relaxed for the first time. He didn't look at the mess on the deck, but at his hands, which now trembled so vigorously that he had to clench them together to make them stop. Bob was on the phone, now, and the sheriff's patrol boat was coming alongside. He had no idea how long they'd been out there. Time meant nothing anymore.

Jack listened from a long, long way off as Bob reported what happened.

"This man shot his wife," Bob nodded to the body. "Mr. Bradley stopped him from shooting Mrs. Hanson. Took the damned gun right away from him and laid him out on the deck. Jack, where the hell did you get the flare gun?"

"While you were in the elevator, I continued counting so I could be heard over the cell phone. I knew I could be heard and not seen so I opened the shuttle craft's emergency kit and took out the flare pistol. Still counting, I dropped a red flare into the chamber and slipped the pistol into the back of my pants. It worked."

All Jack could do was stare out over the placid, sun-dappled lake and into the mountains beyond while a deputy piloted the *Eagle* back to its roost.

Seventeen

Senator Carl Wilder was singing Johnny Cash's "Long Black Veil" in the shower. He liked to sing in spite of his rotten voice, so he'd found it best to sing in the shower. In between chorus and verse he heard the insistent ring of the phone. *It never fails*, he thought.

Phones seem to know when he was crooning in the shower. Maybe phones hated his singing too. Wilder had just finished a heavy head-to-toe lather and placed the bar of Caswell Massey on the soap dish, but it slipped to the marble floor. Wilder put his head under the running water and washed away most of the soap from the shoulders up. He grabbed The Coeur d'Alene bathrobe that was laid out and picked up the extension on the bathroom wall. The room was all tile and mirrors and his voice sounded like he was in an echo chamber.

"Hello, Carl Wilder here."

"Senator, this is Pat Douglas calling from the NFIP in Washington."

Wilder wiped soap from his eyes with the oversized sleeve of the robe.

"The hell you say! It took you long enough to return my call, Douglas!"

The Senator knew Douglas had been informed the exact instant he had called, but Douglas decided to play the age-old power game and make him stew for a while before he called back. It was no secret that Douglas considered himself the head of the nation's most important agency and Wilder just another Senatorial nuisance from a potato state. A junior legislator might have had to wait days, or even weeks, before he'd get a call back from Pat Douglas.

"I'm sorry, Senator, I've been in some crucial meetings and just got your message."

"Bullshit! You've probably been drinking martinis and eating quiche."

Actually, the Senator knew it would have been Heineken and bratwurst, but the jab was enough to draw silence from Douglas.

"I called you, Douglas, because I understand you've got an agent here in Idaho at The Coeur d'Alene Resort asking questions of my friend, Jack Bradley, who manages this place. He's a damned good friend of mine and I don't want him hassled. Now, what's the story?"

"Senator, if we had an agent there I would not discuss it with you on this phone at this time. I'm sure you realize that if one of our people were in place it would indicate an extremely delicate national security mission. And if we had such an agent there, you know very well that I couldn't tell you anything except through an authorized scramble or face-to-face."

"Don't be cute with me, Douglas, I'm the money-man for your agency and I want to know why you're mounting an operation inside the country instead of turning it over to the

FBI as the law requires."

The Senator swiped at his wet hair with the other sleeve of his robe and laid a towel across the bathroom floor to stand on while he dripped and fumed.

"Senator, all I can say is this. It is unfortunate that you're staying at that hotel at this time. I think it would be better if you checked out immediately. I have taken the liberty of dispatching one of our Lear jets from Andrews Air Force Base to pick you up and fly you out of there."

Senator Wilder bristled and felt his face flush.

"Oh, you have, have you?" he growled. "Look, I don't have any desire to go back to DC right now. We're on recess and I'm going to relax a little, right here."

"Senator, I must insist that you evacuate the premises. It simply isn't prudent for you to be there at this time. Look, I respect the fact that you need to take a little time off. We've got an account at the Broadmoor in Colorado Springs that we use for our special agents when they're in need of a little R & R. We'll take you there and pay all your expenses, including golf. Senator, I must insist that you leave The Coeur d'Alene as soon as possible. I can't explain the reasons why at this time and over this phone, but I will give you a complete report at the appropriate moment."

"Send a couple of these expense account agents over here to baby-sit me, if you're worried."

"That would complicate things, Senator. Your presence and additional security presence might turn a nervous man rabbit. I don't care what committees you're on, Senator, and I don't care what you think of me, personally. When that plane arrives, I strongly suggest you get on it."

"Douglas, you pompous ass," Carl said. He kicked his wet towel across the room. "I'll go to Colorado, but you've got a lot of explaining to do. When I get back to my office we're going to have a little inquiry into how you throw your weight around. Then we'll have a look-see at where the hell you get the money to fly Lear jets and maintain agency accounts at fancy resorts. You and your heavy-handed tactics don't scare me, Douglas. I've seen plenty of you come and go and I'll see one more out the door before I'm through."

Wilder slammed the phone into its cradle. *Who the hell does that ass think he is?*

The phone rang again, and startled him. "Wilder," he snapped.

"Senator Wilder? This is Christine in Mr. Bradley's office. He's been delayed by an emergency and suggests that you and the others have lunch without him. He's arranged the private dining room for your convenience."

"I hope he's all right. What kind of emergency?"

Christine sounded pretty excited and he realized she'd been dying to tell him.

"Well, Senator, it looks like we've had our first hostage situation."

"Hostage situation?"

He wondered whether this had anything to do with his conversation with Pat Douglas, but there was no one he could ask.

"I hope it'll be your last one, too," Carl said. "What happened? Is everyone all right?"

"Mr. Bradley is a little shaken up, but he's okay. He and Bob Perkins are finishing their statements to the sheriff right now. One of the kidnappers shot the other one, but no hostages were hurt."

"You mean, this all happened while I've been in the shower?"

He heard a slightly muffled giggle at the other end.

"It happened pretty fast, Senator. None of us had any idea what was going on. Mr. Bradley got the whole thing away from the hotel right away."

"Thank God they're okay," the Senator said. "Listen, tell Mr. Bradley that we'll wait lunch for him. I wouldn't miss this story for the world."

"I'd like to hear the whole thing myself," Christine said. "I'll give him your message, and I'll inform the others in your party."

Carl hung up the phone in time to answer it again. This time it was his staffer, Ron Larson, who had heard rumors of a hostage taking and was worried that it might be his boss. Carl reassured him, then informed Larson that he would be flying to Colorado in a couple of hours.

Ten minutes later Carl Wilder joined Nakamura and Diamond in the private dining room off the main floor of Beverly's. The single table was surrounded on three sides by windows that presented private diners with the feel of hanging out over the lake, with the mountains and skyline all to themselves.

Nakamura and Diamond were already seated when the Senator arrived.

"Senator, have you heard what happened out there?" Diamond asked.

"I heard something about hostages and that Jack saved the day," Carl said. "Any scuttlebutt down here?"

"A couple of bank robbers were hiding out here in the hotel," Clint said. "They got wind of an older couple here who won the Illinois State lottery and decided to pick up some extra cash. Jack stopped them, somehow, and one of them was killed. A woman, I think."

Diamond added, with a wry grin, "I've been looking for a decent script for over a year and now this thing drops right into my lap."

"And I might offer to produce it," Tako said. "My countrymen crave this aspect of Wild West in America. But earlier you said that you already have a producer."

"Potential producer," Clint said. "She may be just a fan with money and that doesn't always work out. If not, I'd certainly like to have my people talk with your people, as they say."

"Done," Tako said as he lifted his orange juice in a toast of agreement. "Now I'd like to hire Jack Bradley away from Von Bueller Industries."

"Neither of you two lets grass grow under your feet, Carl said, joining the toast. Jack's, as much a part of this resort as the lake, Tako, so I don't think you'll have much luck. Now, I wish we had some champagne to liven up this orange juice."

"I can have a bottle sent up for you, Senator," their server said. "Would a Cuvee Dom Perignon be all right?"

She placed a cup of steaming green tea in front of Tako and coffee for Clint and the Senator.

"Two would be better, Susan," Carl said. "Jack may need one all to himself, after what he's been through."

Tako Nakamura picked up his teacup gracefully and sniffed the fragrant steam. He took an unhurried sip and cradled the cup in both hands.

"Excuse me, Senator," he said, "but you have known Jack Bradley for a long time, correct?"

"At least ten years. Probably longer, if I were to think about it. Why?"

"What can you tell us about him? Why is this remarkable man not your country's Ambassador to my country?"

"Yeah," Diamond added with a laugh, "if I'm going to play him in the film, I'll need some background."

Carl laughed, and permitted Susan to pour champagne into his glass of orange juice before he answered.

"He attended the University of Idaho for one year, then joined the U.S. Navy where he excelled, but he just seems to have the hotel business in his blood."

"He gets the best out of his people," Nakamura said. "That's something any businessman can appreciate."

"He can be tough when he has to. He learned that during his time in the Navy. He ran into some tough characters there before deciding to return to Idaho."

"Sounds like old-fashioned hard work and ability," Diamond said. "And good luck for you that he came here."

Carl nodded agreement and doctored his half-empty orange juice with more champagne.

"Don't know what I'd do without him," Carl said. "The place would be just as pretty, I suppose, but not the same. He told me many times that the hospitality field was so attractive to him because it was such an 'up' business. Most people go to a doctor because they're sick. Attorneys handle a constant stream of people with problems. But guests in a resort are here because they want to have a good time, to have fun and to be entertained. He enjoys the upbeat atmosphere of the business."

"Ah-hah! Speak of the devil—here's our boy!"

The Senator had known Jack Bradley for a long time, but he had never seen him pale and shaky. All three men stood and greeted him with warm congratulations and a flush crept into Jack's complexion that seemed to energize him a bit.

"Thank you, gentlemen," Jack said, as they all took their seats.

Bradley pulled in a deep, slow breath and let it out with a heavy sigh.

"Everything's kind of buzzing for me right now," Jack announced. "Clint I don't see how you can handle this kind of action for a living."

Diamond laughed.

"Jack, it's a *game*. The guns aren't loaded and we eat from the same snack bar as the bad guys. Now, please, give us the scoop. What happened out there?"

Then Jack told them the story of how the two lottery winners had gone from being hostages to foster parents in less than an hour and how close everyone at the table had come to being hostages themselves. Carl listened to Jack's story with interest and admiration, but it didn't seem to be the kind of thing that would involve NFIP. Pat Douglas and his goon were up to something else here and Carl Wilder wanted very much to know what that something could be.

Eighteen

Dan Stricklin soaked up the sun on a flat rock outcropping on Tubbs Hill, overlooking the resort and marina. His suntan lotion, thick paperback novel, and boombox completed his surveillance uniform of the day—bathing trunks and sunglasses. Under a thick resort towel he kept his cellular phone, fitted with a Command Communications scrambler and his 9mm Beretta. Only a close observer would note that his headphones did not connect to his boombox, but to a highly sensitive directional microphone that poked its nose from under the towel and took aim at Eric Cannon and his party.

Cannon, Bob Kent and the two women had spent the morning lying around the pool, Cannon drinking orange juice and the others, pina coladas. Stricklin didn't know where Kent had come up with Julie and Rory, but keeping an eye on them was much more entertaining than the usual stake-out in the front seat of an uncomfortable car with stale donuts and bad coffee.

Rory Finley and Julie Adams knew how to move. They

looked like they enjoyed showing off their long, oiled legs and firm breasts. As morning rolled into afternoon, they shrieked and splashed in the pool, their tanned bodies nearly spilling out of skin-tight bikinis. Even the normally ice-cold Stricklin warmed to their delicious inventory.

Eventually, Bob Kent escorted the women back to their rooms and Cannon strolled the boardwalk to the *Bewitched.* As he boarded his yacht, a man with Middle-Eastern features approached. Stricklin risked a quick look with the binoculars and confirmed that it was Mustafa Khadduri, his pick as the Syrian go between.

This guy reeks of amateur, Stricklin thought.

He realigned the microphone and strained to hear what the two men had to say.

"Very nice boat," Mustafa said.

"Thanks," Cannon said, looking the man over carefully.

"Are you Eric Cannon?"

"Maybe," he said. "Who are you?"

"Mustafa Khadduri."

They shook hands and without further discussion Cannon said, "Come aboard."

Bingo!

At that moment, a surprise upset Stricklin's set-up. Lindsey Redding appeared on the boardwalk, just behind two room service waiters who were delivering hors d'oeuvre trays for Cannon's party.

"Dammit!" Stricklin whispered to himself. "What the hell is she doing there?"

Cannon and Khadduri shook hands again as Lindsey stood by admiring the boat. There was too much interference for Stricklin to tell what, if any, arrangements they made to pass the information.

Khadduri left the boat and continued his stroll along the boardwalk as though nothing in the world could be more important. Lindsey Redding had no problem catching Cannon's full attention.

Not now! Stricklin thought. *Damn it!*

He watched and listened for a few more minutes as Lindsey complimented Cannon on his boat.

"You're welcome to join us out on the lake," Cannon said. "There's always room for one more beautiful woman."

"Thank you," Lindsey said, "perhaps another time. I have a business meeting that I can't miss. Besides, I don't care much for being just one more beautiful woman. I'd prefer to be the only woman."

"That can be arranged. You know where to find me."

Lindsey shook hands with Cannon, who followed the waiters aboard. Dan Stricklin activated the local relay on his scrambler and ran his cellular through the hotel switchboard. He punched in the secure number for Pat Douglas.

"This is Douglas, go ahead."

"Pat, this is Stricklin. I've got you on my portable scrambler."

"Wait just one moment, Dan."

Stricklin figured that Douglas' secretary was in his office and he waited while his boss signaled her to leave the room. He heard the soft clunk of the heavy door close. Patrick B. Douglas was at the very top of the National Foreign Intelligence Program. Over the years, he had done a masterful job of promoting the agency and its critical role in the security of the United States. He did this without once giving details to Congress, nor to the five Presidents under whom he had served. Even given the fall of Communism, Douglas had been able to maintain his multi-billion dollar piece of the overall CIA budget. His was one of the few cells of government that received almost no scrutiny. Whatever they needed, they got, as evidenced by the Lear jet that had been directed to pick up Senator Wilder.

The walls of Douglas' office were paneled in oak and hundreds of books filled shelves covering one entire wall. Thick brown-toned carpet accented with blue stripes made the room look even bigger than it was. Double doors opened to a conference room with an enormous oak table and twelve padded chairs. A davenport and two living room chairs surrounded a large square coffee table with a huge globe of the world on one side. His desk of matching oak was positioned so he would sit with his back to two large windows framing the Washington Monument, while he faced the entry door so he would have clear sight of all who entered.

Stricklin heard a telltale *click* as Douglas activated the scrambler in his desk drawer to insure complete privacy.

"Go ahead."

"I've got my man under glass," Stricklin said. "No contact noted as yet, but I expect it may come soon."

"Any clues to a possible handler?"

"Just had a positive with Mustafa Khadduri. I called him in earlier. They shook hands, but got interrupted."

"Anything passed in the handshake?"

"Conversation indicated they didn't have time," Stricklin said. "Besides, that's not Cannon's style. He might have picked up an encryption key from Khadduri, but I doubt it. This Khadduri is unbelievably amateurish."

Stricklin heard the sklick sound the scrambler made when Douglas took a drag on a cigarette. It was against the rules to smoke in a federal office building, but his agency operated under its own set of rules. Besides, two outer offices of receptionists and secretaries insulated Douglas and he didn't give a hoot what anybody thought about it anyway. He was eighteen months from retirement.

"Have we got a file on Khadduri?"

"Just the one I've started here. He lives in Fort Wayne, Indiana, owns and operates a gourmet food store. He moved to this country when he was very young."

"With his parents?"

"Yes."

"How about them?"

"Really, nothing of any consequence. His father, Abdul Khadduri, has since died. There's some hint that he might have had some sort of a relationship with the Baathists in Syria, but it's really pretty vague. Our relationship with Damascus has warmed appreciably, maybe you can get something out of them," suggested Stricklin.

"How about his mother?"

"She's still living but she's quite elderly and no indication that she's a mata hari."

"When did they move over?"

"In the mid 60s."

"Well, Dan, you know that our intelligence in the Middle East at that time was pretty weak. Did you check with Mossad?"

Douglas was of the old school that thought the Israeli espionage organization was the slick new kid on the block. Stricklin did not share this enthusiasm. More and more, he saw Mossad as their competitor in the worldwide information business, more willing to accept information than to dispense it.

"Yes," he said. "Their files gave the hint of old man Khadduri's possible relationship with the Baathists. But it's a side note, nothing more. No substantiation."

"I'll have our people touch bases with our friends in Europe, but if Mossad has nothing, then very probably nobody will."

"I'm sure you're right," Stricklin agreed. He knew the scrambler would not transmit the doubt in his voice.

Douglas let the wires hiss for a moment.

"Dan, I know you know how critical this mission is."

"Absolutely. I fully understand. You know, honestly, I'm half surprised that Cannon's still in line for contact after I took out their first one. I figured neither side would trust the other anymore and we'd be onto a new organization."

"They evidently want what they want," Douglas said. "And Cannon's got it sewed up tight in his skull."

Stricklin had hired a string bikini-clad redhead that night to attract Cannon's attention. The brief distraction was all the time Strickland and his new secret partner needed to eliminate the problem. Douglas didn't know about Stricklin's helper for good reason and with luck he never would. The Arab had carried no identification, but he had carried a hefty little pot of Krugerrands.

Probably to double-cross his own organization, Stricklin thought. He didn't hang onto that thought, since he had neglected to mention the gold nor his new partner to Douglas.

The agency believed Stricklin acted alone of course. Douglas justified Stricklin's actions internally on the basis of national security. The Syrian had been a "deep cover" operative inside the United States for years. Douglas had said he hoped their carjacking ploy would scare off the Arabs and bring Cannon to his senses. No such luck. Stricklin knew there was too much at stake for any of them to call this off.

"Pat, the solution isn't in keeping contacts away from Cannon. That would take an army to accomplish."

Stricklin let the hint lie.

After a few more moments of hiss, Douglas answered.

"Well, let's take it one step at a time. We've got Senator Wilder out of there. We had to give him a freebie vacation, but we sure as hell didn't want him anywhere around the action if this thing comes down hard. Does Cannon suspect you're onto him?"

"Oh, I am sure he doesn't," Stricklin said. "For as smart

as this bastard is supposed to be, he sure lives high on the hog and out in the open. This guy couldn't be more obvious. He and another guy are with a couple of high-ticket gals and everybody in the resort is watching them. Anyway, it's not hard to keep an eye on what they're doing."

"Are you sure you don't need any help?"

"No. This one is a one man job."

Stricklin wanted to keep his new partner to himself, in every conceivable way.

"Dan, I am authorizing a green light on this guy. It's your call."

"I understand," he said. Then he added what he thought Douglas would want to hear. "I'm not about to let Mr. Genius sell out our national security."

"Right. Keep me informed."

Stricklin pressed the *off* switch and slipped the phone under the towel. He checked the reception on the bug he'd planted inside the *Bewitched* then picked up his things and headed back to the hotel.

He glanced back one last time and saw Cannon polishing the brass on his instrument panel.

There is no way this Benedict Arnold is going to get away with this one, Stricklin thought. *And there's no reason why I shouldn't make a little something more for myself in the bargain.*

Nineteen

Eric Cannon knew everything worth knowing about Mustafa Khadduri ten minutes after meeting the man. He had accessed the man's credit history, pitiful bank statements, and his driving record. Mustafa Khadduri had done forty-five in a forty-mile-an-hour zone once in 1992, and as far as Cannon could tell that was the sum total of excitement in his drab little life. It didn't matter. All Cannon wanted from him was his physical presence—and the code.

Cannon wanted Mustafa in the middle as bait, just in case of a trap. And he wanted Mustafa there for another reason, for control. Cannon could have run the whole negotiation electronically, but he wanted BISC to place one of its own on the sacrificial altar as a token of their commitment to him. For this he needed a person, any person who was not him. BISC gave him Mustafa.

Their brief meeting on the dock hadn't given enough time to seal the deal and the false start made both sides nervous. Both sides agreed from the get-go that nothing would ever be written down so a common drop was out of the question. Plan B had to be put into action. Cannon would receive a phone number via his communications system on *Bewitched.* Cannon, himself, would relay the number to Mustafa who would make the call. If the plot was to be detected it would be the butcher from Fort Wayne who would be caught in the sting and not Eric. Mustafa would verbally give Eric the necessary numbers and the two would never again meet. Eric would enter them into his computer and the encryption would be secured. Then, an automatic five-telephone shuffle would eliminate any eavesdroppers before final decryption occurred at base. At each of the five numbers a portion of the formula would be transmitted and a sum of money transferred to Eric's foreign accounts. Plan B would have to work or no deal.

Besides, he thought, *what are a few more hours, after all this time?*

Almost as quickly, Eric realized that a few hours would cost him a bundle in the interest his money could be earning. Still, it paid to be patient.

Money's no good if you're not free to spend it, he reminded himself.

Eric returned to his galley to supervise the preparations for the first of what he expected to be many party cruises.

"These look perfect," he said. "None of them are the drippy kind of hors d'oeuvres that slop all over the boat."

Cannon handed each waiter a folded ten-dollar bill.

"Give the champagne and the ice another hour," he said. He followed them topside and wiped their footprints off the deck with a towel. Eric worried a little about Julie and Rory on his magnificent boat. *They might be great lays*, he thought, *but they're messy as pigs.*

The women had dozens of bags, boxes, cases, tubes, bottles and other armaments of beauty spread out all over the hotel room. He could let it go there, because their suite was housekeeping's problem. *Bewitched* was a different story and he didn't want those two bimbos to screw up his pride and joy.

He checked the bar to make sure that it was fully stocked with liquors the women liked and his favorite tropical juice.

It isn't like we need booze to loosen them up.

Cannon's mind wandered as he organized the galley for the third time. He reminded himself that the touchy part was almost over. Anybody who might be wise to his venture could never prove anything. *And I'll still have the data*, he thought.

Cannon worked out a no competition agreement with the Baathists and he intended to keep it. He would invest his money wisely and live high off the interest. He had no desire to go through anxiety like this again. *But it*'s *good to know that I can*, he thought. *Just in case.*

If he didn't sell it to the Baathists, they'd just get it from someone else, eventually. This was one of those intelligence commodities that couldn't possibly remain secret. Eric hated the waiting and intrigue. All he wanted was his money.

But somebody had screwed up once already and he was likely on a slab in a morgue in Spokane. Cannon would accept the number two bid, or even number three or number twelve, if it meant saving his own neck.

Maybe it was a test, he thought. *They ran a drill Friday night and this is the real thing.*

It's what Cannon himself would have done. His only real regret was missing out on the redhead, who mysteriously vanished from the boardwalk as quickly as she had appeared. Rory and Julie had left him with precious little energy to spare for the redhead, anyway.

Eric secured the boat's cabin door and double-checked the mooring lines. With everything in order for the evening's party, he returned to his room to shower and take a double dose of vitamins in preparation for the evening's festivities.

Twenty

"Mr. Portman," his beeper announced, "Ms. Whitcomb is calling for you from the Juniper suite."

Great! Richard thought. *I fill in as a favor and this is the thanks I get.*

"Connect her to extension 7177, please, Martha," Richard said. He took a deep breath and let it out very slowly before he picked up the receiver. "Yes, Ms. Whitcomb, this is Richard Portman, how can I help you?"

"Have my attorney and Mr. Diamond's representative arrived yet?"

"They have, Ms. Whitcomb. They're set up in Cabin Five, here on the lobby level. It's spacious and comfortable, with a view of the lake and..."

"The only view that interests me at the moment is Clint Diamond. Is he there?"

"He's still in a meeting with Mr. Bradley," Richard said. "Would you like me to call you when he arrives?"

As usual, Veronica Whitcomb ignored his question and

steamrolled right along.

"Are you absolutely sure my suite is not available?"

She tapped the pen from the stationary folder on the parson's table loud enough that Richard could hear it over the phone. This was the second time in two days Richard had heard her call the Bavarian suite her own.

This woman could wear down a diamond, he thought, and then stifled a chuckle as he thought about the unsuspecting movie star.

"Yes, Ms. Whitcomb. I'm so sorry. As I said before, had we known that you were going to be here this weekend, we certainly would have saved it for you."

"I do an awful lot of business here, Richard. You wouldn't want me to take that business elsewhere, would you?"

Oh, God, he thought. *Where's Jack when I need him?*

Richard put on his best front desk smile, even though she couldn't see it.

"Ms. Whitcomb, you are a wonderful friend of our resort. We want to do everything we can to make you happy. I'm truly sorry the suite's not available, but is there anything else that I can do to assist you?"

She humped and clattered her pen across the table.

"Well, first of all, you can find my bodyguards," she said.

"I have this extremely important meeting with Clint and after the horrible goings on this morning I don't intend to leave my room unescorted. Where in the hell are they?"

"You know, I am not sure, Ms. Whitcomb, but I certainly will check."

She slammed down the receiver without any niceties and Richard knew that the lonely heiress meant business. He punched in security on the radio.

"Security, Val."

"Val, this is Richard Portman. Have you seen those two sides of beef who're babysitting the heiress?"

Val knew immediately who he was talking about.

"Roger, unit two," she said. "I think that particular two-some is in the lounge, but let me double check that."

"Roger. Please let me know ASAP."

"Will do."

Richard knew Veronica Whitcomb was the type of woman who got what she wanted, with honey or with mace. Richard didn't want to be the one to make her terminally unhappy, because her usual bill was equal to a tab for a hundred other guests.

"Unit two," the radio squawked, "I'm confirming your party is in the lounge."

Richard thought, *My God, these guys are tossing down whiskeys already.*

He had to admit, if he were with that woman under any circumstances, he'd be drinking at daybreak.

In fact, I'd probably be drinking doubles.

"Roger, 21, I understand. Just let them enjoy themselves. I'll report that they're swimming in the pool and working out in the exercise area. You might notify them that they'll want to return, in their swim suits, in twenty to thirty minutes."

"Roger, I understand."

Richard had always felt that his college education made him smart, but he believed that his job was now making him wise. He was beginning to understand the real world and how to put the right face on any situation. He took another deep, cleansing breath before dialing the Juniper suite.

"Ms. Whitcomb, this is Richard Portman. Your two associates are in the recreation center working out. I told them you called and that your meeting would start in about half an hour. They wanted to finish their workout, since the purpose is to stay in top shape for your protection. I'll call them back if you'd prefer that they return right away."

"No, that's fine. Let them have their workout. Send up four bottles of Dom Perignon. I'm going to take a champagne bath."

"It will be there within five minutes, Ms. Whitcomb." Richard immediately called room service and ordered the champagne. He instructed Donna at the front desk to post a $600 charge for champagne to the Juniper suite folio.

"She must be thirsty. Can she drink that much?" gasped Donna.

"Don't ask," he said. "She's not drinking it, she's sitting in it. Anyway, just post it to her account."

Richard walked into the bar and alerted the bodyguards that they should return to the Juniper suite before too long or plan to hitchhike back home.

Twenty-One

Jack and the room service waiter arrived at the Bavarian Suite just as Lindsey Redding was leaving. She wore a one-piece, French-cut black bathing suit and a white towel over her shoulder. Jack thought she was the most beautiful woman he'd ever seen.

She held the door open for the room service waiter, but her arm across the doorway stopped Jack from following.

"Hello Jack. You've had quite a day."

"Yes it was. I hope I don't see another one like it for a long time.

"The day's not over yet. Meet me at the pool after your discussion with Tako. Bring your camera. We'll see what develops."

Lindsey slipped past him with a coy smile brushing his chest with her own and when she finally let his gaze go she strode to the elevator without a look back.

"Beautiful, isn't she?" Nakamura asked.

Jack was startled by the voice behind him.

"Sorry," Nakamura said. "Didn't mean to startle you."

Tako wore a nail head gray Armani suit, one that might be called gunmetal gray. He extended his hand.

"Guess I'm still a bit jumpy from this afternoon," Jack said and shook hands. "It'll be good to have a quiet cup of tea."

Nakamura led him into the suite's dining room, where the waiter was finishing their set-up for coffee and tea. In spite of his college days and his Navy tour, Jack had never acquired a taste for coffee. He preferred ice water or English Breakfast Tea and he really didn't like tea that much. Nakamura selected coffee. Jack thought it ironic that he, the American, was drinking tea and Nakamura, the Japanese, coffee.

"Tea is much more popular in Japan," Nakamura explained. "But when I travel in the United States, for some reason, I enjoy coffee more."

Nakamura's relaxed posture and quiet voice contrasted with Jack's post-trauma nervousness. Jack's mouth felt like talking even though Jack wasn't in the mood.

"You know," he heard himself say, "coffee has been considered a magic elixir since it was first discovered. The story goes that around the third century an Ethiopian goat herder named Kaldi, discovered his goats had more energy after eating berries from coffee trees. Even his old goats pranced around like kids."

"Is that so?"

Nakamura blew on his coffee to cool it. His eyes said nothing, so Jack continued.

"Yes. Kaldi told his story to an abbot of a nearby monastery who decided to test the power of coffee berries by pouring boiling water on some of them to make a brew. After he discovered that the beverage helped him to stay awake, he and other monks drank the new brew every night to help them stay alert through their long prayers. After that, the word of the magic beverage spread quickly."

"That's interesting. I didn't know it was so magical."

Nakamura stared past the wall of bay windows, looking over the magnificent body of water that lay before him. He dabbed at his lips with his napkin, and set it aside before he continued. When he spoke this time, his solid gaze captured Jack's attention and never wavered.

"Aki has told me a great deal about you and he is very fond of you. He feels you do a great job running your resort. I have several hotels in Japan and I can tell you that my impression of your operation is very favorable. Of course, your actions today are evidence of great decision-making power coupled with the ability to act. I like that."

"I appreciate your compliment, Tako, and consider it a great honor to have you with us here at The Coeur d'Alene."

He has something in mind, Jack thought, *and it wasn't a pat on the back.*

"Let me ask you, Jack, what do you feel is the most important element in the success of a hotel; the location, the physical plant, or the people?"

"That's a bit like asking what is the most important leg on a three-legged stool. Success is a combination of all three, but in any great hotel, the people make the critical difference."

"Jack, I need to tell you that I'm here for more than simply a relaxing weekend."

Jack sat up in his chair, his interest piqued.

Here comes the pitch, he thought. At least he didn't dance around it for an hour, like some people do.

"As Aki told you, I have been very fortunate and found great financial success in Japan. My father was heavily influential in the Japanese Yakusa many years ago. It's no shame to admit it. He amassed great wealth and power."

Jack knew that Yakusa was bad news. It was the dreaded and powerful Japanese mafia that, in spite of Japan's structured economy, was among the worst group of criminals in the world. He let Nakamura continue.

"When I completed my university training here in the United States, I returned to Japan and became involved with my father's many businesses—his legitimate holdings. Soon, I learned the truth about other family investments. My father was not much different than many successful and powerful people who did what was necessary to build wealth and take care of a family. He had stepped on some people, but this was no different than many other leaders worldwide. Politicians were no better, even in this great country. Who died in Vietnam? The sons of rich, influential people? Or the poor, uneducated black and white sons from Harlem and Appalachia? Well," he waved it aside, "no matter. His way was not my way. After I took over, our businesses were completely legitimate within seven years. We have diversified our holdings and become heavily involved in real estate worldwide, something precious in Japan.

"My father's greatest wealth came during World War II when, as you know, Japan and Germany were Axis partners. The war was a disaster for both nations but not for two families—one in Japan and one in Germany. A great many weapons and ammunitions were traded between the two nations at great profit. The Japanese family was Nakamura and the German family Von Bueller."

Jack's face must have shown his surprise that Nakamura would reveal this information so openly. He tried to keep a straight face. Nakamura looked like he thought Jack knew nothing about his relationship with Von Bueller.

"That's right," continued Nakamura, with a grin. "It is the same Von Bueller family that today owns your beloved Coeur d'Alene Resort. Von Bueller's industrial empire was based on ammunition, weapons and of course the poisonous gas. The Soviet Union fell and a relative peace has broken out in the world, so the demand for weapons and ammunition has fallen off. Many third-world nations have made other arrangements, Guatemala put in a new highly classified weapons plant, for example, as a joint venture with the Israelis. Times are tough for the arms business."

"I can't say I'm sorry," Jack said.

Nakamura waved off the comment. "No matter," he said. "It's a cyclical business in a temporary slump. The Von Bueller family has diversified over the years; this resort is a small example, while they were still wealthy and powerful. Now, their major industry, arming countries to fight each other, is cracking under enormous financial pressure."

Jack remained motionless and, he hoped, expressionless. *If Nakamura's in the mood, let him tell it all,* he thought.

Nakamura set his coffee cup down but his gaze never left Jack. "Max Von Bueller called me several weeks ago. He knows I want to diversify my own real estate holdings and asked if I would be interested in the purchase of The Coeur d'Alene Resort. I knew Aki was acquainted with you and asked him to introduce us. You should know for Aki's sake that he had no knowledge of my real purpose in coming here."

Jack sat in stunned silence. *So, it's real!*

His relationship with Max Von Bueller was excellent. As excellent a relationship as one could have with a rich recluse. Von Bueller knew that Jack had always wanted the opportunity to put together a joint venture to buy the resort whenever Von Bueller wanted to sell. Though he had learned of Nakamura's purpose on his own, Jack was still flabbergasted that Von Bueller said nothing to him personally about selling The Coeur d'Alene. Jack determined that the best reaction for now would be noncommittal.

"Mr. Nakamura, I am at a loss for words. I don't know

what to say and I should probably call Max before we continue this conversation."

Tako Nakamura nodded his head in a stylized bow of respect.

"You are loyal and courageous. Your actions today will be rewarded."

Nakamura's grin broadened into a triumphant smile. He removed an envelope from the breast pocket of his suit and placed it carefully on the tabletop in front of Jack.

"Max anticipated your response. He gave me this letter, authorizing you to talk to me about intimate details of the resort. I already have all of the pertinent financial information. My staff and our American consulting firm have completed the due diligence work. My own director of hotel operations, Mr. Ogura, has been helping me analyze this situation from Tokyo and I will require his personal inspection. I believe I can justify a very handsome price for the resort and all of its properties. I am prepared to wire this amount to Von Bueller Industries in Cologne, Germany next week. I am sorry to surprise you with this information, but Max agreed with me that it would be best if I gave you this information first hand."

Jack placed his teacup back into the saucer. His hands had not lost their tremble from the morning's events and now they felt as numb and cold as his heart. Once again, he waited politely for Nakamura to continue. Nakamura's grin faded as he waited in vain for Jack's response. Finally, the tycoon cleared his throat and got down to details.

"It is now 4:30 PM and with the seventeen hour time difference between here and Tokyo, it is time for me to make some phone calls regarding other pressing business. I'm sure this meeting has given you a great deal to think about and I would like to meet with you again tomorrow morning for a more formal discussion and a detailed tour of the properties."

Nakamura gulped the last of his coffee and Jack stood to leave.

"Very well, Mr. Nakamura," he said.

The easy camaraderie of the golf game was gone and Nakamura would never be "Tako" to him again, no matter how this came out. Jack said nothing more. He merely bowed slightly and left the Bavarian suite. His shock gave way to practical speculation about his own status at the resort and that of the excellent staff he had meticulously put together over the past ten years. Jack recalled something that Aki had told him many years ago: "Controlling land is the only real power of a shogun."

And now Tako Nakamura will control The Coeur d'Alene!

Jack had precious little time to remedy this situation and the enormity of the day's events had him too disoriented to think clearly. He stopped at the front desk to talk to Richard Portman before going on to his office.

"Richard," he said, "let's make sure we keep the Smith room under quarantine just in case the authorities want to take a look at it."

"Okay, Jack. It's still doubled-locked and housekeeping has been instructed not to touch it. You know we are full tonight, though, and it's going to cost us some revenue."

Jack shook his head.

"I know, but with a homicide involved, we'd better make sure that everything is handled properly."

"Yes, sir," Richard said. He looked Jack up and down and said, "Are you all right? I mean, you've had a helluva day Jack. Shouldn't you treat yourself to some time off?"

Jack rubbed at the tension at the back of his neck to hide his trembling hands. He shook his head.

"I'll treat myself to finishing up my paperwork. That'll be a relief in itself. But thanks for asking."

As Jack entered his office, the mound of paperwork he had left neatly stacked on his credenza was still staring him in the face. Before tackling it, though, he thought he'd best use his time to get updated on the Smith incident. He pulled up the security log on his screen but the only notation reported that room #523 was double-locked and was not to be entered by any member of the staff, including housekeeping. Jack noted Perkins had called to say he'd check in with his report later.

Jack switched from security to the computer's newspaper news line, which gave him the developing stories for the morning edition of *The Coeur d'Alene Press.* The headline blasted out at him: FUGITIVE KILLS WIFE.

The front-page story included a color photo of Perkins and a pair of deputy sheriffs lifting the body from *Eagle* to the boardwalk.

Several articles described the situation in graphic detail, including interviews of the Hansons that painted Jack as the greatest hero since Audie Murphy. Page two had an early mug shot of Smith side-by-side with a photo of an EMT treating the massive burns on his chest. The history of his life of crime was a long and violent one. Smith was first arrested in Odessa, Texas, at the age of eighteen for stealing a car. In his mid-twenties he was tried, but acquitted, of a gas station hold-up in which the attendant had been badly beaten. The attendant had been too terrified to name his assailant on the stand. Smith's latest spree placed him as the chief suspect in the murder of a Federal Marshall near Memphis, Tennessee. The account did not give many details about his wife and only mentioned the child in passing. Jack assumed that the newspaper was running close to deadline and more information would be forthcoming.

An additional article on page two showed a blurred picture of what appeared to be Smith in the act of robbing the

First National Bank of the West, captured on film by the bank's security cameras.

Jack switched off his screen and turned to the small television on his bookshelf. The evening news was interviewing the FBI officer in charge of the investigation.

"Federal fugitive, Ronald Wheeler, also known as Ronald Smith, fatally shot his wife Rebecca Wheeler this morning at approximately 11:45 AM after the couple took four hostages and fled from The Coeur d'Alene Resort by boat. He was disarmed and subdued by Jack Bradley, General Manager of the resort and one of those held hostage. An infant child of the Wheelers was not harmed during the incident and will be turned over to the state's Child Protective Services. Wheeler was a suspect in the shooting of a federal Marshall in Memphis, Tennessee and in the robbery of the First National Bank of the West in Colby, among others. Full charges on Mr. Wheeler will be filed upon completion of our preliminary investigation. None of the hostages were harmed."

Jack's head buzzed and he felt a little chilled and sweaty. The announcer reported that an investigation of the incident was continuing.

Television news cameras showed the massive pool of blood on *Eagle's* deck and the burn marks where the flare fell after Wheeler clawed it out of his chest.

Jack turned the TV sound down, folded his arms on his desktop and rested his forehead on his arms.

"That was an awful thing today wasn't it?"

Jack looked up, embarrassed to be seen in a moment of weakness. It was Peter Harding, his food and beverage manager.

"Pardon me, Peter?"

"That Wheeler thing. That was awful." Harding shook off a shudder. "I took them several meals myself, it could have been any of us. I guess we were all lucky it was you and

Bob, who knew what to do, or one of us might be dead right now."

"Oh, yeah. Lucky. Bob Perkins was a cool cookie all the way through. That Smith guy, whatever his name was, was as twitchy as they come."

Jack didn't feel lucky. He was tired and a little depressed. Flashbacks to his Naval Intelligence days had been nibbling at him for hours. He thought he'd left those behind him years ago.

"That's what I've heard," said Peter. "We may never get Bob back down to earth."

Jack didn't want to talk about it. He'd already given enough depositions, reports, and statements to last a good long while.

Peter cleared his throat.

"Well, Jack, could I introduce you to a new member of our team here at Coeur d'Alene?"

Jack perked up. What he needed was something routine to ground him before he drifted into that thousand-yard stare of post-traumatic stress. He had seen it in others and felt the lure of it now.

"Sure, Peter."

Jack stood and straightened his tie while Peter summoned in his newest employee. It was standard operating procedure at The Coeur d'Alene for all new members of the staff to spend at least a couple of minutes with Jack Bradley so that he could evaluate them and so they could get a feel for the operating philosophy of the resort.

"Mr. Bradley, I'd like you to meet Carl Wagner who is the newest member of our room service team here at the resort."

Jack offered his hand to the obviously nervous young man.

"It's nice to meet you, Carl. Welcome to our family."

"Mr. Bradley, I am very pleased to meet you. I'm certainly excited about being a part of The Coeur d'Alene Resort."

"Do you live around here?" asked Jack.

"Well, actually I'm from Kellogg."

His posture was good and his appearance clean and neat.

"I've completed my sophomore year in college," he continued, "but I'm sitting out this semester to earn enough money so that I can go next semester without having to work part-time."

"That's great. Remember that your income and the success of our resort go together. The way we all move forward is by creating happy guests."

"Yes, sir. Mr. Harding said the same thing. I'm anxious to get started."

Jack realized why the young man stared at him in obvious awe.

He's heard about the hostage thing, he thought. *He must think I'm some sort of Rambo in a suit and tie!* That thought brought Jack his first real smile of the afternoon.

"Remember, it's teamwork that gets the job done," Jack said. "The boat won't go unless we all row!" He reached out his hand again. "It's a pleasure to have you aboard and I look forward to seeing you again soon."

Carl's grip was firm, but a little sweaty.

"Thanks a lot, Mr. Bradley," he said, and went into the outer office to wait for Peter.

"Good job, Peter," Jack said. "I think you have a keeper there."

"Thanks," Peter said as he turned to leave.

As he reached the door, Jack said, "By the way, you'd better give him a few days before you have him take an order to Veronica Whitcomb's suite."

"Very funny."

Jack didn't get a chance to get back to his paperwork. Before the door had a chance to close behind Peter, Bob Perkins knocked and stepped into the office.

"Well, we got the job done, boss. I can't believe we're still alive!"

Perkins had changed from his bloodied room service disguise into his starched security uniform. Jack had felt better himself, after a long, hot shower and a change of clothes.

"It's just catching up to me too, Bob. Have a seat. How did the wrap-up go?"

"Body's at the morgue. Wheeler—you heard his name was Wheeler?—he's in restraints and under guard at the hospital. He'll go into surgery in about an hour to repair the damage you did to his chest."

"What about the Hansons and the baby?"

"They were checked out at the hospital and they're fine, physically. A counselor has been talking with them about the emotional stuff. Betty and the baby have taken to each other, so they're leaving them together for now. I hope you didn't mind that I asked for a crib to be moved into their room."

"Not at all Bob. I read your entry in the security log and I think you did the right thing. You were cool up there in the room, too. That guy was ready to blow and I'm just glad it didn't happen in the hotel."

"I appreciate that, boss. It was bad luck that he remembered me from his check-in, but good luck that things turned out okay. Except for the wife, that is."

Jack saw the same fatigue in Bob's eyes that he felt in his own.

"I appreciate you coming in and giving me this first-hand report, but you really ought to go home and take it easy for the next day or two. You've been under a fair amount of stress yourself."

"I'll take time off if you'll take time off, boss."

Jack laughed. "Got me there. Well, at least get home and get a good night's sleep."

"Okay, you know I think I'll do just that. After a double shot of scotch. Oh, and after I drop off my room service uniform over at housekeeping."

"Just leave it right here," Jack offered. "I'm heading up there now anyway and I'll take care of it for you."

Jack was restless again and a walk through the hotel was just what he needed to calm down. He tucked the bundle of clothes under his arm and strolled toward housekeeping.

On his way he noticed a maid's cart outside one of the guest rooms. The room door was open and Jack stuck his head inside to say hello to the room attendant.

"Oh, Kristeen. It's you . . . how are you this afternoon?"

"Fine, Mr. Bradley. Thank you."

Kristeen Gallager had been with The Coeur d'Alene for over fifteen years and she wore her service pin to prove it. She was an excellent housekeeper who took great pride in her work.

Jack glanced around the room, which was a stay over. It was a connecting parlor suite and the large folding door between the two rooms was wide open. The furnishings were in good shape, but boy, was the room a mess. He could see that these two rooms were going to be a challenge even for Kristeen.

Some people are sure thoughtless, Jack thought.

As he walked out of the room toward the hallway, he noticed a five-dollar bill on the pillow of one of the beds. "It looks like these people have left you a pretty good mess, Kristeen but at least they're thoughtful enough to leave a small thank you on the pillow."

"They're messy, but they're nice people. They've been here a couple of days and I've had a chance to talk to them. They're just young people having a little fun. They're out at the pool so this gives me a chance to give their rooms our clean, fresh Coeur d'Alene touch."

"Kristeen, you're a great one." She was one of the most positive people he knew and she always made him smile.

As Jack left, he noticed the room numbers—362 and 364—and he realized who was staying there—the traitor. Jack thought it ironic that Cannon was kind enough to leave Kristeen a tip, yet selfish enough to betray his country.

Jack dropped the bundle of clothing onto the counter in the laundry and headed back to the lobby. As he returned to his desk his secretary was anxiously waiting.

"Senator Wilder has called three times since you left. He says it's absolutely urgent he talks to you as soon as possible. He had to step out of his room for a few minutes but will call back shortly. He seems quite upset!"

Now what?

Twenty-Two

Mustafa Khadduri was pacing his room, wondering what to do about making contact with Cannon, when his phone rang. His stomach clenched and his pulse quickened.

Maybe it's over, he thought. *Maybe he didn't like my looks and they're sending me home.*

"They" were the only ones who could be calling, besides Cannon, and he didn't think Cannon would risk it. He was wrong.

"Hello?"

Mustafa heard a lot of background noise that he couldn't place.

"In front of the electronic reader board listing the resort's daily events . . . just across from the bell desk. Five minutes."

The caller hung up and Mustafa's pulse raced so fast his hand clattered the phone when he set it down. He took a deep breath and tried to visualize his wife and children having a picnic down by the river near their house.

So it begins, he thought as he left the room.

It couldn't have taken him more than a couple of minutes to get to the resort's front entry. He scanned the red letters on the reader board directing guests to the location of their particular event. He turned and watched three people maneuver through the resort's revolving door. He glanced out the window to search the grounds for a sign of Eric Cannon, but saw only the comings and goings of guests and staff. The ring of the pay phone next to him startled him. He let it ring twice before he realized that it must be for him.

"Yes?"

"I will give you a number," the voice said, "do not write it down. Call the number and ask for a permit for a wide load. You will receive a permit number. Do not write it down. Repeat it back to make sure that you have it correct. This is most important. Make your call from a different pay phone."

The voice—he was sure it was Cannon's—gave him a phone number and Mustafa repeated it. Again, the dial tone. For safety's sake Cannon had decided he wanted one more layer of protection. He had decided not to risk the phone number that the voice had given Mustafa back home in Indiana. He wanted a fresh, new number that neither the voice, nor any other interested party, could bug or tape. Hence, the last minute switch. The voice hadn't liked it but followed the instructions that Cannon had electronically demanded. Cannon, himself, would control the transfer of information and would route Mustafa's call using his own electronic phone interlock.

Mustafa decided a pay phone in the hotel lobby would be too risky, so he walked to the nearby shopping plaza, repeating the number all the way. He found a pay phone in the walkway near Tito Macaroni's Restaurant, inserted his money and made the call.

A soft-voiced woman answered.

"Department of Transportation."

"I would like a permit for a wide load," he said.

By this time Mustafa was sweating profusely and trying desperately to think of nothing so that there would be room in his mind for this precious number.

It was a long number, a *very* long number. Mustafa repeated it successfully, the lush voice of the woman gave it to him again and Mustafa repeated it again, for insurance, before she hung up.

What now? He wondered, fearful that numbers already leaked from his ears.

He turned and looked up and down the corridor of shops. A blind accordion player was entertaining some tables of coffee drinkers nearby and one of those was Eric Cannon. Cannon motioned him forward with a flick of his eyes, left a tip for the musician and timed it so he left the table as Mustafa walked past.

"The number?"

Mustafa recited it as they walked and Cannon repeated it to him without hesitation and without error.

"Wait in your room." Cannon ordered. "You will receive a call when everything's clear."

"But. . .

It was no use. Cannon walked away briskly, heading for the marina. When Mustafa turned to go back to the hotel, he nearly bumped into the solitary guest who seemed to crop up everywhere.

"Excuse me," he said, but the man ignored him and hurried out of the plaza in the same direction as Eric Cannon.

Mustafa hoped his family was now safe, but he couldn't help the dark, heavy feeling that pressed him down. He felt he had saved his family but doomed his adopted country. The ease and the magnitude of his betrayal stunned him. He quickly returned to his room just in time to vomit profusely in the nicest bathroom he had ever seen.

Twenty-Three

Dan Stricklin watched Cannon hurry along the boardwalk to his boat and decided that following the man furthered nothing. He was sure Mustafa was his contact, but he had seen nothing pass between the men except a few words of hurried conversation. Stricklin didn't know much about nuclear physics, but he did know that the formula in Cannon's head could not be passed that quickly.

They never touched, he thought, *and neither of them picked anything up or set anything down.*

The accordion player's enthusiasm had kept Stricklin's earpiece from picking up anything but a couple of numbers.

Probably a phone number, he thought, *for contact later*.

He decided his best course would be to monitor all parties from the set-up in his room and returned there as quickly as possible without appearing to hurry. Thanks to Bradley, he'd had the opportunity to install some ears in the hotel's phone system. Stricklin was not disappointed. Cannon's electronic system had been quiet, but Jack Bradley had received a very interesting call from Senator Wilder.

"Senator, how's it going?"

"Well, could be better," the senator said. The old man's breathing was labored and wet. "You're okay after your little experience today?"

"A little shaky, Senator, but coming around."

"I find that Mr. Daniel's, in Tennessee, makes a decent remedy for that condition."

Bradley laughed.

"I'll have one for both of us, Senator, as soon as I get out from under this paperwork."

"Jack, when I checked in, we had a little conversation about a certain agency of the government."

There was a moment of silence on Bradley's end.

"Yes. I remember the conversation very well."

"We didn't have the chance to talk at lunch, so I couldn't bring you up to speed. I've been contacted by that certain agency and it was strongly recommended that I vacation elsewhere for the next couple of days. Hell, they even made reservations for me at the Broadmoor in Colorado Springs. I'm at the airport in Hayden Lake now. They're sending a Lear jet to take me there to play some golf. Jack, I don't know what's going on, but you and I have been good friends over the years and I didn't want to leave without talking to you. I'd better follow their lead until I find out what they're up to, but I'll be back before too long. I was told not to discuss this so please keep it under your hat."

"I won't say anything, Senator. You can count on me."

"Jack, you be careful. I'm not sure what's going on, but watch yourself." Wilder coughed and his voice became more excited and angry.

"When I get back to the hill, I'm going to convene a little investigation into the activities of Stricklin and his boss, Pat Douglas. If they've got the kind of money lying around to bring a Lear jet here to take an old broken down Senator to Colorado, then they might just have a little bit too much petty cash. Hell, we've got enough budget and tax debates going on to choke a horse. They think we've got a bottomless pit. It might finally be time to cut those boys' purse strings back a little."

"Well," Bradley said, "at least you'll enjoy the Broadmoor. It's a fine place."

"Not as much as The Coeur d'Alene. This is home to me and I've been away too long. This is the kind of jaunt that my opponent will spread all over the papers, saying I'm the one wasting our money. Congress is supposed to be the dog that wags the tail, not the other way around."

Bradley and the Senator rung off and Stricklin scribbled a few notes even though he had the whole thing on his little Sony digital handheld wired into the hotel system. Protecting the agency's free flow budget was Douglas' passion. Stricklin placed an immediate call to Douglas. He reviewed his notes with the director on scramble and played the cassette recording.

"Play it again," Douglas ordered.

Stricklin quickly rewound the cassette and played it again.

"That son of a bitch," snapped the director. "Who the hell does he think he is?" Stricklin was silent. He knew the director wanted no answer to his question. "I've got a file on that drunken bastard that would choke a horse. We'll just add a final chapter to that two-bit politician's book and he'll shut his mouth for good."

Stricklin, of all people, knew that Douglas played for keeps. During his long career, he and his boss had blackmailed dozens of congressmen, bureaucrats and even a pair of Presidents. No tinhorn Senator from the back woods was going to undermine his empire. Stricklin felt himself grinning.

"There's another Lear that will land three minutes after

Wilder takes off for Colorado," Douglas said. "I'm putting Andrews on it, so he won't be available for your backup. Wilder's pilot will take the scenic route, so Andrews will have plenty of time to arrive at Broadmoor ahead of the old fart. If you wind up your business early, join him there. Andrews will be sleeping right across the hall from Wilder. Wilder's suite is one of our regulars, so it's already wired. Andrews will have the gear in his room. What's the buzz on Cannon?"

"Looks like he's setting up to make a move," Stricklin said. "I expect it to come down tonight."

"Remember," Douglas said, "you have a green light on this one. Don't take chances."

"I'll cool his jets. Don't worry about that."

Douglas was already gone. Stricklin called the resort's Boardwalk Marina and rented the fastest boat he could get his hands on. Then he made a scramble call to his secret partner and made arrangements to pick her up after he secured the boat.

Stricklin slicked back his hair in the mirror and smiled.

Cannon, he thought, *you'd best just bend over and kiss your sorry ass goodbye.*

Twenty-Four

Carl Wilder's reception at the Broadmoor afforded him VIP treatment, but not the same personalized attention Jack Bradley gave him at The Coeur d'Alene. He'd let his staff stay on an extra day in Coeur d'Alene. They deserved a day off. Besides, they could report back later on whatever it was that Pat Douglas and his goon were up to. There'd been plenty of Jack Daniel's on the Lear and it was just as well. He couldn't get any business done even though they provided him with a phone, computer and fax.

No way am I going to use an agency phone, he thought. *If they want something from me, they're going to have to work for it.*

So, he drank their Jack Daniel's and felt the flash of anger he'd started with grow to a white-hot heat. The Senator finished the two tiny bottles of Jack in his suite's mini-bar within twenty minutes of his arrival. Before his luggage had been delivered, Wilder discovered more reserves in the Terrace Lounge located in a quiet corner of the resort. Senator

Carl Wilder's mood was as black as a JD label.

The weather was as bad as his attitude and he soon discovered the golfers had flown south to the sun. The Terrace Lounge was nearly empty. Within two hours of his arrival, Carl had to admit to himself that he was on his lips.

"Hello," a voice said at his elbow, "aren't you Senator Wilder?"

Carl turned to see a well-dressed and well-groomed young man at his shoulder. He automatically shifted into his "public servant" personality.

"That's right. Have a seat."

The young man sat down and crossed the legs of his white and tight Chap's trousers. He wore deck shoes with no socks and a purple Polo shirt with Ralph Lauren's familiar "Player" embroidered in green. He had a well-trimmed mustache and styled, mid-length blond hair. His tan said "outdoors" but his build said "trust fund baby." Carl had met thousands in his day. A well-manicured hand reached out for a greeting. "I'm Randy, from Florida," he said as he smiled broadly.

"Carl Wilder," Carl said and shook the hand. He caught the slur in his voice and straightened at the stool. "But you already knew that. Have we met before?"

"Recognized you from the news. You're pretty popular in Florida, with your legislation for the elderly."

Carl realized, through the Daniel's fog, that Randy included him in there with the "elderly."

Oh, well, he thought, *I suppose I am.*

"You a golfer?" Randy asked.

"Damn right," Carl said. "But it looks like I picked the wrong time to vacation."

Wilder turned and motioned with two fingers to the bartender. "Another Jack, Jack. And whatever Randy's drinking."

The two engaged in small talk for a couple more drinks

and decided to do dinner. Randy called his friend, who was the maître d' of the Penrose Room, and reserved a table for two. The restaurant was perched on top of the resort's south building and they were seated at a table that let them view and be viewed. Randy seemed to have a limitless cash flow with tips to make sure they were seated at the best table and little green thank you gifts to the servers with every fresh round of drinks, which he ordered in rapid fire all night. Randy was a great conversationalist and his jokes and stories kept Wilder entertained throughout the evening. All in all, the two strangers got along very well.

The Senator felt his eyelids drooping by the time he pushed his plate away. He was very warm and very full.

Randy ordered the obligatory "one for the road." When the waiter delivered the check a mock fight to pay the bill ensued. Randy insisted harder and hosted the entire tab, but none too soon. Wilder's head began to bob up and down fighting the booze and fatigue, so Randy put his arm around the Senator and walked him slowly past the other patrons and down the hallway to the suite. Carl's body was numb and he dimly thought that he would have hell to pay in the morning.

"Never been so drunk," was what his mouth tried to say, but what he heard come out was a barely audible gurgle.

By the time Randy got Carl to his room, Carl felt like he was having one of those out-of-body experiences he'd read about in the tabloids. He floated somewhere above the bed and watched Randy undress him as though his wrinkled, pale flesh belonged to a stranger.

Carl was sure he was dreaming when Randy bent to kiss his forehead, then the young man lingered in the room for a bit and had another nightcap. As he left, he slipped the "do not disturb" sign between the door and the doorframe, defeating the lock for anyone who might want to come inside. Already Carl was forgetting the young man's name and this bothered him because Carl Wilder never forgot a name or a face.

Carl knew it was important for him to pull that sign free and let the door lock, but with the alcohol and the altitude, his body didn't seem to work anymore and it was all he could do to keep breathing.

Twenty-Five

Jack found he couldn't keep his mind on his accounts, so he opted for a late afternoon stroll. Veronica Whitcomb and her two escorts lounged with a tray of drinks beside the pool. Veronica was trying her best to play the temptress and Jack had to laugh to himself.

If she'd just learn some consideration for other people, he thought, *she'd be a very attractive woman.*

Veronica was lying on her stomach on a chaise lounge, reading a book through sunglasses with the top of her one-piece swimming suit down to her waist. Her dark-haired bodyguard rubbed suntan lotion gently across her back and legs. He was a handsome guy. His biceps bulged and his pectorals were perfectly developed. It was funny to see such a physical specimen trying so hard to be genteel. He wore oversized red and white striped shorts covering most of his thighs but accentuating his muscular calves. From the look on the young man's face, Jack could tell he was thoroughly smitten by his spoiled, egotistical employer.

Jack was hesitant to go over and talk to Veronica because Richard Portman had filled him in on her unhappiness at not having "her own suite" available. However, she was a tremendous guest, financially speaking and the hotelier wanted to be sure not to snub her. Besides, he had to admit to curiosity about her meeting with Clint Diamond. For once, the heiress had told the truth. Suddenly, her familiar shriek shattered the relaxed air around the pool. Jack was still jumpy and his heart rate tripled in the blink of an eye.

"What are you doing, you idiot?"

Veronica clutched the top of her suit to her nicely curved chest and glared at her bodyguard over the top of her sunglasses. Unfortunately, to more readily cover the palm of his huge hand with lotion, he had removed the squeeze top from the Chanel bottle and inadvertently dropped it on Veronica. Her back was bare and while most of the Chanel splashed on her skin, several ounces of the lotion spilled onto Whitcomb's suit.

"You idiot!" she repeated, trembling with anger.

"I am sorry, Ms. Whitcomb. It was an accident."

She swiped at her back with a towel, momentarily freeing her left breast to bobble in the young man's face.

"You imbecile!"

"It should come right out of your suit when you get into the pool," he said.

His body was tremendous, but his demeanor meek. Jack thought her bodyguards would be dangerous to cross. They experienced so much frustration from the mouth of their boss that they had to take it out on somebody.

Whitcomb grabbed the bottle of Chanel, which had fallen to the pool deck. Reading the label, she blurted out what Jack knew to be yet another untruth.

"See here?" She demanded. "It has titanium dioxide which will bleach out the delicate material of this suit!" Of course, she didn't know titanium dioxide from Alka Seltzer. Her voice rose for the benefit of the other guests. "Don't you realize that a Givenchy suit is not for swimming? It's for looks and sunning. It costs a fortune and this one was specifically designed for me!" *Another lie.*

Jack decided to step in when Whitcomb slapped her bodyguard's wrist. It would have been his face, but he was so quick to block the slap that Jack never saw his move.

"Good afternoon, Ms. Whitcomb," Jack said. "Is there a problem here?"

Veronica Whitcomb instantly changed her tone upon seeing the General Manager. Sitting upright on her chaise lounge and pulling up the front of her swimsuit, she slapped the hand of her sunscreen applicator again as he tried to wipe away his mistake.

"Just forget it, idiot,"

She turned to Jack with a smile that would have put Delilah to shame.

"Oh, Mr. Bradley. It's so nice of you to stop by and say hello."

"Ms. Whitcomb, it's always a pleasure to welcome you back to The Coeur d'Alene. I hope you're enjoying your visit."

Jack knew she measured the success of her visits by a body count of people she'd inconvenienced, so he hoped she wasn't enjoying herself too much.

"Well, thank you so very much. I'm pleased to be back here at my favorite resort in the world, even if I was put into someone else's suite."

Jack shook his head in what he hoped was a sufficient show of sympathy.

"I'm sorry the Bavarian suite wasn't available for you this time. Since *Conde' Nast* picked us as the number one resort in the country, we've been booked full for weeks in advance."

"Well, I understand," she said, in a rare gesture of magnanimity. "The Juniper suite is very nice and I'm making do with it."

She turned and slapped the hand of her bodyguard again who was still trying to cover up his blunder.

"Just forget it!"

"Ms. Whitcomb, I would be very pleased to have Paula, in our laundry, take care of the lotion that spilled on your beautiful swimsuit. She is an extremely capable professional and I'm confident there isn't a stain made that she can't remove."

Veronica waved a limp hand, dismissing the whole thing.

"No, it's fine. I'll just give it to my neighbor back East. Of course, she'll never be able to fit in it, but it will look good in her closet."

"Well, accidents happen," Jack said, trying to get the man off the hook.

"Well, all I can say is I'm glad I hired these two for their bodies and not for their brains."

Jack couldn't believe anyone would work for someone who treated them so poorly in public.

Or in private, he thought. *Surely whatever she does for them in bed can't make up for this!*

"You two go and get me a glass of chilled Chardonnay while I talk to Mr. Bradley. After what happened today, I think he can protect me adequately while you're gone."

Both men walked away, looking more energized with every step out of her sphere of influence.

"Really, Jack—may I call you Jack? —Everything is very nice. I had an excellent dinner delivered to my suite from Beverly's last night and it was perfect."

"Yes. Peter Harding mentioned to me he had the pleasure of personally serving you last evening."

Jack couldn't help himself and it was out before he knew

it. Now Veronica Whitcomb knew that her lewd performance with her bodyguards had been discussed throughout the resort, reaching as high as the office of the General Manager.

Non-plussed, Whitcomb continued.

"My friend, Martin Hofer, is starring in the Phantom of the Opera, which is presently playing in Seattle. The purpose of my trip was to see Martin perform the lead in Seattle for pleasure then meet Mr. Diamond's people on business. Martin was a backup on Broadway and has considerable talent. Hopefully, if he can suffer through the embarrassment of having to perform in Seattle, he'll return to New York and gain a role there, which he so richly deserves. I've watched the Phantom many times and, of course, the cast has come to my apartment in the city for after opera theater parties. This is where I first met Martin. I called and told him I would not be able to make it to Seattle because of the dreadful fog. He was mortified because he was so looking forward to my visit, but I told him I would try to come back when I could work it into my schedule."

"I hope your meeting with Mr. Diamond was fruitful," Jack said. "He seems like a nice, down-to-earth gentleman."

Veronica put on her pouty face.

"I wouldn't know. His people would hardly let us talk between ourselves. I'll fly to Los Angeles next week to firm up details. Once I've signed on the dotted line, they'll let us talk. You'd better believe it!"

The faithful bodyguards re-appeared with the criminal lotion spiller carefully carrying a glass of Chardonnay as though it was nitroglycerin. Jack took his leave as graciously as he could manage when he saw Lindsey striding towards the marina. He hurried to the boardwalk as quickly as he could while still being discreet, but gave it up when he saw her step into a little Boston Whaler that pulled up to the dock. She barely had the chance to sit down when it roared off and

Jack could have sworn he saw Dan Stricklin at the helm.

Stricklin and Lindsey Redding! What the hell is going on here?

Jack stood, stunned, as people brushed past him and the Whaler joined another dozen boats heading out on the lake. He and Lindsey had made a casual date for dinner, since Nakamura would be taking care of his Tokyo business.

Two bits says she left a message at the office, he thought. *"Unexpected business . . . blah . . . blah . . . blah . . . regrets."*

Jack ran a hand through his hair and realized he was trembling. He didn't like the connections his tired brain was making. Stricklin meant Cannon and national security. Lindsey meant Nakamura and weapons interests.

I'll bet they're not heading for chicken salad sandwiches on the beach.

Cannon's boat had left the boardwalk and Jack shook his head. Something big was coming down out there on the lake and his gut told him it wasn't good. He hurried back to his office and found the expected apologies from Lindsey Redding on his message service. Immediately, Jack called the Senator in Colorado.

"I'm sorry," the operator said, "Senator Wilder doesn't answer. May I take a message?"

"Yes, tell him Jack Bradley called. Tell him 'The traveling salesman is a dirty joke.' He'll know what I mean."

Wilder was on the intelligence committee and Jack was counting on him knowing the lingo. A "dirty salesman" is an agent who has turned and he hoped Wilder would get the reference before it was too late. He picked up the phone again and called Bob Perkins at home. He got the security chief's answering machine.

"Bob, its Jack Bradley. If you're there, please pick up."

The receiver clicked on. "Yeah, Jack. Reporters have been calling nonstop, so we decided to screen calls. What's up?"

I'm not sure. Are you still technically a deputy sheriff in this county?"

"Yes, I am. Now what do we have?"

Jack hesitated. *What if I'm just being paranoid? What if this is all just flashback stuff?* He blew out the breath he'd been holding. *Then I'll be out a nice evening boat ride on the lake, is all.*

"Jack?"

"Bob, this might be nothing. Can you meet me at *Double Eagle's* slip in fifteen minutes?"

"I don't know, Jack, I'm really done in. Is it important?"

"I can't say over this phone."

"Look, Jack," he said. "You've had one helluva day, we both have. Get some rest.

"This is important, Bob. . ."

"Then go to the sheriff. Let the pros handle it, that's what they're paid for."

Jack felt his temper swell.

"They wouldn't believe me and there isn't enough time to convince them."

The line crackled for a moment between them as neither man spoke. Finally, Bob broke the silence.

"Jack, do you realize that you went off like a rocket out there today? For a couple of minutes you were a raving madman. Something set off a switch in you and that switch is still on. You get me? Now, I think you should call Dr. Mathes, get something to help you sleep, and go to bed. We can talk in the morning."

Jack ran a hand through his hair and noticed he was sweating profusely. "Okay. Maybe you're right. I'll see you tomorrow."

"Promise me you're not going to do something stupid," Bob said. "Promise me you'll get some sleep and look at this thing fresh in the morning."

"All right, it's a promise. Thanks."

"Jack, by the way, I found out something interesting this morning, something you should know about Nakamura."

Jack felt his belly go cold. "What is it?"

"It's that Redding woman," Bob said. "She's not Nakamura's PR director at all. She's Nakamura's security chief for all of his North American operations."

Jack gritted his teeth. *Taken in like a stupid teenager in heat*, he thought.

"Thanks," Jack said. "We'll talk tomorrow."

Jack hung up, tossed a pencil across his office and stuffed his gym bag with two sweatshirts and a pair of sweatpants. He wished that he had time to go home for his old 9mm Colt and a box of cartridges, but he'd wasted enough time already. He locked his office and hurried to the dock and the *Double Eagle.*

Twenty-Six

Eric Cannon locked himself inside the communications center of *Bewitched* and switched on his bank of screens. He balanced the keyboard across his knees and entered his telecommunications program. He started with the critical numbers Mustafa had given him and they unlocked the passage for Cannon's data. While the computers clicked and booted Eric thought of his friend Bob Kent. There was no doubt in his mind that Kent would not tolerate the betrayal of his country. If Kent knew what Eric was doing tonight, it would cost Eric a lot more than their long friendship.

Bob Kent never was the nosey type. He was a private man who didn't talk much about himself and didn't ask personal questions.

Eric and Bob were plebes together in the U.S. Naval Academy at Annapolis. Bob flunked out of the academy in their second year, but completed three hitches as a Chief Petty Officer on nuclear subs. Eric was a Lieutenant, but the two of them had remained close friends despite the difference in rank. Cannon's genius in electronics and nuclear engineering set him on a fast-track career path, which led him inside some of the country's top military secrets.

Cannon and Kent had partied together for years, beginning when they first met and their friendship had continued after discharge. Kent was the fast-talker who always came up with the women. Cannon came up with the cash.

Frustrated with his Navy pay, Bob Kent didn't re-up after Cannon's medical discharge. He vowed to make his fortune in real estate. The fortune had not yet materialized, but his lifestyle was far from uncomfortable, thanks to his hustle and Eric's constant infusions of cash.

Cannon was forced to resign because of his allergies, which had been only a minor nuisance when he was younger. For some reason they kicked into high gear in his senior year at the academy and deviled him more every year. Eric requested submarines, even though it meant giving up the cushy life he'd cultivated as a bachelor officer. They turned him down because his skills were more useful topside. His resentment over the Navy's pettiness and the money were what drove him to betrayal.

Even though Bob Kent was Eric's only friend, Eric took great pains to see to it that Kent was not involved in any way in his personal mission. He knew Bob Kent as a party animal and a screw-off, but a genuinely patriotic screw-off who wouldn't tolerate any compromise of national security.

If he knew, he'd kill me, Eric thought. *But he doesn't want to know, so it's no sweat.*

Eric finished encrypting the first of five installments of the three-page formula and keyed the cellular modem through his computer. He pressed enter and the high-pitched squeal of data transfer verified that the preliminary text of the formula was on its way.

Eric clicked on Video Input and turned on CAM 1. Eric

had four video cameras installed in strategic locations and camera one was located in the yacht's elegant head. The image of two women, elbow to elbow at a makeup mirror, appeared on his screen. He slipped on his headset and cranked the squelch out of the analog line while he fed the digital into memory. Eric leaned back and watched the two women primping on the other side of his wall. He had other fiber optic lenses installed above the master bed and above both guest berths.

Julie and Rory could have been showgirls in Las Vegas. They had met Bob a couple of weeks earlier at a lady's night bar promotion and Bob introduced them to Eric.

"Eric seems nice," Rory said, "but he's the only person I've met who parties hearty and doesn't drink."

"He doesn't need any artificial stimulation, " Julie said.

"Remember that first night, when you pulled your little white powder kit out of your purse?" Rory asked. "You would have thought it was rat poison, the way he looked at it."

Julie rested an elbow on the countertop to steady her hand as she painted on thin eyeliner.

"I thought he was a narc," she said. "But now I think he might be one of those big-time dealers who never uses, you know? He has all this money and no job."

"You didn't waste any time packing your bags when he invited us here to the resort," Rory pointed out. "You were out the door before the ink was dry on the airline tickets."

"Yeah, but I was still behind *you*."

They giggled as Cannon zoomed in on the reflection of Julie's firm butt with the black lace thong underwear. None of the foursome had been married before, although Julie had been living with a bar manager for a couple of years. She left on Bob Kent's arm with the clothes on her back and, as far as Eric Cannon knew, she never looked back.

Both women related to men through their bodies. Eric

liked it that way. *No muss, no fuss*, he thought.

Everyone had an addiction, and for some people that addiction was sex. Eric knew this first hand. If he wanted to keep his precious gift, he couldn't afford alcohol, or drugs, or even a bad diet. But he could afford sex and it rounded out the aerobic leg of his daily fitness program.

Experience made it obvious to Eric early on that both girls subscribed to the same conditioning philosophy. Rory and Julie had even posed for a spicy magazine spread. Rory gave Kent a copy of their issue on the night they met and he passed it on to Eric. Eric appreciated a woman with a versatile tongue and now he had the pleasure of two.

They admitted to Kent that they had enjoyed their photo shoot, but their true motivation was money, coupled with the long-shot possibility for Hollywood discovery. Cannon and Kent never paid the women directly for their services and the women never asked them for money. They enjoyed each other and were having the time of their lives satisfying their bottomless hunger for action.

This fantasy island trip means big bucks, Eric thought. *So, why not spread my good fortune around?*

The women gave both men everything they could have hoped for. Now, on the screen, Eric watched Julie as her shaky hand tapped two fat lines of white powder onto the countertop. Rory unscrewed one of the hotel pens and snorted half of one line into a nostril before Julie had the other prepared. Rory switched nostrils and passed the pen barrel to Julie.

Eric was worried about Bob Kent. Julie was leading him around by the nose—literally—and this made Eric nervous. He didn't like any loss of control himself and he didn't understand it in others, particularly in his one and only friend. Cocaine had taken Bob Kent by storm. Eric didn't like it. Still, he wouldn't criticize his friend's vices unless they interfered with his own.

The women would live like pigs if he let them. Even though the parlor suite at the resort had double bath areas, the two primped over the same vanity so that they could talk and gossip together and it was a good thing. They had to step over every swimsuit, tank top and twitch butt skirt they'd worn for the past two weeks just to get to the toilet. Other than the twin sinks, the Corian counter top was covered from one end to the other with brushes, curling irons, mirrors, and enough make-up to fill the cosmetic department of Neiman Marcus. Eric did not relish the damages that these two would inflict on his precious, spotless *Bewitched.*

He turned up the volume so that he could hear their conversation better.

"How did you enjoy Kent last night?" Julie asked.

She spoke over the whine of the portable hair dryer that the two shared.

Julie ought to know everything there is to know after their little fling two nights ago, Eric thought.

Rory didn't answer Julie right away. She was squinting and tight-lipped as she carefully painted her eyelashes with thick mascara. "He really topped off my tank," Rory said. "He's really something. But Eric's more . . . inquisitive."

The women were silent for a moment and then Rory added, "We made love all night. Volume counts. I'm tired but wonderfully so!"

The hair dryer delayed conversation, then went silent and Eric listened to the small sounds of the women as they brushed, powdered and painted themselves for another twenty minutes. Finally, they clambered up on deck and Eric took the opportunity to lock up his communications and to use the head. They left their mess in the head as Eric predicted, including a tube of K-Y jelly. He smiled as he peed, thinking of all the ways he could help them use it up.

Eric glanced up the passageway and saw the women topside talking with Bob Kent. The women stood arm in arm, still giggling from the buzz of the pina coladas they had sipped all afternoon around the pool. Both women wore tight, white short-shorts that contrasted with their darkly tanned legs. The shorts fit so tight they appeared to be painted on. Julie wore a blue, low cut silk blouse thin enough to gather provocatively in all the right places. She wore it with the tails tied together just above her navel, exposing lots of skin. Rory wore an admiral's jacket, with braids and piping on the shoulders, wide open in the front with a V coming together at one button over her navel. Eric knew from experience that she never wore underwear, top or bottom.

The giddy twosome paced the deck, giggling and laughing all the way. Rory's blonde hair was ablaze with the highlights of the setting sun. It was layered with soft curls that framed a rounded face. Her flashing blue eyes seemed to add to her brazenness. She was blatantly sexy.

Julie was slightly taller, with long, jet-black hair. Her frame was small but her bearing, confident. Her large green eyes were perfectly enhanced by just the right blend of make-up. She was not as buxom as Rory, but her appeal was not only in her beauty but by the way she moved her long legs and carried herself. Her personality vacillated between modesty and wildness, which made her a master in the art of seduction. The modesty was for show because Julie knew quite well just how to move and maximize her particular magic.

When Cannon first met Julie and Rory, he was excited by Rory's flagrancy, her shameless "come one, come all" attitude towards sex. As time went on, Eric and Bob both found themselves drawn more and more to the intoxicating Julie, whose appeal was much more subtle and intriguing. She was desirable because of her personality as well as her body. Alas, with Rory, what you saw was all you got but that, too, had its place. Both women possessed their own unique attractiveness and sensuality. Julie's appeal grew with time, while Rory's was shorter-lived, but hot, very hot.

Eric Cannon fired up the two big Cummins diesel engines from below decks, then went topside as they warmed up. Kent was helping the women down from the flying bridge, embracing them both with a squeeze of each arm, as they jumped onto the deck and pushed their bodies against his chest. They both hugged back. Eric received the same full-body press.

"What a great boat!" Rory said. "I feel like I'm on a cruise to Fantasy Island."

Cannon smiled coyly and said, "That's exactly the plan. Welcome aboard the love boat."

Kent popped the cork on the first champagne bottle and filled 3 glasses. As usual, Cannon's drink was ginger ale. The four toasted "fantasy" and then three began to get toasted themselves. Cannon untied the lines holding his new yacht to the guest dock and removed the three oversized, spotlessly white fenders that were protecting the side of the boat. Kent steadied the big Carver while Eric climbed to his captain's perch on the flying bridge. By placing one of the dual electronic throttles in forward and the other in reverse and then quickly switching the two to the opposite position, Cannon was able to "walk" the boat a few feet from the padded dock. He then moved both throttles into the forward position using his right hand and turned the steering wheel with his left.

The big diesels purred as smoke puffed out of each exhaust and the magnificent vessel surged forward.

Rory climbed the steps to the captain's chair and wrapped her arms around his chest. She pushed her firm breasts into his back. Eric felt like he was on top of the world. Absolutely nothing could go wrong tonight and he would wake up in the morning a very wealthy man.

I've got it made now, he thought, *just a few one-minute*

phone calls left in this operation.

Bewitched picked up speed and pulled out of the harbor. Behind him Eric sensed Rory slipping out of her top.

He was aroused. Never had he been so excited to find an all night berth for *Bewitched* where he could drop his anchor.

Twenty-Seven

Dan Stricklin peered through his binoculars as the boat, captain, and party crew, headed into the oncoming night. The freshly painted name, *Bewitched,* was brightly illuminated by the stern light and Stricklin could read it clearly through his binoculars.

"Bewitched," he whispered. "I'll bewitch his ass."

The agent had changed out of his third-rate suit and tie to black sweatpants and a dark blue T-shirt. A wetsuit, scuba tank and other diving gear were hidden in the fish cooler at his feet. The twenty-foot Boston Whaler he had rented for tonight's mission didn't give him much room, but his new partner didn't seem to notice. She scanned the hotel, marina and the lakeside with her own binoculars, searching for anyone watching them or the *Bewitched.* Under a canvas, in the open bow, Stricklin had stored his radio, electronic listening devices, scrambler and night vision scope.

Within minutes, *Bewitched* was nearly out of sight. Stricklin smiled when his monitor picked up the yacht's radar and recorded its course and speed.

Gotcha!

Stricklin fired up the little Whaler's ninety horsepower Johnson. He knew his fishing boat could run circles around the big yacht. The Boston Whaler's low profile was perfect for surveillance. He could stay far enough behind the yacht so as to not be noticed, but close enough to stay in range of his bugs.

"I don't understand why you're letting him broadcast," Lindsey Redding said. She half shouted so he could hear her over the scream of the engine. "How is this formula valuable to us if somebody else has it?"

"It's not." Stricklin admitted, "So we see that they don't get it. He's transmitting in five stages. I got that much from his initial setup on the World Wide Web. We intercept the first four transmissions, relay them through, and let him see his money transferred as planned. For the fifth transmission, we intercept but don't relay. We'll have the final and critical part of his formula and be in the driver's seat to negotiate our own deal."

"And if the parties of the first part don't want to negotiate with the parties of the third part?"

"They will," he declared with great confidence. "It would take them years, if ever, to crack the formula if they don't have the final chunk. Besides, I understand your boss has persuasive means of negotiation."

"Indeed he does," Lindsey said. She held tight to the grab bar behind Stricklin and leaned closer to make sure he could hear. "And your boss has an excellent record for hunting down agents who turn on him. What are you going to do about that?"

Stricklin shrugged.

"He's a bastard. He's one of those jerks who takes credit for everything. I'm good at what I do and if Douglas can't pay me what I'm worth, I'd at least like a few strokes. But, not only don't I get strokes, he's passed me over for promotions in favor of younger agents who're still wet behind the ears with no clue. He's about to get his nice cushy retirement with all the glory and I'm the good ol' civil servant left with nothing but jack-shit." Stricklin tried to lean his cheek against hers, but she flinched away. "Besides," he said, "I'm the one he sends to hunt 'em down. There's nobody as good as me out there."

"I am," Lindsey said.

"But you don't work for Douglas. And if I thought for a second you did you would already be dead."

"Charming."

"Don't lay that shit on me, sister. I've seen you work. Remember the Syrian?"

She shrugged it off.

"What happens when Cannon doesn't get confirmation for his last broadcast?" she asked. "Won't he just try again, or go to a backup plan?"

Stricklin smiled and zigzagged the boat for the fun of it, forcing her to grab him for support.

"Not if he's dead." He grinned, winked and reached for her waist.

Lindsey spun his wrist around and pressed his arm up behind his shoulder blades. She did it all smoothly, without a grunt or flush of effort. The boat went into a tight turn and Stricklin backed off the throttle.

"Now, I said 'None of that' when we made our deal," she said. "If I have to tell you again, they'll call you 'Lefty.' This is business and only business. Got it?"

"It's cool," Stricklin said, through clenched teeth. "It's okay, it's cool."

Lindsey stepped back and let go of his wrist and Stricklin shook it hard to get the circulation back. He swung them back on course and pursued the yacht into the night, keeping well out of sight. He rehearsed his plan as Lindsey Redding stripped behind him and pulled on her own black wetsuit. He caught a flash of skin reflected in his gauges and peeped at the well-turned curve of her magnificent ass.

In a couple hours we'll be rich, he thought. *What the hell.*

Twenty-Eight

Jack Bradley pulled the blue canvas cover from the cockpit of the *Double Eagle* and tossed his bag aboard. He switched on the blower for the bilge and released the dock lines before starting the engines. Both Chevy 350s fired with the first press of the switch. In less than a minute Jack was racing south, following the course that the Whaler and the Carver took. Light was fading fast and he wanted at least a glimpse of them before nightfall. He did not like the position he'd put himself in. For that matter he wasn't sure why he had put himself there.

Unarmed, in pursuit of two boats that I can't see, with innocent people right in the middle.

Jack grabbed the boat's cell phone and called the hotel.

"This is Jack Bradley. Tell security I'm checking out that outdrive problem that Paul was having on *Double Eagle*. I'll have it back at the slip in an hour or so.

"Okay, Mr. Bradley," Angie said. "I'll let them know."

Jack worked out his strategy as he sped towards a faint

white dot moving just outside Kidd Island Bay.

Cannon's set up for a big party, Jack thought. *That means he'll find himself a cozy spot to anchor. Stricklin will be hanging just out of sight. I'll have to skirt Stricklin without being seen and then use Cannon's boat as cover when I approach. I'll hug the shoreline so they can't see me.*

Jack reached for his binoculars. He could tell the white dot was a Whaler, but he couldn't be sure it was Stricklin. Two people were in the little boat that was circling slowly outside the mouth of the bay.

Suddenly, Jack wanted to do exactly what Bob advised—have a drink, go to bed, think it all out fresh in the morning. He shook it off.

I'm out here now, it's a beautiful evening and I'm not tired.

Many a night like this saw him out on the lake, so why not this one?

Because tonight he was hunting humans, something he'd promised himself years ago that he would never do again.

Jack cranked the helm, taking *Double Eagle* off the Whaler's course in a flanking maneuver. Once or twice he thought he could see the stern light of Bewitched bobbing in the gathering dark. This was a perfect night on the lake—warm, pine-scented air and a scattering of stars. This would be a great night for romance.

That's probably what Cannon's thinking.

Jack eased his iron grip on the helm, shook out one hand and then the other to relax. He dug a sweatshirt out of his bag and pulled it on. He tried not to think about how Lindsey Redding was staying warm in the Whaler with Stricklin.

"Nakamura is screwing us front and back." Jack whispered. "Stricklin's not here to stop Cannon. He's going to steal this secret for Nakamura."

He agreed with himself and pulled on the sweatpants

against the growing chill.

Then Nakamura will cut a deal with Von Bueller for the resort. Stricklin will probably kill Cannon. Maybe the whole boatload of them!

Jack shook his head. He was sure that the rest of them were cover for Cannon—just an innocent, but not too bright, party bunch.

Jack glanced at the dim, distant speck that was the Whaler. It wasn't moving. He checked them again through the binoculars, but there was too little light and the glasses weren't powerful enough. He wished he had Bob's set of night vision glasses. He wished he had Bob.

Twenty-Nine

Mustafa stood at the balcony of his room with his shoulders hunched up like a turtle trying to pull his head into his shell. He watched Jack Bradley roar out of the marina in the same direction Eric Cannon took, and he prayed Mr. Bradley wouldn't do something that would cost Mustafa his family. Mustafa pounded the wall in frustration. Never in his life had he felt so helpless.

"All this, just for some numbers," he whispered.

Mustafa knew that, even with so many numbers to remember, he would never forget them as long as he lived. They were burned into his brain for eternity.

He had watched the news clip about Jack Bradley and was surprised to hear he had been an intelligence officer. Mustafa had tried to get up the courage to speak with Jack Bradley after that, but decided it was not worth the risk to his family. Now he was ashamed. The one thing he could have done was impossible now. He wanted to take a long walk away from the hotel, but he didn't dare leave the room in case a crucial phone call came.

Mustafa sweated profusely and tried to relax by praying. His prayer was more like begging, pleading with Allah to spare his family. Mustafa continued to sweat, then he began to tremble as though from a great chill.

The phone rang and a real chill descended as Mustafa answered.

"You have done well."

A man's thickly accented voice praised him, but there was no sign of joy in the voice. It was the voice that he remembered from his deli in Fort Wayne.

"What about my wife?" Mustafa asked. "My children?"

"Shhh," the voice hissed, just as he had done in Fort Wayne.

"All in due time. Room service will arrive momentarily with a meal. On the tray will be a set of keys and on the keys, a tag. The tag will direct you to a vehicle waiting for you on the third level of the resort's parking garage. Drive to the airport in Spokane and present your ticket for your seat assignment. Then return to your car, it *is* your car, by the way, a token of our appreciation. You are free to drive it home. When you arrive, you will find your family safe and happy. You have talked with your wife so you know we are behaving honorably."

"But . . . "

The man hung up. Mustafa hurriedly gathered his new clothes and toilet articles and stuffed them into his bag, then waited, pacing, for the room service knock. He thought it took five years for the knock, but his watch proved it had been only five minutes.

Mustafa stuffed a wad of crumpled bills into the waiter's hand and shut the door. He didn't lift the food covers. He was only interested in the car keys, the keys to his future, his freedom. He hurried to the garage, afraid that at any moment the mysterious voice might change its mind about letting him go free.

The car was a small gray Ford, two years old, with only eight thousand miles on the odometer. It smelled like a new car and it was certainly newer than any car Mustafa had owned. The car came with Indiana license plates, a registration with his own name on it, and a full tank of gas. It also came with a package on the seat. Mustafa opened the package.

More money!

A cursory inspection proved they were all twenties. Most were older bills that had been bound together. He tried to open the glove box to place the money inside, but it was locked and neither key worked. Mustafa stuffed the money into his bag, took a deep breath, started the car and set out for the airport in Spokane.

He was a little over five miles from the resort when a dark blue car came up behind him and flashed its lights. Then the driver pulled alongside and motioned for him to pull over to the side of the road. The man turned on his interior light so that Mustafa could see him clearly. He was Middle-Eastern and did nothing that seemed threatening. Mustafa found a streetlight and pulled over, but he made sure the doors were locked.

The other vehicle stopped directly in front of him. The driver left his car running and walked up to Mustafa's window.

"Mustafa, please follow me. I am Habib and I am your friend."

The friend, Habib.

The mystery man turned without waiting for a response and got back into his car.

The two drove about a mile and Mustafa followed the other car into the parking lot of a small grocery store and gas station. The station and store were dark except for a security light in the back.

"Please come with me," Habib said and walked Mustafa to a pay telephone booth, which was located outside on the corner of the grocery store property. The streetlight above them was out and the light in the phone booth didn't work. Their only illumination came from the neon "Coors" sign in the store window.

"One moment," Habib said.

He took out a small penlight and punched in several numbers on the telephone pad.

Habib spoke for a moment in Arabic, too fast for Mustafa to catch it, then he turned and handed the phone to Mustafa. He spoke Arabic poorly on his best day and today was not one of his best days.

"Hello?" said Mustafa, his voice cracking in a dry throat.

"Mustafa, what has happened at the resort?"

This was now the third time in his life that Mustafa had heard this particular voice—three times more than he wished. Mustafa turned to see if anyone was watching. There was no one in sight except Habib, who stared up the road blankly with dark, heavy lidded eyes.

"What . . . what do you mean?"

"Is there anything we should know?" Mustafa heard a cigarette deeply inhaled at the other end.

"There . . . There . . . was a man. He seemed to be watching Cannon and me."

The voice cleared its throat, "And?"

"When Cannon left on his boat tonight, that man followed him in a smaller boat. There was a woman with him. I would have told you but . . ."

"Yes," the voice interrupted, "I know. You didn't know how to contact me and I didn't give you the chance on the hotel phone. You have done well. Have you considered the possibility of working for us?"

Mustafa was stunned. He wanted nothing more to do with this matter, these people. What would they do to him if he said "No?"

"I . . . I don't think I could," he stammered. Suddenly the night air seemed cold, penetrating. "I like the deli business."

"And a good business it is," said the voice. "Very well. As agreed, I will not contact you again. Your father's promise is fulfilled. Praise Allah."

"Yes," Mustafa said to the voice, "praise Allah." Mustafa handed the telephone back to Habib who continued a conversation with the voice. It was mostly one way as Habib said little and listened intently. He hung up the phone softly and walked to the Ford.

Mustafa looked at Habib who was now standing next to Mustafa's car. The man probably had been tailing him all along. Mustafa was no longer surprised. He didn't know whether anything would surprise him again.

"Well, where were you going, Mustafa?"

"I was going to the airport, as instructed," he said. "To check in and then leave."

"I can save you that trouble," Habib said. "I have to go to the airport to turn in my car. Give me your ticket and I'll present it. To most of these devils, one of us looks just like the other. If you're driving east, it will save you an hour over and an hour back."

"Yes, I understand," Mustafa, said.

Anything, he thought, *just get me out of here!* He handed Habib his tickets.

"I trust you received the package on the seat?" Habib asked.

"Yes. Thank you."

"There will be more waiting for you at home. Now,

there was a phone call and some numbers. Do you remember them?"

Mustafa swallowed. His throat was parched and his stomach flipped.

"Yes," he said. "Do you want them?"

Habib shook his head and waved off the question with his slender hands.

"No, no. I am not authorized. Just forget them and do not write them down, ever. Now, Mustafa, do you think anyone knew why you were at the resort or had any suspicions about you?"

"There was the man following Cannon, but I don't think he was interested in me. And Cannon seemed unconcerned."

"That is very good, Mustafa." Habib jingled his car keys and Mustafa saw that they were attached to one of those car alarm transmitters. "Your father prepared you well for this service. Thank you for your efforts and have a safe trip home."

The two men shook hands. "Good bye," Mustafa said. "And thank you for saving me the airport trip."

Habib simply waved, jingling his keys and fingering the transmitter as he quick-stepped to his car putting distance between himself and the Ford.

Mustafa buckled his seat belt and, with trembling fingers, slid the key into the ignition switch on the steering column. It would be good to leave the intense tension of the weekend and return to his loving family and deli in Fort Wayne. With his eyes closed he slowly turned the key. He gripped the steering wheel with both hands at ten and two o'clock and inhaled a grateful gush of air. He exhaled a prayerful sigh of thanksgiving and hung his head forward chin to chest as he heard the car's motor come to life. After a few seconds he composed himself and with his right hand, still trembling, placed the car in gear and turned east.

The assassin, Habib, was standing outside his own car when he heard the crunch of gravel under Mustafa's tires. He turned for one last look at Mustafa and gritted his teeth. He placed his thumb on the transmitter and pressed——the automatic door locks on Habib's car released. He opened the door and entered the car in preparation for his journey to the airport.

The obedient, Habib, had received a pardon for Mustafa. The voice was convinced the council had been well served and that Mustafa had fulfilled his Father's promise. Another Habib in Fort Wayne would secretly remove the explosives hidden in the Ford's glove box and Mustafa would be none the wiser.

As he sped toward Indiana, home and family Mustafa prayed to Allah and his father, *promise fulfilled.*

Thirty

Eric Cannon guided *Bewitched* into Kidd Island Bay, just a short cruise from the resort, where he anchored. His music system piped Jimmy Buffet tunes throughout the dozen speakers that he had built into the cabins, berths and the flying bridge. His guests were well into their second bottle of champagne already.

"Save one for me," Eric said. "I might join you later."

"You?" Rory mocked. "My goodness, Captain, what's the occasion?"

Eric smiled.

"A business deal. It should be final in a couple of hours, then I'd like to celebrate in style."

"Well, Eric," Julie said, and swept a hand to indicate the yacht and its appointments, "this is style."

"You go ahead and do your business, Eric," Bob said. "We'll manage the celebration."

"Good," Eric said, "I wouldn't want you to be bored. Why don't you start on this first tray of hors d'oeuvres and

I'll be back shortly. I still have some last minute negotiating to do."

"At this time of night?" Rory asked.

Eric frowned and bit back the snapping "mind your own business" that came too quick to his tongue.

"It's always banking hours in the electronic world. And somewhere the sun's always rising on a new business day."

Bob Kent caught the edge in his friend's voice. He deftly steered the conversation to music and the women to the hors d'oeuvres.

Eric locked himself into the communications shack and checked his messages.

"Message received," the screen reported along with the date and time. He called up the appropriate offshore bank on his screen and saw that the first installment had, indeed, been made to that account. He entered a phone number and transaction code, then the code for the offshore bank and electronically transferred the money to a third account in Belize.

"Instant millionaire," he whispered. "Ba-boom!"

When the night was done, he would make one last set of transfers, distributing his gigantic paycheck among a dozen banks in as many countries. Fifty percent of his money came in the last installment. Eager as he was for the money, he reminded himself not to hurry.

You've been years setting this up, he thought. *Don't blow the game plan now*.

Eric entered his second installment, a schematic element that complemented the piece of formula in his first transmission, entered his encryption code and pressed *send*. As his electronics squealed in the background, he opened a screen to the activity in the main cabin.

Julie had taken a plate of hors d'oeuvres and her drink to the outside deck. Rory had Bob in a passionate lip-lock, backed up against the table. Both of her hands rubbed at his crotch, and Eric could see that Bob's shorts had developed an incredible bulge. Eric felt a swelling of his own and decided to do something about it. A few keystrokes placed his electronics on standby.

Rory and Bob didn't even notice Eric when he entered the cabin, loaded up a plate and squeezed past them to join Julie on deck. She leaned against the rail, her hair rustling in the evening breeze.

"They seem to hit it off lately," Julie said.

"Jealous?"

"Glad," she answered. "That gives me more time with you. And you?"

Eric was surprised. Except for a couple of wham-bam encounters, he hadn't thought she was particularly interested in him.

But then, a boat like this can make an impression, even when the owner doesn't.

"World's too big for jealousy," he said, around a mouthful of food. "It's about as useful as water wings on a bat."

He wiped his hands and lips with a towel, brushed the few crumbs from his impeccable deck and started up the ladder to the bridge.

"Going so soon?" Julie asked as her hand slid up the inside leg of his shorts and tickled his privates. Eric stopped on the ladder for a moment, enjoying the play of her skillful fingers.

"I'd like to check out a couple more bays before anchoring for the night. Too many houses around here, I'd like a little more privacy. But, if you insist, there's one hors d'oeuvre that's not on the menu."

"They built here for the view, after all. The least we can do is give 'em one." Her hand explored further, then she followed him up the ladder.

The bridge was lit softly by the instrument lights and

Julie insisted in her persuasive way. It was another half-hour before Eric roused himself from the cushions on the bridge to flick the anchor switch and move on.

The foursome had eaten most of the hors d'oeuvres by the time *Bewitched* approached Arrow Point. Rory, Julie and Bob had moved from sipping champagne to quaffing Cuervo Gold tequila and Stolichnaya Russian vodka. Still, they saved two bottles of champagne for the moment when Eric would finish his "business."

Kent stocked Eric's Sony compact disc player with a full load of ocean-going Reggae. The volume and beat of the music seemed to grow in intensity along with the passions of the night.

Eric, cautious as ever, scanned the horizon one more time. His binoculars picked up a flash of white halfway across the lake, a small fishing boat bobbing in the waves.

Night fishing, he thought, *isn't that illegal?*

Then he chuckled to himself. Selling nuclear secrets to the Baathists was a little more illegal than night fishing! At least it meant that whoever was poaching on that boat wouldn't give him any trouble.

Eric piloted *Bewitched* past Moscow Bay and then south into Beauty Bay. Mount Coeur d'Alene loomed to the south, shrouded in silver from the rising moon. Lights from the resort disappeared as Eric hugged the west end of the bay and found an anchorage free of human influence. His only worry was cellular transmission, with the mountains rising on both sides, but a quick check of his equipment found it functioning perfectly. All they had for company here were stars and a stark white moon.

"This is it, folks," he announced "This is the spot for us. It'll be just right for a spectacular sunrise."

"I might even be ready for some sleep by then," Bob said.

"Not if I have anything to say about it," Rory countered.

This time, as Eric shuffled his second deposit to Antigua and transmitted his third message, he watched, on his monitor, as Julie took her sunglass case out of her purse. To anyone else, this might seem strange in the middle of the night, even with a full, bright moon. Out of the designer case, she removed a small amber-colored glass vial filled with a white powder—not sunglasses.

"Oh, it looks like it's going to snow tonight," said Rory, pointing to the vial in Julie's hand.

"You bet!" Julie rocked a little more than the wave action called for and had to steady herself against the table. "I found the snowman and got enough for all of us."

Julie removed the plastic cap from the vial. She used the tiny plastic spoon attached to the cap to put several little piles onto her compact mirror and cut them into three thin white lines with a Nordstrom card.

Eric put his private cabin on standby and joined his three guests at the table.

"How many Colombians do you think it took to stomp enough coca leaves in kerosene to take care of your little party tonight?" Eric asked.

"Only you would wonder something like that, Eric," Bob said. "And you don't even use the stuff."

"I don't use the stuff because when I do something I'd like to hang onto it long enough to figure it out," he said.

The other three weren't listening as usual. Sometimes, when they got too drunk or too far-gone on their other party favors, Eric wanted to just walk out and leave them to their pitiful selves. But then, the sex was always wildest when the women were loaded, so he stayed.

"Well, my friends, be my guest for a little magic," Julie said.

She handed each of the others a small straw from the galley.

Rory was the first to take a hit. Eric knew from experience that a little coke greatly increased her sex drive and revved up her energy level. She immediately turned the cabin into a dance floor and ground her pelvis to a wild beat. Kent and Julie each closed one of their nostrils and snorted their share. Julie was generous. Her vial held two grams, which cost her all of the money she had saved for rent.

"There's plenty more for the rest of the night," she yelled above the music. "Eric, I'm saving some for you, to go with your champagne."

She carefully replaced the cap on the vial and hid it once again in her sunglass case. The combination of drugs and alcohol moved the cruise to a fever pitch. Julie and Rory both began to shimmy to the sensuous beat and the Carver rocked to the dancing on the main lower deck.

Kent, seizing the moment, skipped the CD player ahead to a disk he had strategically placed in the player, and the familiar music of a striptease began to blare over the twenty-four, high tech speakers and woofers of *Bewitched.* The night Bob met the women, Rory had won an amateur strip contest to this same tune. Neither woman missed a beat and, as if on cue, began an erotic, face-to-face strip. Rory's single Admiral's button slipped free and she threw off the short jacket to expose herself. Julie was a step behind for only a moment. She pressed herself against Rory and the two women danced chest-to-chest, their eyes full of each other. The sensuous focus of the two naked women stimulated Eric and Bob Kent to join them.

Eric didn't care that he was a lousy dancer. This wasn't about dance. This was about sex, something Eric understood thoroughly. As the men rubbed and bumped the sweaty bodies of the women, Rory and Julie helped them peel off their clothes. The foursome, overheated in the cabin, moved their dance party out to fresh air on the aft deck.

"Hey, let's skinny dip," Rory suggested. "I haven't done that since I was a kid."

"Yeah," Julie agreed, "we can water dance."

Eric lowered the swim ladder and the women dove over the rail. Eric loved to swim and yelled to Bob, "Last one in sleeps alone!"

He surfaced between the women treading water easily. Julie kissed him long and deep, like she meant it, and Eric realized that this was no longer just a fling for her. He would have to do something about that, but he vowed not to worry about it tonight.

The lake water was warm and on a night like this he thought he could probably swim forever. But swimming was something he could do alone. It was not his plan to exhaust himself in the water, no matter how warm and calm the night. Bob joined them and the four revelers played like a troop of otters. Their giggles and shrieks carried across the water as the men chased the women teasing and taunting them with little underwater grabs.

Julie tired first. Kent gave her ankle a jerk and her head ducked under before she was ready and she came up sputtering and coughing and a little pissed.

"Enough!" she said, and wiped her face with her hands. "I want to play a game where *you* go down until you come up coughing."

"I know that game," Kent said. "It's not something I can play in the water."

Julie scrambled up the ladder with Rory close behind. Kent tried to dunk Eric, but he was too fast for him. They followed the women onto the deck and Eric tossed several towels to the dripping revelers. He used his own towel to dry the deck.

"Eric, you're such a perfectionist," Julie muttered. "Boats are made to get wet."

"It's slick when it's wet. I don't want some stupid accident to ruin our night, that's all."

Julie grabbed his hand and placed it on her slick, wet breast.

"This night will be perfect," she whispered. "I promise."

She tugged him toward the king-sized bed in the master bedroom at the bow. Bob and a giggling jiggling Rory followed close behind.

Thirty-One

Senator Carl Wilder woke up, vomiting violently and almost choked to death before he could get his head over the side of the bed. He gasped for breath and his heart pounded so hard he thought it was going to explode.

"What. . .?"

He heard himself say it out loud, but that was all his voice could manage. His body didn't want to move on command and he didn't know where he was.

Am I having a stroke? He wondered.

He'd quit taking his blood pressure pills months ago because they made him get up too often in the night. His doctor warned him, maybe a stroke . . .

"Hey!" he croaked.

The Senator wanted one of his assistants, but now he couldn't remember any of their names.

"Hey!"

This time a little louder. He thought he heard footsteps at the door, but when he started to holler, he vomited again and had to concentrate on breathing. Every heartbeat felt like a hammer driving a spike into his skull.

Jesus! He thought. *How much did I drink?*

The last thing he remembered was playing golf with Clint Diamond at The Coeur d'Alene Resort.

Or was that a dream?

Everything was so fuzzy and his muscles felt like water. The nausea passed and he found enough strength to lift his head back to the pillow, but his pillow and bedding were fouled with vomit.

I'd better call Jack, he thought. *Get a doctor. Get my staff on the ball.*

He fumbled for the switch on the bedside lamp. The glare of the light felt like shards of glass piercing his eyes. When his vision recovered and he looked around the room, he was shocked.

This isn't The Coeur d'Alene! Where the hell am I?

He checked the bedside table and found a tent card advertising the Terrace Room at the Broadmoor. Then some hazy images started coming back—the Lear jet, his evening in the lounge, dinner with a wealthy young stranger. "Shit!"

The Senator sat up too fast and the nausea returned.

"Douglas," he muttered, as he held his head. "Douglas, you son-of-a-bitch!"

He shouted because it finally dawned on him what had happened. He'd been set up like a tenderfoot and Pat Douglas was behind it. The last image he remembered before sleep was the young man placing the "do not disturb" card between the door and the frame and blocking the lock. He leaned forward and looked at the door.

Gone!

A surge of adrenaline shot strength to his legs. He held onto the bed and slid over to his trousers draped across the vanity. His wallet, with his money, credit cards, and ID was still there. This was Pat Douglas's game, all right. Senator Wilder was scared for a moment. Then he was angry. Angrier than he'd been in a long, long time.

He would call the airport and get a flight out to DC even if he had to charter one. He'd call his staff and have them on line when he arrived. Douglas was up to something and it smelled worse than the bedding. Senator Carl Wilder had a gut feeling that he was in for the fight of his life and he could barely stand on his own. He gagged with dry heaves for a few moments, then caught his breath.

"Shower," he mumbled and shuffled to the bathroom.

By the time he stepped out to dry off, he had a plan. He would fix that son-of-a-bitch Douglas and his freewheeling agency once and for all. He left a message for a special consultant to the Senate Intelligence Committee. Someone who knew the ins and outs of all the agency dirty tricks and someone who owed Carl Wilder a very big favor. Favors meant a hell of a lot more than money on the hill and it was time Senator Wilder cashed some in.

Thirty-Two

Dan Stricklin crouched behind the helm of the Whaler and unwrapped a piece of cold fried chicken. He always got hungry before an operation and this was no exception. Besides, it kept his mind off the wait, off his silent, sultry partner and off the passionate moans and music riding the night wind from the cabin of *Bewitched.* A chilly breeze kept his mind clear. Lindsey reached under the canvas at the bow and put on a tight-fitting foul-weather coat.

She toed the open lid of his captain's case that held his notebook computer and the STU III cellular intercept.

"Are you absolutely sure this little toy can intercept Cannon's message without tipping him off?" she asked. "Doesn't his call go out to everybody else at the same time it goes to us?"

"Not exactly."

Stricklin tried unsuccessfully to talk with a mouthful of chicken. He gulped a big swallow of lukewarm coffee to wash it down.

"It goes out to us and to the relay station at the same time. There's an Opto Electronics card in this computer that intercepts his call even if he switches frequencies. I installed a similar unit at the relay station, these puppies run ten grand apiece, by the way. Once he starts broadcasting, our unit detects and identifies the frequency. I click out trackball here and the relay station ICOM receiver locks on and blocks relay of that signal. It all stops at the nearest mountaintop."

Lindsey hugged herself against the chill.

"What if his target is within range, like we are?"

"All his numbers have been international calls," Stricklin whispered.

"Still," she said, "the numbers could be a decoy. Maybe somebody here on the lake is monitoring, just like we are."

"Then we're screwed. I've done all I can."

Stricklin was interrupted by the wakeup of his notebook's screen, indicating that it had locked on to Cannon's fifth and final portion of the formula and schematic. He notified the relay intercept at the click of a button and the whole thing was over in less than two minutes. He confirmed that the data had been dumped to his computer and the relay had successfully blocked transmission of Cannon's call.

"Okay, we've got it. Now, I have to get to Cannon before he checks for confirmation. If he transmits again before I get to him, you'll have to block it. The screen will start up like you've seen. When that little phone icon lights up, put the arrow on it and click once. Got it?"

"Yes," she said. "Hurry up and let's get out of here."

Stricklin removed something from the side of the computer and inserted something else.

"What's that?" Lindsey asked.

"The hard drive," he said.

Stricklin triple sealed it inside watertight pouches and placed it into a container attached to his belt.

"I wouldn't want to go to all this trouble just so you could freelance without me. Now, at any sign of trouble on that boat, you get your ass over there with the artillery. The agency gave me a green light on Cannon, so he's a legal kill. But if I get into trouble, we'll have to take out the lot of them. Questions?"

"No."

"Good."

Stricklin blew into his mouthpiece to clear the regulator, then slipped into the black water without a sound.

During the short swim to *Bewitched,* he imagined himself with the best of all worlds—rich, retired and a national hero. He saw the ceremony in his mind, with Pat Douglas placing a medal around his neck. Hell, maybe it would be the President himself and the Medal of Freedom. The TV boys would be filming away and rows of journalists would be scribbling on their pads. Tom Brokaw might cover it himself. Stricklin would be the man who foiled the Middle East monsters single-handedly. There'd be big parties, the promotion he'd deserved years ago and a big raise. And, somewhere in the Caribbean, a big retirement account.

The bone-white hull of *Bewitched* loomed ahead and he worked his way toward the stern. Stricklin thought it very accommodating of Cannon to leave the swim platform down.

Thirty-Three

Bewitched had rocked wildly for almost two hours before Eric Cannon extricated himself from a tangle of sweaty bodies and staggered to the main cabin. The muscles in his legs didn't want to hold him up and the thick musk of sex permeated everything. He found it hard to breathe and he rummaged through the pile of women's things in the head to find his inhaler. A couple of squirts opened his wheezing lungs.

Julie and Rory had started the love marathon with a reenactment of their magazine spread. Then, when the two-man audience was at the bursting point, they pulled them into the action. It started out as action, indeed, but it ended up with Julie saying "I love you, Eric," into his ear. This was a complication he didn't need and he would have to settle it quickly.

"I'm going out on the aft deck for some air," he called back to the master cabin. "It's boiling in here."

He pushed his tired, naked bones through the galley and

living area of the yacht out to the teakwood deck and the refreshing night air. The low lying moon painted a silver highway across the lake. Cannon folded the towel he had used to wipe the deck and hung it over the rail to dry.

Things are going perfect, just perfect, he thought. *New yacht, great women, even if one of them is getting serious. And a lot more to come.*

Eric's inhaler always made him a little dizzy, and he was woozy anyway from the two hours of sexual aerobics. He leaned over the starboard rail of the open stern deck, drinking in fresh air, and tried to force oxygen into his wheezing lungs. He thought he heard one of the women behind him and as he turned to look, he tumbled headfirst over the rail into the middle of the moon's silver highway. He only had time to yell something unintelligible before he was driven under. He thought at first that Kent had dunked him for a joke and he was instantly peeved because he didn't like this kind of horseplay on his boat.

Cannon caught some water in his throat as he hit the lake and his reflexes wanted desperately to cough. He focused all of his energies on suppressing the cough that might kill him, so it was only after a few moments that he felt a strange pressure around his waist. He tried to turn upward, towards the fading moonlight, but he continued his headlong plunge into the darkness. He thought that the inhaler must have him confused because there was no way that he could be sinking without a weight belt. Swimmers often became disoriented underwater after dark and Eric presumed that, no matter what his senses told him, he must have been floating to the surface.

But his lungs burned hotter and the pressure became too much. Eric held out as long as he could and then coughed. Immediately, his nose, throat and lungs sucked in lake water. It tasted a little like blood. He could see nothing in the blackness and no matter how hard he kicked his legs and swept his arms upward, his body continued to plummet straight down. The pressure at his waist let up, but now he didn't have the strength to turn and the surface was a pinpoint, seemingly miles away.

Eric tried to recall the survival training from his Navy days. He hadn't listened carefully because he was an excellent swimmer and good swimmers don't drown.

He repeated that lie to himself, to get it clear in his mind.

Good swimmers don't drown!

He remembered that if his arms were held above his head, his body would very probably sink deeper into the water. In just a few short seconds he tried to employ every survival technique that he had learned, but it was to no avail. No matter how hard he tried, excellent swimmer that he was, he sank deeper and deeper into the abyss. As he began to lose all sense of reality, he sensed someone behind him. He remembered that a drowning victim was best approached from the rear and he felt that Kent was there, after all, to rescue him. His last thought was that of his friend coming to his rescue.

Cannon's body convulsed a few times and, had he not been drowning already, he would have asphyxiated on the vomit that clogged his airway. His arms and legs quit their futile struggle. His heart continued to serve him well for several minutes after his body achieved stasis, floating motionless under the water.

Bob Kent had heard Cannon's yell as he went overboard and ran naked to the aft deck to help his friend. As his feet hit the wet deck, they slipped out from under him. His feet went above his head and he fell directly on his left wrist and the back of his head. He wasn't quite knocked out, but he was dazed and his vision was blurry. His wrist hurt like hell and his hand wouldn't work.

By then, the two women had joined him on deck and they too, had trouble keeping their footing on the wet, polished teak. Eric's immaculate deck was puddled with water. The three looked out over the rails and called Eric's name. Kent saw what he thought was a series of bubbles trailing away from the yacht into the moonlight, but because of the blood pouring out of the back of his head and his left arm useless, he was in no condition to jump in after his friend. The women searched the water on the port side but saw nothing. Julie started crying.

"It's a joke, isn't it?" she asked him. "He's playing some kind of lousy joke?"

"He can't be in trouble," Rory told her. "He's an excellent swimmer. And he doesn't even drink."

A groggy Kent broke into the communications shack and radioed a "man overboard" distress call on the CB radio. The three survivors continued to search the black water and call Eric's name while they waited for the sheriff. Their fantasy island party was over.

Thirty-Four

Jack Bradley had dozed off on the cushions under the copper dome of *Double Eagle* when he heard shouts across the water. Noise had been coming from *Bewitched* all night, but these shouts had an urgency that was very different from the party sounds. With painstaking difficulty, Jack had put *Bewitched* between himself and the Boston Whaler. He was far enough away to avoid notice, but close enough to hear that the shouts were panicked and calling Eric Cannon's name.

Jack got to the helm and saw sweeping flashes of spotlights across the water. He fired up the engines but approached *Bewitched* cautiously. He remembered the first rule of emergency service, "Never rush into trouble."

A red flare went up, then another, by the time he pulled alongside.

"What's the problem," he hollered.

One of the women pushed forward. "It's Eric Cannon, the boat's owner," she said, her voice choked and hoarse from shouting. "He came out alone to get some air, we heard a splash and now we can't find him."

Jack estimated the shoreline to be a few hundred feet away.

"Maybe he decided to swim ashore for some reason."

"No," Kent said. "He wouldn't do that he . . . he . . . didn't have any clothes on."

Jack heard the screaming sound of an outboard motor heading 180 degrees away from them. The sound faded as the speeding boat rounded Arrow Point. It turned south heading down the main channel of the lake *away* from the resort.

"Do you have a radio?" Jack asked. "I have a cell phone aboard, if you need to call for help."

"I've already done that," Kent said. "I got somebody on channel nine who said they'd call the sheriff." Kent's knees gave out and he slid to the deck with his back supported by the cabin bulkhead. He held a towel to his bleeding head and stared blankly into the night.

Jack had to concentrate on keeping the two boats from bumping each other. The waters had roughed up with his approach and with the swift departure of the Whaler. He looked at the pathetic sight of Kent, "Are you all right?"

"I slipped on the deck and hit my head," Kent said. "I feel kind of sick right now, but I'm all right. What can we do about Eric?"

His voice was slurred and Jack couldn't tell if it was from the fall or booze, but figured it was probably some of both.

More than anything, Jack wanted to go after the Whaler. He suspected that Eric Cannon, or Cannon's secret, was racing away from him in the night. But he couldn't take a chance on leaving a drowning man. He switched on *Double Eagle's* powerful twin bow lights and motioned to one of the women who held a spotlight.

"Come aboard," he said. "We'll circle out from the boat

and see if we can find him."

The woman was unsteady but determined. She'd been crying and wore only a T-shirt. The first thing she did was shine her light into Jack's eyes and ruin his night vision.

"Please," he said, shading his eyes, "point that thing out over the water."

"Okay. I'm sorry."

She shined her light into the water and they searched the black waters in a spiral, with *Bewitched* at the center. With every circuit they made, each one about twenty feet farther than the last, Jack's hopes diminished for finding Cannon alive.

He could be aboard the Whaler, he thought, *and this is a diversion to give them time to get away.*

Jack and Julie exchanged names, but other than that they didn't speak. Julie, and the others aboard the yacht, continued to call Eric's name until they couldn't shout anymore. Jack was relieved to see the lights of the sheriff's patrol boat turn into the bay. He returned Julie to the yacht, gave a quick report of his search to the deputy, then raced off to see if he could catch the Whaler.

He knew it was hopeless, but he had to try. When he was well past Arrow Point and saw nothing, he shut down his engines and listened.

Nothing.

As he listened to nothing, Jack realized that it made no sense for Cannon to be on the Whaler with Stricklin and Redding. Jack couldn't figure out what Redding was doing but he knew for sure that Stricklin was tailing Cannon and certainly wouldn't be his co-conspirator. Stricklin and Lindsey had pulled something off right under his nose—possibly a murder—and he couldn't do anything about it. He headed back to the resort, hoping they'd return there under the guise of a late-night cruise, but there was no sign of the Whaler in the marina or the public boat launch next door.

Jack tied the *Double Eagle* in its slip, pulled the canvas covers into place and carried his duffel bag up to the resort. He called the hotel operator and asked for Stricklin's room. No answer. He stopped at the bell desk and asked a valet if Stricklin's car was still in the parking garage. The valet checked the key control board and quickly confirmed that it was.

Good, he thought. *He's playing it cool.*

That meant Stricklin would stay around a day or two for cover and he'd use Lindsey Redding as an alibi, if he had to.

Very neat.

Jack put in a call to the Senator at the Broadmoor and was surprised to find that he'd checked out in the early morning hours. He left his number with Wilder's service in D.C., hoping the Senator would call him first thing and get his people working on this fiasco. There wasn't anything more Jack could do. A booming headache had come on and he tried breathing in the night air to shake it. Deep breathing didn't work and Jack shook off the temptation to get roaring drunk. It was a good thing.

Jack didn't remember the ride home. He seemed to have arrived in his driveway by magic. Exhausted, he flopped onto his bed with all of his clothes on and fell immediately into a fitful, dream-torn sleep of blood and betrayal.

Thirty-Five

Redding and Stricklin stayed hunkered down out of sight in the Whaler just outside Driftwood Point until the wee hours of the morning. Stricklin wasn't particularly happy about it, but Redding insisted on lying low until they were sure *Bewitched* or any other boats were long gone.

All night she'd had the feeling that there was another boat interested in *Bewitched,* but every time she said something to Stricklin he told her she was hearing things. It wasn't so much hearing as a feeling and that feeling included Jack Bradley. She'd been nervous ever since she heard the details of the afternoon events, particularly the detail that he had been a naval intelligence officer. When she talked with Stricklin about it, he said it was unimportant

"I knew that," Stricklin said, with that annoying, know-it-all smirk. "I already talked with him about Cannon."

"I can't believe you did that," Lindsey said. "You tipped your hand and you don't even know whether he's still working or not."

Stricklin spat over the side in disgust and said, "He had a little taste of this business on his last mission and he quit. He's not a problem. Besides he's a do-gooder. He's harmless. Let's get the hell back to Coeur D'Alene before the sun comes up.

"You've done your thing. Now it's my turn to handle the show. I wanted to be sure nobody followed us," Redding said.

She started the engine after another half-hour under the caution flag. "We'll hug the shore and work our way back to the resort slowly." When he started too object, she said, "I've handled boats since I was a kid. I'll take care of it."

Stricklin grunted disapproval but said no more. He took the hard drive out of his belt and secured it with the computer and the STU III in a set of water tight bags.

Lindsey shut the engine down just outside of Mica Bay.

"Now what are you doing?" Stricklin demanded.

"Something we used to do at the end of every run when I was young. I spent all three of my high school summers deck handing on my aunt's charter boat. I can fillet anything that swims before it even knows it's dead."

With a swift backhand slash, Lindsey cut Stricklin's flabby white neck, severing his right jugular, carotid artery, and his trachea. Her forehand slash caught him on the left side and he hit the deck with a thud. Except for a few last gurgles, he didn't make a sound.

"Idiot," Lindsey whispered.

She started the engine and very slowly worked her way along the shadows of the shoreline. Redding thought about going farther up the lake, to Rockford Bay where the lake looked wide and deep. With the 90 horses behind her, she could be there in ten minutes if she let them loose. She decided against it when she remembered the Club at Black Rock was located there. Fancy homes with big decks can have powerful telescopes. The views of the lake from the estates would leave her too much in the open. Redding decided to stay north of Black Rock.

She shredded Stricklin's clothes and diving suit a piece at a time and then left the cover of the shadows and headed for deeper water. In the middle of the lake between Carlin Bay and Turner Bay, she stuffed the cut-up clothing in a heavy bag and tied it and the Whaler's anchor to the corpse. Lindsey grunted as she pushed Stricklin's body over the side and into the deep, placid lake. The anchor hooked the side of the little boat and almost capsized it but Redding was able to break it free. She hoped it hadn't ripped away from Stricklin's body. *Even if it did, the heavy bags of clothes will keep him down,* she thought.

Redding circled in the open water for a time, rinsing Stricklin's blood out of the Whaler with a bucket. She secured the computer and its hard drive, but sunk the rest of his equipment. Redding then jammed the Whaler's throttle forward and headed full speed, back toward the resort. She was careful to steer as wide as possible from Arrow Point with its classy condos. She didn't need to be noticed or caught in some camera angle. She beached the Whaler behind Tubbs Hill and set the computer ashore. Turning the boat around, she put it in slow forward gear and jumped out. She turned and walked quickly up Tubbs Hill trail leading back to the resort. The little Whaler putted into the darkness with its running lights off.

Thirty-Six

Senator Wilder's chartered jet touched down at Andrews exactly two hours and forty-five minutes after its liftoff from Peterson Field in Colorado. He had called Douglas and demanded a meeting. With luck, Douglas would be his usual confident, arrogant self and he'd get right down to business. Years of political experience paid off and Carl Wilder was right.

Director Pat Douglas was sitting in the back of his black Lincoln limousine waiting to escort the Senator to his home in Virginia. The Lear taxied up to the Lincoln sitting on the tarmac and the doors of the Lear and the limo opened at the same instant. Wilder took eight unsteady steps and he let himself be ushered inside the Lincoln.

"What the hell is going on here?" Wilder snapped.

"I came to show you my respect, that's all," Douglas said. "And, of course, to make sure you had a nice vacation."

"Well, how thoughtful. I've got some questions to ask you and I want some straight answers."

As the Lincoln drove through the airport security gate and turned northwest onto Brandywine Road, Douglas rolled up the limo's privacy window. The two were seated side by side in the back seat. Douglas poured Wilder a Jack Daniel's on the rocks and a glass of ice water for himself. It was eight-thirty in the morning. Douglas played his opening card when he didn't have to ask the Senator his drink of choice. Obviously this was just another tidbit available in the agency dossier.

"I don't want that," Carl said and he meant it.

His stomach was barely under control and if he'd had to walk more than the eight steps from the jet he'd have collapsed on the tarmac.

"You'll need it." Douglas handed the drink to Carl, then reached into his briefcase and pulled out a file. "I understand you have some questions about our budget."

"I sure as hell do. I'm calling an emergency session of the Intelligence Committee specifically to pick your budget like a dead chicken."

Pat Douglas smiled and set his drink aside.

"Before you call your committee, you may want to take a peek at this file." When Carl didn't take it from him, Douglas dropped it onto his lap.

Carl opened the cover and there was a picture of Randy, the young man he had met from Florida, and the Senator, sitting close to each other in the Terrace Lounge. Even though this was the line that Carl had expected Douglas to take, the reality of it, the sleazy black-and-white, made his skin crawl. It was one thing to suspect that he had been violated, manipulated. It was quite another to know it for a fact and to have the perpetrator smiling his cocky smile and sitting right next to him.

The Senator flipped through the file. It wasn't a file, just a pile of pictures, pictures of the two of them eating together, drinking and laughing. Innocent enough. Carl knew what was to come and he was right. Next, Randy had his arm around the Senator, walking him to his suite. Then, a scene of the naked Senator in compromising positions with an equally naked Randy. Wilder was shocked. He knew he'd been drugged and that Randy must have returned after he was out, but this. . .

"This is bullshit, Douglas," he said. His stomach flipped again and he swiped at the sweat on his lip. Could he go through with this? The truth wouldn't matter if these pictures got back to Idaho.

Douglas said nothing. He didn't have to. The pictures were good.

They should be, Carl thought. *My committee okayed the funding for them.*

The set-up was clever enough so it didn't appear that Wilder was gone to the world. They looked real. Randy was all over him and Carl already knew it wasn't the first time Randy had been so used. The Mormons and the conservatives in Idaho would never punch the Wilder name again in the ballot booth and his career would be over. This was going to be a hell of a fight, but fight was what Wilder was born to. He let Douglas have his say.

"Randy is Randy Nance, arrested several times in Fort Lauderdale for sodomy, the last time, with a thirteen year old boy. You want to hear the tapes that go with the pictures?"

Now that the cards were face up, it was time to give Douglas a little rope.

"This is a set-up, Douglas, you lousy bastard. Nobody will believe this. I voted against letting gays in the military and everybody knows it."

"Only because your constituents demanded that vote. Everybody also knows that you've lived alone for twenty years and that your staff is usually young and male. I'll bet there's a question or two out there."

"Leave my staff out of this," Carl snapped. "They don't deserve this kind of treatment and you know it. This is between you and me."

Douglas raised an eyebrow.

"All's fair in love and war, Senator. Which is it going to be?"

The limo pulled up in front of Wilder's Virginia home and Carl didn't answer. Douglas dropped the file folder into his lap. "This is an extra. I have plenty more. Let me know when your committee is going to convene, Senator. I'll be sure to bring you a copy of the next morning's *Washington Post*. They'll have a heyday with this."

Douglas slapped the file with his knuckle and laughed.

Cocky-bastard! Carl thought. *We'll see who nips whose nuts.*

Wilder opened the door of the Lincoln and threw his full glass of whiskey on the floor. Then he leaned over and vomited into Douglas' lap. As Douglas cursed and squirmed to brush himself off, it was Carl's turn to laugh. It was hoarse and wheezy, but a laugh.

"Thanks for the lift, Douglas. I'm feeling much, much better."

He slammed the door hard and walked toward his front door, as steady as he could muster with his shoulders thrown back.

The tires of the limo squealed as it sped away.

Wilder was in the middle of collecting messages from his service when he got Jack Bradley's warning: "The traveling salesman is dirty."

"If Jack knows that much, he's in trouble," Carl muttered.

He made some coffee, got on his own scramble phone, and started rattling cages from sea to shining sea.

Even if you've got only one horse, you're a cavalry, he thought. *And when you're a cavalry, you charge.*

Thirty-Seven

Jack woke up before daylight. His brain kept going over and over the events of last night. He remembered telling the two deputies about the possibility of Cannon being a traitor and about him being under surveillance at the resort. Cannon may have pulled this dramatic stunt to shake Stricklin. Jack didn't want whatever Cannon knew falling into anybody's hands, including Nakamura's, so he didn't feel bad about blowing Stricklin's cover to the deputies. They only listened because they'd known Jack for years and because of the recent news about his intelligence past. Even with that, they looked pretty skeptical when they sent him home.

His phone rang and moved him from awake to wide-awake. "Jack Bradley," he answered.

"Mr. Bradley," a worried voice said. "This is Brent Dickson, night auditor at the resort. You'd better come in right away."

Jack winced, "What is it?"

He heard Brent's swallow over the line. "It's a body,

Mr. Bradley. Security just discovered a body washed up on the beach." Jack pressed the cool handset of the phone to his forehead. "Mr. Bradley?"

"Yes, I'm here. Where's this body located?"

"On the beach just below hole number three at the golf course."

"I'll be right there, Brent. Thanks for calling. You did the right thing. Tell them to call Bob Perkins, if they haven't already. I'll be right there."

Jack didn't bother showering or shaving and he dashed out the door in his sweats.

By the time he arrived at the resort Vernon Webster, one of the deputies he'd talked with the night before, was already at the scene. He and Officer Phil Riley had responded to Kent's distress call and they'd searched all night in their marine division jet boat, with no luck. They had also debriefed Kent and the two women and had taken their statements.

Jack had known Deputy Webster for several years and liked him. He didn't know Riley and Riley, obviously, had never encountered a "floater" before. He was standing well away from the body, staring out on the lake, trying to get his color back.

"Hey, Jack," Vernon said. "Long time no see. We have to stop meeting like this, my wife's getting suspicious."

They shook hands and Vernon rolled his eyes towards Riley.

"Green," he said in a low voice, "in more ways than one."

The two of them stood with the corpse between them. The body was covered with a soft-beige blanket. The lump underneath looked too small to be a man. The morning birdsongs were just starting up around them, proving that one less man still meant business as usual for the rest of the world.

"This might be your man Cannon, Jack. You ready to

have a look?"

"No," Jack said. "Do I have a choice?"

"Of course," Vernon said. "We can get his buddy down here. But I'd rather it was you. I'm sorry to do this to you but we need a positive ID. His friends are in shock already and probably just got to bed. They'll have to deal with other details soon enough. It would speed things up immensely if you'd take a look and see if this is Cannon. When he washed up on shore he didn't have a stitch of clothes on, which corroborates their story that he'd just got up out of bed. And what a story that was! But, no jewelry, no tattoos. So, you know the drill. Want a cigar?"

Jack had seen his share of floaters in the Navy. A lot of the crusty old mariners smoked cigars to cut the smell, but if this was Cannon he hadn't been in the water long enough for that.

"Okay, Vern," said Jack. "But you can keep your cigar. Let's see him."

Deputy Webster reached down and slowly peeled the blanket away from the face of the corpse.

"This him?"

Jack looked down upon a pale, flaccid face, a little waterlogged but not yet tight with bloat. The face and body were white to the point of transparency and Jack could see individual blood vessels like blue spaghetti in his arms and legs. Cannon's eyes were half open but hazed over with edema. If there was a look to the face at all, it was one of surprise.

"The eyes are the worst part," said Webster. "That's the part that goes first. Even though he's only been in the water five or six hours, you can see they're already going."

"Yeah."

"Is that, 'Yeah, they're going' or 'Yeah, that's him?"

Jack looked the body over for another moment. No cuts

or wounds visible on the front, no finger bruises or other signs of a struggle.

Of course there wouldn't be, if Stricklin's *involved.* Jack had a strong feeling that Cannon's demise was no accident and that, in fact, he'd been whacked. *But with no signs of a struggle "how" and by "whom" and how would he ever prove it?*

He sighed and ran a nervous hand through his tangled hair.

"Yes, Vern, that's Eric Cannon."

Webster kept the corpse exposed as he reviewed the statements of Julie Adams, Rory Finley and Bob Kent with Jack.

"They didn't seem to be hiding anything," Vern said. "They were up front about who'd been doing what with who and how much they'd all had to drink. Sounds like a helluva party. Kent's got a thing about that wet deck."

"Kent was really woozy when I got there," Jack said. "And the back of his head was bleeding pretty bad. Do you think he didn't get hurt in a fall. . .?"

"No . . . no," Vern said. "I tend to believe him. It's just that he thinks Cannon had some help drowning. Riley, tell Jack what Kent told you."

Officer Riley was reluctant to step up to the body and once there he chose not to look at it. Vernon offered him a cigar and he took it. But the young officer didn't light the cigar, he just moved it from one hand to the other.

"They heard a yell," Riley said, "and Kent saw some bubbles along the starboard side of the boat that could have been air from Cannon's lungs. The women heard only the one yell, too. Kent made a big deal out of the water on the deck. All three of them testified that this Cannon guy was meticulous as hell. According to them, he had wiped the deck dry after they took their swim. The group then went into the bedroom up in the bow."

"Cannon," Webster said, gesturing at the body, "must have made a heck of a splash when he hit the water. That could have soaked the deck."

"Did you check into the little matter I told you about last night?" Jack asked.

"I did," Webster said, "and we have some calls out. Your man hasn't come back to the hotel, his car's still there, his rental boat showed up out of gas just the other side of Bennett's Bay."

Jack hesitated, then asked the question he feared the most. "And the woman?"

"Says she never left the hotel. Her Japanese boyfriend agrees. They had room service very late, quite a spread. Claimed they were doing business on Tokyo time."

Al Dunlap entered the roped off area to examine the scene and the corpse. No one could look as much like a coroner should look as Dunlap. He could have played the undertaker part in "B" westerns. His thin face seldom smiled and he combed his thinning black hair over a huge bald spot. The lakeside breeze peeled the thin hair loose and waved it out from the side of his head like a tattered flag. Dunlap had the responsibility to sign the death certificate after the postmortem.

Webster introduced the group."Coroner Dunlap, you know officer Riley and I am sure you know Jack Bradley, General Manager of The Coeur d'Alene Resort."

"Of course, gentlemen, how are you?" Dunlap's voice was casual, as though they were talking baseball. The lump of dead flesh at their feet could be a pitcher's mound. Dunlap squinted at what was left of Eric Cannon.

"What have you got here?"

The body was still exposed and Jack caught himself thinking that Cannon might get pretty cold and wet uncovered like that.

"We didn't find any bruises or evidence of a struggle of any kind," said Riley. "The body was laying on its back with its feet toward shore and head toward the lake."

"We pulled the deceased about two feet in this direction to get him out of the water," Vern said.

Cannon's left arm lay across his belly and his right above his head. All of the skin of his chest and body was soft and white. His exposed testicles, legs and feet had a dusky cast. The tips of his fingers and toes were heavily wrinkled, as though he'd taken a long, hot bath.

"Let's turn him over and take a look at the other side," Dunlap said. He made a tight circle with his hand to accentuate the request.

The officers did as they were instructed and as the body turned on its side, water trickled out the corner of the dead man's mouth and nose. The back of his neck, buttocks and shoulder blades were a dark bluish purple and appeared as though they were heavily bruised. Jack had seen this before, but Riley evidently had not.

"He was beat up," Riley said.

"No, son," Dunlap said. "In a corpse, blood settles to the low areas and there's no pump to pump it out. When the heart stops the blood turns a purplish blue and that's what we're looking at here."

"Then it turns black, right Doc?" Vern asked.

Jack thought the question was more to get Riley's goat than anything else.

"That's right. Let's turn him all the way over, please."

They did, and Riley lit his cigar.

"Yes," Dunlap said in his casual way, "by the looks of what we have here, death occurred some time during the past twenty-four hours, maximum. I don't think it was that long ago because of the condition of the body . . . it's certainly not a floater. Stomach contents will tell the tale."

Riley stepped up to Dunlap so he wouldn't have to face the corpse.

"What do you mean, he's not a floater?"

"You're not used to those cigars, are you son?" Dunlap said. "What I meant was, people who have been in the water for several days or longer usually come up to the surface and we call them 'floaters.' When lungs fill with water, that takes all of the buoyancy out of 'em and they sink. Eventually, unless they're in real deep cold water, gas forms 'cause of decomposition. When that happens, the body fills with gas and rises."

"Vern," Riley said, still not looking at the body, "I'd better get the clipboard out of the car."

"Yeah, Riley, we'd better have that clipboard," he said, tossing a wink at Jack. Riley was already making his way through the trees. "Take your time," Vern hollered after him, "as long as you're back in a couple of minutes."

"I'd speculate that the heavy underwater currents in this part of the lake, pushing the lake water toward the mouth of the Spokane River, took the body and washed it here on the beach before it could sink all the way," Dunlap mused. "Did you get any pictures yet?"

"Not yet," Vern said, then he hollered after Rilcy, "Hey! Riley! When you're done yelling at the grass, bring the Polaroid!"

"We'll get pathology to do a complete autopsy as well as toxicology tests for blood alcohol and drugs," the coroner said.

"He didn't drink," Jack said.

"No?"

"Not at my hotel, anyway," Jack said. "His pals drank enough for a dozen people, but he stuck to ginger ale and Virgin Marys."

"Well, we'll see," Dunlap said. "Drugs?"

"I don't know," Jack said.

"Well, gents, based on everything you've told me and my examination of the body, it appears to me that we have an accidental drowning on our hands. I'd like some pictures here to document the scene, then let's get Yates to get him down to the county morgue for the pathologist."

"Riley!" Vern hollered, "have dispatch call Yates. Then get your ass over here with that camera."

Vern shrugged at Jack and the coroner.

"Sometimes coming down on 'em a little hard helps 'em get over the first one," he said. "Truth is, I've seen more than my share and I still don't have the stomach for it. But I do my puking at home."

After a quick series of pictures of both sides of the body, the four men helped the undertaker from Yates Funeral Home slip Cannon into the black zippered body bag. After placing the corpse inside and with both zippers secured they lifted the bag onto the funeral home gurney and tied the body to the framework so that it wouldn't slide off going up the steep hill.

"To be honest with you, I'm glad he washed up over here," Jack said. "This way we can keep the body out of sight of the resort guests, even though most of them probably aren't up yet."

"We're all professionals, in our way," the coroner remarked. "I worry about documentation, Vern worries about motives, Riley worries about his stomach and you worry about your guests."

The mortician opened the back door of the unmarked white Ford Aerostar Van. The wheels of the gurney folded themselves neatly underneath as they pushed it into the bed of the van and the restraints clicked into place.

As the vehicle drove off toward the county morgue, Jack glanced at his wristwatch and was surprised to see that it was already a quarter past seven in the morning. He had an eight o'clock meeting with Nakamura.

"Call me if you need anything else," Jack told Vern. "I've got to get cleaned up and into a meeting."

"I'll keep you posted. Let me know if your man shows up."

Jack waved acknowledgment as he hurried up to the parking lot. He didn't want to show up for this morning's meeting unshaven and in sweat clothes, in spite of his new contempt for Nakamura and Lindsey Redding. No matter how loud he played the car stereo, it wouldn't blast the image of Cannon's corpse out of his mind.

Thirty-Eight

Senator Carl Wilder represented a western state and he looked for western solutions to his and the country's problems. He'd leave politics someday, but he would never be driven out. Carl Wilder would take a stand and make the enemy take him down with his six-guns blazing. He would not be staked out like a goat as cheap bear bait.

By daybreak, Senator Wilder had called in every major favor owed him during his lifetime of public service and he called in a fistful of minor favors as well. He set up an emergency meeting of his Intelligence Committee and managed to get a quorum on a holiday weekend. For the first time, he opened the meeting to public scrutiny. He personally invited the ten hottest young members of the press corps and promised them major fireworks. Even the young pups knew that whatever Senator Wilder promised, he delivered.

Some of the old dogs promised to be there, as well. Helen Thomason, the Post's toughest capital conscience, heard him out and offered her services as his personal super-sleuth. Carl had access to the best spies in the country, but he trusted Helen. She could be a royal pain, but she was honest and whatever she printed was inarguably the truth, well researched and in plain English.

The committee convened in the Caucus Room of the Russell Building. Nine Senators, all men, sat as an elevated panel, two feet higher than the witnesses and the rest of the world. Their perch served to emphasize their superior wisdom and judgment. Green tablecloths draped the head table and a witness table, which sprouted a heavy crop of microphones. The floor was carpeted in a gaudy red, which clashed mightily with the tablecloths. A pack of reporters, with cameras and notebooks, crouched on the floor directly in front of the Senators. Shutter clicks and the whirr of cameras rolling drowned out the backhand whispers among the dignitaries.

A row of aides sat in chairs behind the head table, ready to serve their Senators. The rest of the room was filled with rows of empty chairs. Helen Thomason sat stiffly and long faced in the second row.

Senator Carl Wilder was the ranking majority member of the committee and his seniority allowed him plenty of latitude to conduct the inquiry. Both sides of the isle had come to hate the agency. Douglas had practiced his intimidation for many years without regard to political affiliation.

At the last minute, Agent Wendell Phillips threw open the heavy double wooden doors of the meeting room to allow the grand entrance of Director Pat Douglas. Douglas entered the room with his briefcase and entourage. He took a prime seat in the front row directly behind the witness table and face-to-face with Senator Wilder. Douglas turned to agent Phillips and whispered, "That shithead doesn't have enough brains to blow up a balloon. We'll chew him up and spit him out."

Douglas opened his briefcase and pulled out the blackmail. Carl Wilder used a handkerchief to blot away the perspiration that dotted his upper lip. The director was flanked on both sides by agents and he tapped the intimidating file on his knee with his gaze firmly on Wilder. The Senator nodded and motioned for Douglas to look behind him. Douglas turned and dropped the file folder.

Randy was strategically seated in the second row precisely behind him. Randy leaned forward with a big smile and put both hands on the Director's shoulders. With his lips close to the Director's ears, he whispered, "I have never met Senator Carl Wilder and will be glad to testify that those pictures are fakes, sweetheart. Oh, and I've taken the liberty of telling Ms. Thomason there, about the close personal relationship that you and I enjoy."

Douglas tried to jerk free, but Randy held him firm.

"She promised me she'd keep it quiet unless you or I agreed to make it public."

Randy kissed Douglas on the ear and as the director pulled away a file dropped into his lap. He opened it to discover a picture of himself and Randy in an intimate position—a *very* intimate position.

"A picture is worth a thousand words," Randy whispered. "I might be gay but I'd much rather be that than a power hungry blackmailer like you."

Douglas looked at Helen Thomason. She glanced at him with a look of pure disgust and began scribbling intently in her famous notebook. Douglas looked up at the old Senator, who winked at him.

"I understand that you wanted to announce your resignation," Senator Wilder boomed. "Consider it accepted. This committee has a busy agenda, Mr. Douglas, please don't waste any more of our precious time."

Douglas said nothing. He placed both files into his briefcase, closed it and latched both of the clasps. As he stood, so did his shocked entourage. He led his flock from the committee room like a mother duck and the huge double doors slammed closed behind him. The room began buzzing and reporters ran to call in the sensational resignation story. Senator Wilder gave Randy a firm thumbs up, Helen applauded and the staffers smiled. Randy leaned back on the two rear legs of his chair with his hands and arms behind his head and a satisfied smirk of righteousness.

Chairman Wilder gaveled the meeting to order. "Now," he said, "we have the matter of some freelance intelligence work in Idaho to discuss. Gentlemen, may we call the Director of the CIA and get this meeting under way?"

Thirty-Nine

Jack's commute to work was only about ten to twelve minutes along a beautiful, tree lined county highway. His classic golden Porsche hugged the road and was a treat to drive.

The car was a birthday present to himself. Jack reached to the dashboard and pushed the button to activate the computerized phone, which he had installed in the classic car.

"Name please?" asked the computer.

"Resort."

"Thank you."

He appreciated a polite machine. Within seconds, the phone was ringing.

"It's a great day at The Coeur d'Alene Resort."

Jack recognized the friendly voice at the switchboard.

"Linda, this is Jack Bradley. Last night I asked Peter Harding to make sure our executive boardroom was set up for a breakfast meeting for two for Mr. Tako Nakamura and myself at 8:00 AM. I'm in my car now heading back to the resort, but I want to make sure that it's done."

"Mr. Bradley, Peter wanted to make sure the set-up and the service was perfect, and he's been here working on it for over an hour."

"Great, Linda. Thanks. Tell Peter I'll be there in seven or eight minutes."

"It will be my pleasure, Mr. Bradley."

That damn Peter is really something, he thought. *He was probably working until the wee hours of the morning and he's already back to make sure my breakfast with Nakamura goes well.*

Peter was going to be one hell of a hotelier. Jack also hoped that both he and Peter would still be employed after this morning's meeting.

Jack quickly stopped by his office and dialed Stricklin's room, but there was no answer. He looked at his watch again and decided he'd just have to call him after the meeting, because he wasn't about to be late for this morning's session. Jack asked the telephone operator to turn Stricklin's message light on and ask him to call Jack as soon as possible.

Jack's own messages included a couple from Senator Wilder. They said, simply, "Dirty salesman, dirty boss," and "Audit in progress."

Jack smiled and felt the strain on the tight muscles of his face.

We might win this one yet.

Peter was in the executive boardroom wiping the silverware one last time. A suitable Japanese flower arrangement graced the center of the table. Jack noticed the table was set for three. He didn't have to wonder very hard about what that meant.

"Have you seen Nakamura yet?" Jack asked.

"No, sir, not yet. But he should be here any minute. He called down to say that his associate would be joining you. I hope that's okay."

"It'll be . . . interesting."

"I'm glad to see you," Peter said. His frown of concern was genuine. "Sounds like you had a rough morning after a rough day."

"Yep, Peter, not too enjoyable. I'll fill you in on the details a little later."

"I'm not sure I want to hear them."

Tako Nakamura entered the room in a crisp blue suit with a perfectly starched and pressed white shirt and formal tie. His distinguished gray hair was perfectly combed and his greeting to Jack was stiff and formal. Lindsey followed, all smiles and innocence, elegantly dressed in a gray power suit that showed off just enough of her legs to break his concentration. She carried a black leather briefcase which Jack did not remember seeing as part of her baggage. The scent of "Poison," one of those irresistible perfumes, hung about her. Jack felt very bad vibes. He held out a hand to Nakamura in greeting and prepared himself for the worst.

Nakamura had drunk coffee the day before because it gave him more of a feeling of America, but this morning he selected Japanese green tea. His expression was somber. The three of them completed a near silent Japanese breakfast of rice, dried fish, raw egg, miso soup, nori, and Japanese pickles, which Nakamura had specified. Finally, Nakamura spoke, slowly, and in a steady, calculated manner.

"I do not need to take a further tour of the resort, Mr. Bradley. Because of the seventeen-hour time difference, I was up very, very early this morning and walked through much of the property. I have called and instructed my financial people to fax the proper paperwork to Von Bueller Industries. Von Bueller and I will meet later today at his home on the lake to finalize matters."

Nakamura paused for a response, but Jack simply held

his gaze and out waited him.

"Jack, as you know, I have my own hotels in Japan. We do things very differently and I need to be sure that with an investment of this magnitude, it is properly and profitably operated. I have considered expanding my holdings outside of Japan and have been preparing my staff for additional responsibilities. I have made my decision and I took the liberty of calling Aki and informing him earlier this morning. My decision has his full support and I would appreciate having yours, as well."

Jack's head spun and his inner eye saw the handwriting on the wall. The collar of his shirt seemed to tighten around his neck and he felt his face flush with frustration and anger. Nakamura was going to bring in his own people, which was the style of many Japanese companies that invest overseas. Jack was out. What fate awaited his great staff for which he cared so much?

"I understand. Congratulations," Jack said, his voice dry and flat.

He avoided looking at Lindsey Redding only with great effort. She pulled a sheaf of papers from her briefcase and set it on the tabletop. Jack's gaze slipped down to the black briefcase that leaned against her slender ankle. What he saw there stiffened his spine and sat him straighter in his chair. The top of the case was unzipped and inside was the small, black specialty computer that Jack remembered seeing in the hands of Dan Stricklin.

Oh, shit! Jack thought. *This isn't a money deal, it's a trade, whatever Stricklin got from Cannon for The Coeur d'Alene!*

"Thank you," Nakamura said and nodded. "I have asked the Managing Director of my Japanese hotels to travel to Coeur d'Alene early next week."

My God, Jack thought. *He's wasting no time. The re-*

sort is gone. Maybe I can, at least, keep them from turning over that computer?

"His name is Kyosin Ogura and he is now making the appropriate arrangements. Even though I have only been here a short time, it is very easy for me to see that this resort is a trophy hotel."

Nakamura leaned back in his chair, tented his hands on his belly and looked beyond Jack to the lake and mountains beyond.

"I wish Ogura-san to come and personally meet you and the members of your management team and review the hotel's operations. Even though Japan is thousands of years older than your country, we have a great deal to learn about the modern world's hospitality industry.

Jack clenched his teeth and looked at neither of them.

"I see," he said.

"Perhaps you don't," Nakamura said. The tycoon leaned forward, forcing their gazes to meet. "Mr. Jack Bradley, The Coeur d'Alene Resort is the finest operated facility that I have ever seen anywhere in the world. I would like The Coeur d'Alene Resort to become the international headquarters and flagship of our new company, 'Nakamura Worldwide.' In the twenty-four hours that I have known you, I have been very, very favorably impressed." Nakamura slid the sheaf of papers from Lindsey to Jack. "I am offering you today, to become the president of this new venture and to oversee the operations not only of The Coeur d'Alene, but of our existing hotels in Japan and our expansions internationally. I have funded a large credit draft into my Bank of America account in San Francisco. It is my desire that you begin to plan, immediately, an expansion of this facility. Von Bueller has shared with me the exciting plans you have developed over the years. I took the liberty of calling your designer to meet with you this afternoon. In addition, as president of Nakamura Worldwide, you will start at a salary which is over two times your current compensation. In addition, you will be tied to bonuses based on the operating profits of all of our hotels and will become a very close advisor of mine. I am an unmarried man, unusual in Japan, and have no children or living relatives. It is my desire to develop a relationship with someone I can trust, someone who knows this industry, so that Nakamura Worldwide will continue to move forward for many decades, as my father and grandfather would have wished."

Jack was stunned. He fingered the paperwork without reading it.

Is this the way it always ends, he wondered, *with the one offer that you've waited for all your life?*

Lindsey Redding smiled at him with the same warm, seductive smile she wore yesterday morning, the morning that began one of the longest days in Jack's life. He couldn't help one more glance at the open briefcase and the reminder that he was dealing with people who were inhumanly cold and vicious. Jack took a deep breath and ran a hand through his hair.

"Mr. Nakamura," he said, "frankly, I'm flattered and a little stunned. I thank you for your confidence in me. I'm honored and don't know quite what to say."

"Good," Nakamura said, and he smiled for the first time of the day. "I'll take that as a willingness to proceed. Look over this agreement. I think you'll find it satisfactory. I have a very important meeting in New York this evening, but I would like to work out these details with you at my office in Japan in ten days. You will fly back with Mr. Ogura and we will have a traditional Japanese ceremony celebrating Nakamura Worldwide and its new president, Mr. Jack Bradley."

With that, the confident Nakamura stood, shook Jack's hand and gave a slight bow. Jack returned the bow, suitably lower, as a sign of respect, which he no longer felt for Nakamura or for Lindsey Redding.

Lindsey reached out a congratulatory hand, which Jack ignored. Instead, he handed her the black briefcase, but when she reached for it he didn't let it go.

"I was noticing your computer," Jack said. "I'm looking for something very small that I could use to get work done at home and on the road."

For the first time Jack saw a flaw in her well-played role. While her expression didn't change, her color went very pale, in spite of her perfect make-up.

"Yes," she said, glancing at Nakamura for help, "It's very handy."

She gave the slightest tug, but Jack didn't let her have it. He looked into the briefcase as though admiring the computer, but in reality he was verifying that, at least externally, it was identical to the one that Stricklin had brought into his office, the powerful black computer with no manufacturer's identification anywhere on its surface.

"I'm sure we could provide one for you, Jack," Nakamura said. "Anything that makes your job smoother affects our bottom line, right?"

"That's true." Jack said. "Unfortunately, I'm not very computer literate. In fact, I've been having some problems learning all of the ins and outs of our new system, which I understand, is the best on the market. Who manufactures this one?"

This time Jack let her tug be successful, but obvious.

"I don't remember," Lindsey said, "I . . ."

"We have a meeting in just a few minutes Jack," Nakamura interrupted. "We're finalizing some paperwork with your local Idaho Independent Bank. It is most important, as you Americans say, to get our ducks in a row before we meet with Von Bueller. Perhaps Lindsey can demonstrate her machine for you another time under less pressured circumstances."

Lindsey's color and composure returned. But Jack couldn't quite let it go.

"We don't have much luck with evening meetings, but leave word with my secretary and we can arrange something suitable."

With that, Tako Nakamura and Lindsey Redding hurried out of the dining room. Jack threw his napkin onto the tabletop and startled the busboy that was reaching for the dishes.

"Sorry," Jack mumbled. "Sorry about that."

He hurried out of the dining room and uncharacteristically did not return the greetings of the employees he met on the way to his office. His mind was elsewhere, on the computer, on Von Bueller and on the relentless ticking of a great clock way out of his control.

Forty

When Jack returned to his office he had messages to call his favorite guests, the Hanson's, and his least favorite, Veronica Whitcomb. Though he was curious about how the Hanson's were getting along after their traumatic day yesterday, Jack couldn't bring himself to call. Veronica Whitcomb could wait until hell freezes over, as far as he was concerned. *I'll call them but I just can't right now.* Jack turned to his voice mail and the only message was from Senator Carl Wilder.

"Cavalry dispatched to your location," the Senator's raspy voice advised. "Meantime, watch your back."

No shit. The image of that small, black computer kept popping up in his mind. *What if they've copied that data already?* He thought. *What if they've transmitted it to Japan, or worse?*

Jack ignored his ringing phone and chewed over some logic. They probably wouldn't risk transmission. This was something that they most likely would keep between themselves and close at hand. Lindsey would be a fool to keep the only copy of a billion dollar formula on one computer. Lindsey Redding might be a liar and a traitor, but she was no fool. Jack called the concierge.

"Lily, this is Jack Bradley. Did Mr. Nakamura or his associate request any services last night or this morning?"

"As a matter of fact they did Mr. Bradley," Lily said. "First thing this morning Miss Redding asked me to find her 3 computer diskettes. A couple of hours later she asked me to prepare a Federal Express package for shipment to her office in Portland. One moment." Jack listened to the background shuffle of paperwork.

"Yes," Lily said, "here it is."

"I know that this sounds unusual, Lily, but do you know what she's shipping in that package?"

"Why, yes. She prepared it right here. The package has one of the three computer discs that I had gotten for her earlier this morning."

"Lily, this is very important," Jack said. "Hold that package and if either Mr. Nakamura or Miss Redding asks, tell them you've already sent it."

Lily hesitated before answering. "Mr. Bradley," she said, her voice low, "I can't do that. It's illegal isn't it, to mess with the mail?"

"Don't worry, Federal Express is not U.S. Mail" Jack reassured her, "and the police will bring in a search warrant for it within the next couple of hours. Please keep this confidential."

"Yes, of course, Mr. Bradley. Will you . . .?"

"I'll tell you the whole story as soon as I have it. Take my word for it, this is important."

Christine opened Jack's door enough to stick her head into his office. "The phone's been going crazy for you this morning, Mr. Bradley," she said. "This time it's Vernon Webster. He says it's urgent."

What now?

Jack picked up the phone and heard Vernon speaking to someone else.

"Tell them of course we'll cooperate," the deputy said. "Tell them to get us a list of equipment that they need and an estimate of manpower. Jack, is that you?"

"It's me Vern. What's going on?"

"I'm busier than a long-tailed cat in a roomful of rockers," Vern said. "The FBI's on the horn, they have a team on the way. We've got ourselves another floater and he may be the MIA you told me about who calls your hotel 'home sweet home.'"

"What?" Jack swallowed hard. "Who?"

"The Avista boys down at the dam in Post Falls fished him out of one of their turbine inlet screens. He's a real pretty one."

"What do you mean?"

"Well, somebody didn't want him identified real quick," Vern said. "They cut him up pretty good."

Cut him up—knife—the morning of arrival in Nakamura's suite Lindsey Redding turned an apple into a peacock with a knife. She was incredibly good with that knife. Jack sucked in a breath and let it out slowly.

"Teeth?"

"Yeah," Vern said, "but we'll have to know where to look for the dental records. This boy's about six-one, two-twenty, short brown hair going to gray. Sound familiar?"

Jack hesitated. He didn't want Vern to talk him into looking at a second body in one day—especially a body as mutilated as this one. But it did sound like Stricklin and if Lindsey Redding did something like that to Stricklin what might she have in store for Jack Bradley? Suddenly, remembering the Senator's warning, Jack's shoulder blades felt very, very naked.

"Jack? Are you with me?"

"Yes, Vern, I'm here. Your description sounds like Stricklin, all right. His dentals should be on file with CIA, Langley. Look, I think I know who killed him. Can you get a search warrant up here to secure some evidence?"

"Given our body count in the past several hours, I think I could get a search warrant on the President of these United States. Which reminds me, do you know anything about an FBI team that's on its way?"

Jack recalled the Senator's message about the cavalry.

"Not really," he said. "Why?"

"They've asked us to have you on hand. A couple of agents are driving in from Spokane and they have a support team of heavyweights comin' from Seattle. They want some answers and fast. You want that meeting here or at your hotel?"

"If I have a choice, I'd rather keep this out of the resort."

"Fine," Vern said, "come over here then. We'll get going on your warrant. Anything else you might feel like telling me? I mean, so far this last twenty-four hours involves only two bodies, two pain-in-the-ass federal agencies and a shitload of paperwork and you seem to be smack dab in the middle of it all."

"I told you what I could tell you last night, Vern. I'll make a phone call before I come over and maybe I'll have some more for you by then."

"Lucky me," Vern Webster said and hung up.

Jack called Senator Wilder's office in DC, and after being passed through three staffers he finally got through to the man himself.

"Jack Bradley, I've had one hell of a day!" the Senator announced. "How about you?"

"It's been a big one, all right. We have two bodies on

slabs and it's not even lunchtime yet."

"*Two?*" the Senator spluttered. "What the hell, boy?"

Jack filled him in and asked if the Senator could arrange to have Stricklin's dental records faxed to the sheriff's office.

"Absolutely," Wilder said. "Seems that Pat Douglas has given his notice and he plans on being mighty cooperative in his final days. I'll find out more about that computer, too, but I think you can rest easy. All of our intelligence units are password-protected on several levels. Someone might break that code, but they're gonna have to put a big computer on it for quite some time. The disk-copy feature is protected, too. The machine tells them a copy's made which is still password-protected, but the real data's never copied. If they do translate those disks, they'll find a copy of the Declaration of Independence, or something. Now, about the cavalry."

"The FBI?" Jack asked. "Yeah, what should I tell them?"

"Most of it they've already been told. They were expecting to come in there and tangle with Stricklin and Cannon. You'll have to update them as to what's happened and on Nakamura and your girlfriend. Are you sure that Nakamura's in on it? If you're wrong and the Redding woman is freelancing, there could be some international shit in the State Department fan."

"I'm not absolutely sure of anything, anymore, but Nakamura's whole manner was different today. And when I started talking about the computer, Nakamura got her off the hook. He might not know that two men are dead over this, but I think he knows what he's got in his hands."

"Well, Jack, if we can get Nakamura, Redding and Von Bueller together making this deal, then I'd say you might get a shot at buying your dream hotel, after all."

Jack laughed. "It would have to be bargain basement prices, Senator. We're talking huge bucks."

"Jack, you might be surprised at the kind of money that's

lying around for the asking. Hell, an old Senator might even kick in his life savings if you'd consider a joint venture. You're on a first name basis with guys like Clint Diamond and sweethearts like Veronica Whitcomb. But, we don't want to get the cart before the horse. Get over there and brief the FBI boys. I'll fax those dental records and anything else I can think of that might be useful. And, Jack?"

"Yes, Senator?"

"Watch your back. You're still on the hot seat."

Jack didn't even get a chance to hang up before Bob Perkins strode into the office.

"I hear you identified Cannon's body this morning. Vern just called with another. What's happening?"

"A whole lot, Bob. Do you have a spare sidearm?"

"Now, wait a minute, Jack. This is big time. Let's leave this to the heavies. They'll take the credit, anyway."

"So," Jack said, moving for the door, "if you're not interested, then I'll have to explain everything later."

"Whoa, there, Boss," Bob said as he stopped Jack with a hand on his arm. "I didn't say I wasn't interested. I just don't want you getting yourself killed, which you damned near did yesterday. Why do you want a gun?"

Jack looked at his watch.

"We're due at the sheriff's office right now. We're meeting the FBI and they're here because of Cannon. Stricklin was a Fed and he was after Cannon, only it looks like he decided to freelance once he got Cannon's information. I think Lindsey Redding killed Stricklin, took that information for Nakamura and is now trading it to Von Bueller for the resort."

Perkins whistled. "No shit?"

"No shit," said Jack. "I'm sure that the FBI's going to try to nab Nakamura, Von Bueller and Lindsey together with a certain piece of evidence. They'll want somebody familiar to talk with them. I'm the logical choice. I don't want to go in there without at least a backup piece."

"Sounds like it goes by the manual. Why the hardware?"

"Because this one won't go by the manual," Jack said. "Lindsey Redding's writing the manual on this one and we have two bodies so far that illustrate her methods."

"That sexy blonde? What makes you. . .?"

"It's a long story and we don't have the time. And I don't want to count on anybody else for my personal protection."

Bob Perkins sighed and slipped his left pants cuff up far enough to reach a small, black automatic.

"It's not much," Bob said. "Twenty-two, six-shot. Just don't shoot me with it."

Jack checked the safety and the chamber then snuggled the little pistol between his belt and the small of his back. He put on his jacket and clapped Bob on the shoulder. "Okay, let's hit it."

Jack opened the door to Christine's office and nearly bumped into Mrs. Hansen, who had the Smith's infant slung over her shoulder.

"Oh, Mr. Bradley," she said, "I'm so glad to see you."

"Hello, Mrs. Hansen. I'm afraid we're in a bit of a rush. . ."

"Well," she said, "I won't keep you. I just wanted you to know that this baby is a dream come true for us and it looks like we'll be able to keep her."

The baby delivered a grand burp, impressive for her size, then flashed Jack a big, toothless grin.

"She's a cutie," Jack admitted, "and she looks right at home. Maybe you could fill me in later on the details."

"I'd love to," Mrs. Hansen said. "We're going to extend a few days to take care of paperwork. Thanks, again. And thank you, Mr. Perkins."

Christine was on the phone. She waved at Jack to get his attention and silently mouthed, "It's Vernon."

"Tell him we left already," Jack whispered, then he and Bob Perkins hustled out the door.

Forty-One

Lindsey Redding stepped aboard the elegant green and white houseboat and let Tako Nakamura guide her by the elbow to the bow rail. A crewman untied the dock lines and the elderly charter skipper eased the houseboat away from the pier. Lindsey would have preferred to pilot the boat herself and she would have preferred that only she and Tako make the journey to Von Bueller's mansion, but Tako was in one of his take-charge moods. This mood had been brought on by her late return the night before, a return she obliquely blamed on Jack Bradley. Nakamura wanted time to savor his upcoming conquest and arranged with the boat captain to travel up the main channel of the lake toward Harrison before turning back to return to the meeting place.

Lindsey had known Tako for many years and she knew his quirks. One such quirk forced Tako to surround himself with elegance and servants before every major negotiation. He was an otherwise painfully independent man for one so wealthy. Lindsey interpreted these occasions as a cross between dramatic appearance and confidence building.

He's nervous, she thought, *and he wants to impress Von Bueller.*

"We have an excellent opportunity ahead," he said, "but you don't look happy."

"You see this as an opportunity. I see we have a problem."

"What problem have we not covered?"

A gentle breeze ruffled her hair and Lindsey smoothed it back into place. She used the movement to accentuate the ample contents of her silk blouse.

"Meeting the man on his own turf," she said, "amounts to a concession that he is the greater man. That gives him a negotiating edge, much like an incumbent politician deflecting a challenger. Meeting him here will cost you money."

Tako smiled that confident, reptilian smile he wore when he knew he had a deal cornered.

"You do play chess, Lindsey, do you not?"

"You know I do."

"And what is the optimum situation in a game of chess?"

"To have multiple moves available, any one of which puts the opponent into checkmate."

"Precisely. And I have those moves set up. If Max wants to place conditions on our deal, over and above those we've discussed, I will simply walk away. He will fail, the price will fall and I will buy it for less. There are disadvantages, given time and chaos, excellent employees may choose to leave."

"Jack Bradley, for instance?"

Tako took Lindsey by the shoulders and turned her to face him.

"I believe you when you tell me that nothing happened between you two last night," Tako said. "I think that Bradley is the true pearl of this resort and I intend to work with him. I do not intend to suffer indignity due to indiscretions on your part. Is that clear?"

"You have nothing to worry about. I have never given you cause to worry about that."

"Until last night. And you didn't answer my question."

"Yes," she said, "that's clear."

He let go of her shoulders and she turned again to the rail. She nodded toward the large 3-story house barely visible against the shore adjoining the resort's golf course.

"Von Bueller may be bitter," she reminded him, "and sell to someone else."

"Then I will buy from someone else. I will have this magnificent resort by the end of the year, one way or another."

"For a higher price, of course."

"Perhaps. Perhaps for a *much* higher price. But, as Max knows, I would prefer to keep this between our two families. He intends to remain in the arms business and I do not. The Nakamuras and the Von Buellers have made 'gentleman's agreements' before and I'm confident that we can make one now."

Lindsey accepted the brush of Tako's hand across her chest. Business made Tako passionate and she had found long ago that it was wise to play to his hormones. It was no accident that she had chosen the elegant little houseboat to transport them to Von Bueller's. Besides the buffet spread on the galley table, the boat offered a cozy bedroom. Tako led her to it, as she knew he would.

"About twenty minutes to Mr. Von Bueller's," the skipper said, as they passed the helm.

"Perfect," Tako said. "And what a beautiful day, don't you agree?"

"Yes, sir," the skipper said, but Tako wasn't listening.

Lindsey placed her briefcase beside the bed and Tako

tapped it with the toe of a perfectly shined shoe.

"By the way, you didn't bring this computer with you on the flight. Where did you get it?"

Lindsey felt a moment of breathlessness, a drop in the pit of her stomach.

"I had it Federal Expressed from my office when I realized that I'd forgotten it. It arrived yesterday evening." She smiled. "Would you like a demonstration?"

"Yes, but not of the computer."

Lindsey quickly slipped out of her clothes and joined him on the bed. The chop of the lake water accentuated Tako's aggressive lovemaking. Within fifteen minutes she was slipping back into her clothes, relieved that he had forgotten about the computer. They had finished just in time for Tako to commence his assault on the German and achieve his newest business climax. He triumphantly disembarked. His confident strides down the dock and up the path to Von Bueller's were leading him to the conquest. A conquest to satisfy his lust for the resort.

Forty-Two

Jack and Bob Perkins arrived at the sheriff's office just as the two special agents from Spokane stepped out of their gray, four-door Ford. The driver was a lanky young woman, about five feet eight inches tall, with wiry black hair and a grim expression. Her partner looked old enough to be Jack's father and what little gray hair he had was buzzed close to the back of his head. Vern met them at the door and, after the introductions, Special Agent Lolanne Flakita did the talking.

"For the record, I hope you all recognize the international possibilities we're facing here," she said. "We're about to serve warrants on two of the wealthiest industrialists in the world, the equivalent of Mossad arresting William Randolph Hearst and J. Paul Getty. No matter how this comes down, we're all in for a very hard time."

"Everything I told you is true," Jack said. "And my suspicions are sound. Two people are dead and a vital nuclear secret is up for grabs. We can't let them get away with this."

"Maybe three dead," the older agent said. His name

was Phil, and his manner was impatient. "A Syrian was mysteriously shot in Spokane a few days ago. Could be connected."

"That makes me feel so much better," Vernon said. "Now, warrants are cut for the package at the hotel, Cannon's two rooms, Nakamura's suite and any safe deposit boxes they might have used at the resort. We have warrants specifically for Von Bueller's residence and grounds and for Nakamura and Lindsey Redding's personal effects. How do we serve them?"

Special Agent Flakita didn't waste time taking charge. She was of American Indian heritage, a proud member of the Kootenai Tribe of Idaho. The agent was a strikingly attractive woman whose bloodline and upbringing made her courageous and decisive. She had distinguished herself at posts around the country and was now home in her own backyard.

"You and Perkins know the hotel and its grounds," she told Vernon, "you serve those warrants. Phil will stay here as command coordinator for the rest of your people and the incoming team. Mr. Bradley and I will drop in on the party at Von Bueller's."

Phil's complexion flushed red from the neck of his white shirt to the top of his head.

"Lolanne, you're making a mistake," he said. "It's inappropriate for you to take a civilian in there."

"Phil, you've seen the sheet on Bradley. He's experienced in this kind of operation and he's in a unique position to get us in there without trouble." She turned to Jack and asked, "You *can* get us in there, can't you?"

Jack felt something wash over him—a confidence and calm from the past. "Absolutely. I'll tell Max that I have a joint venture partner and I want a last minute chance to bid on the resort. Marko Rivers can fly us over there in a matter of minutes."

"This is bullshit!" Phil interrupted. "You don't know what kind of security he has and we can't get backup in there fast enough to cover your butts. Now you're talking about bringing a civilian chopper into the middle of who knows what."

"Marko knows what he's doing," Jack said. "He flew . . ."

"I don't give a damn if he flew wingman for the Red Baron. When I want to hear something from you, I'll squeeze your head." Phil turned his fury onto Flakita. "This op has been cockamamie from the start. I say that you and I should go in, deliver the warrants by the book and sort it out from there."

Special Agent Flakita developed a flush of her own, but didn't so much as blink.

"We'll wire up," Flakita said, nodding towards Jack. Her voice was calm; she could have been ordering a burger. "Call your chopper. Phil, if you hear trouble, come on in with Baker team. Mr. Bradley, can you give us the layout of Von Bueller's place and his security arrangements?"

"Sure," Jack said, and he stepped up to a map on Vernon's wall. "As you can see, there is only one private road to the house. Helicopters have landed by the pool before and there is a dock and boat slips here. A fence with a gated entry surrounds the entire place. Max is careful, but not paranoid. His two full-time caretakers do carry side arms, but he relies on his isolation and his extensive electronics and cameras for protection."

"How does he feel about drop in visitors?" Flakita asked.

Jack ran a hand through his hair. "I've never known him to have many. He prefers to keep his life completely private."

"So," she said, tapping a finger on the desktop, "meeting Nakamura like this is highly unusual?"

Jack shrugged and said, "Their families have been in business together since the last century. He may consider Nakamura to be family. I would guess that he doesn't want any part of this deal to be public."

"That's exactly what I object to here," Phil said, "There's

too much guesswork and not enough hard evidence."

Flakita raised her eyebrows as if to ask, "Are you through now?" Phil turned away in disgust.

"There's a steep cliff behind the house adjoining the golf course." Perkins said. He stepped up to the map and ran a finger from the roadway to the back of Von Bueller's property. "A few of us could head up there, just in case, and rappel down the cliff in a couple of seconds if we were needed."

Flakita nodded. "Good, let's send a few deputies up that way. I'd still like you to assist at the hotel, Mr. Perkins. I want Baker team's chopper available for a chase, in case anybody tries to fly out of there. Now let's get some wires on and coordinate our frequencies. I want this to be quick, before they have a chance to hide the computer." Special Agent Flakita turned to Jack and with a hard, level gaze said, "I want you to understand one thing, Mr. Bradley. If you're wrong about this thing, your ass is mine."

Just then, the receptionist called back to Vernon.

"Vernon! It's Al Dunlap calling from Yates. Line two."

"It's our coroner," Vern explained and picked up the phone.

"Yeah, Al. What have we got?" The background chatter in the sheriff's office quieted to a faint rustle of paperwork as Vern nodded twice. "The short version, Al," Vern said. "We're in a bind here."

Vern nodded again, hung up and looked Jack straight in the eye.

"Well, Jack, the dentals match up. Our stiff's confirmed as Major Daniel Elton Stricklin, late flunky for the CIA. He must have some mighty valuable fillings; a couple of AP's from Fairchild are on their way to fly what's left of him back East." Special Agent Flakita flicked a glance of reappraisal over Jack, tossed him a slight nod of approval and said, "Okay, gentlemen, let's get our butts in gear. Mr. Bradley, the phone's all yours."

Jack ran a hand through his hair again.

"We'd better call Max from my car phone. He has caller I.D. on his switchboard."

"Good thinking," Flakita said. She stared at the sheriff's map as a deputy clipped a tiny microphone inside her lapel. "If you'd like a job when this is all over, Mr. Bradley, I can get you an application."

Jack hesitated, his hand on the doorknob. "No, thanks. I've already got a job." *He hoped he'd still have it after today.*

Jack hurried to his Porsche. Once he sat in the familiar leather and shut the door, he took in a huge breath of air and exhaled it slowly and out loud. He calmed himself for the call to Marko Rivers.

He pushed the phone button. "Name," the computer said.

"Chopper."

Bob Perkins came out of the sheriff's office, tossed Jack a quick salute then climbed into the patrol car with Riley. Riley waved an envelope full of warrants and the two of them drove off towards the resort.

"Rivers Aviation," Marko said.

"Hello, Marko. Jack Bradley. Can you fly two to Von Bueller's right away?"

"I suppose I could. I've got four hours before I pick up your big shots in Spokane."

"Big shots?"

"The Senator and three government people," Marko said. "You want me to stay out there at Von Bueller's, or do I just drop you off?"

"We'll want you to stick around. This might be an arrest situation. Are you okay with that?"

"Just so it doesn't take more than four hours and nobody shoots my bird. You at the hotel?"

"No, Sheriff's Office. How soon can you be here?"

"Ten minutes."

"Good," Jack said and pushed the "off" button. He unplugged the phone and took it inside. Phil, still red-faced and unhappy, rushed up to him. "Did you call Von Bueller?" Phil asked, his voice snappish and surly.

"No. I didn't. I'll call as we're setting down, so everything goes down fast."

Phil grunted a reluctant approval. "Sheriff's got your wire," Phil said. "Better get it on."

Vernon wired him up and loaned him two pairs of handcuffs, then Phil said, "Your bird's down," and Jack followed Flakita under the blades and into the chopper. He sealed the door and the racket subsided to a high, warbling whine. Marko lifted off and Jack put through the call to Max.

"Jack," Max said, "you've called me away from a very important meeting. Your new boss will not be impressed."

"I have investors," Jack said. "One of them is with me now. I have a prospectus and a bid for the hotel."

"Jack, it's a little late for . . ."

"What can it hurt?" Jack pressed. "Even if you don't sell to me, we might bid the price up and make it worth your while. You promised me a crack at it, remember?"

The line crackled while Max seemed to think it over. "Yes, I remember. You realize you're risking everything? Nakamura won't have you, after this."

"I know."

"Come in then. I will sell to the highest bidder.

"Thanks, Max. You won't be sorry."

"I'd better not be," Max said as he hung up.

Marko was spiraling in on Von Bueller's front lawn. He skillfully made a steep vertical approach to the grounds because of the high trees standing between the house and the lake. Special Agent Flakita had her skirt pulled up to the tops of her long, tan thighs. She finished checking the draw on her back-up piece, strapped to the inside of her left knee and smoothed her skirt back into place. She caught Jack's glance and blushed. He was the first to look away and he saw, through the Bell Long Ranger's thick glass, that both of Von Bueller's maintenance men were trotting out to the pool to meet them. Both men wore holstered weapons. One stationed himself at the nose of the chopper, the other waited a few paces back from the loading door.

"Ambush positions," Jack said.

"Nose man will be on the pilot," Flakita said. "I'm going out first. If they make a move I'll take the nose man and you two get your asses out of here.

"What about inside?"

Flakita brushed a stray strand of black hair out of her face. "Once we're inside and you identify Lindsey Redding, I'll arrest her immediately. If we don't seize the computer materials right away, I'll serve the search warrant and call for backup to come immediately. First priority is to secure the Redding woman. Questions?"

"None," Jack said. "I'll watch your back."

"I'm counting on it, Mr. Bradley, but I hope there is no need for your gun."

Marko touched the Bell down gently. The turbine started to wind down and Jack's heart rate picked up. He worked up some saliva in his dry mouth.

"You knew all along that I had a piece?" he asked.

Flakita gave a disdainful little laugh. "Vernon wasn't the only one checking your wire," she said. "You saved me the trouble of arguing with Phil over giving you a weapon. If you could call that dinky thing a weapon." Flakita flung open the copter's door and yelled to Jack, "Follow me, its show time!"

Forty-Three

Lindsey Redding heard the chopper settling onto the lawn as Max Von Bueller came back into the sitting room. Something was very wrong. With a highest-level meeting like this one, interruption was unheard of. Von Bueller's step and bearing held a new confidence and he called his housekeeper aside. As the woman hurried off towards the kitchen, Lindsey turned to a corner of the room where two banks of windows met. From that corner, she had a view of Marko's chopper resting on the lawn. She sucked in a hissing breath when she recognized the second person to exit the chopper.

Jack Bradley!

Out of reflex her eyes focused on the black briefcase, which leaned against a sofa in the sitting area. Tako and Von Bueller sat close on the sofa, talking together in low voices. Lindsey took a couple of deep breaths to maintain composure and then walked slowly to the two men.

"Tako, should I notify your staff that there will be a delay in your New York flight?" Lindsey asked.

As she put the question to Tako, she toed her briefcase under the side of the sofa.

"Thank you, Lindsey. That won't be necessary, yet. We'll hear what Mr. Bradley has to say, but I doubt that he will delay our negotiations significantly."

Max Von Bueller rose as Jack Bradley and a tall, business-like woman entered the room.

"Jack, I believe you know Mr. Nakamura and Miss Redding," Max said.

"I have not had the pleasure of meeting your associate." Jack shook hands with Max and with Tako Nakamura and recognized Lindsey with a barely perceptible nod.

"This is Lolanne Flakita. Lolanne, this is Tako Nakamura, Max Von Bueller and Lindsey Redding. I'll leave it to Lolanne to explain our mission here today."

The housekeeper arrived with a tray of tea, lemonade, coffee and three different kinds of biscotti. Conversation halted as she placed the refreshments on the tabletop, arranged napkins and silverware, then bowed to Max before leaving.

The men proceeded to shake hands with Lolanne Flakita, but Lindsey hung back. All of her instincts screamed "trap!" but she could see neither the cage nor the spring. She sat in an overstuffed chair facing the sofa and affected a casual posture.

"Please," Max said, "have a seat, both of you. Jack, you said you have an offer to make on the resort. This is very unusual, of course and Mr. Nakamura has another appointment. Would you brief us now?"

Both Jack and Lolanne Flakita remained standing. Jack never took his eyes off Lindsey Redding and Lindsey imagined straps binding her arms to the chair. She measured the steps to the sofa and the front door. A conundrum. She had the Hobson's choice of briefcase or escape, but not both.

Flakita opened her pocketbook and took out a small,

black wallet. She stepped up to Lindsey's chair and opened the wallet to reveal a photo ID. Somehow a pair of handcuffs appeared in her left hand.

"Special Agent Lolanne Flakita, FBI. Lindsey Redding, you're under arrest for the murder of Major Dan Stricklin. You have the right to. . ."

Lindsey scissored her legs between Flakita's feet and upended the FBI agent. The agent's pocketbook tumbled across the carpet and Lindsey heard the satisfying *thunk* of a pistol as it fell to the floor. Flakita rolled on her side to gain leverage to fight back but before she could right herself Redding delivered a snapping kick to the throat. She grabbed Flatika's pistol and pointed it between Jack Bradley's eyes.

"Don't even twitch," she said to Jack who had drawn his weapon. "Let that little gun drop and step away from it."

Bradley let the pistol drop and took two slow steps backwards.

Tako took a step towards her. "Lindsey, I. . ."

"You'll do exactly as I say," she interrupted, her sights still on Jack. "You can't follow directions if you're talking. Max, you lie face down on the carpet. Don't anyone make me say anything twice."

Out of the corner of her eye, she saw the German kneel, then sprawl facedown beside the FBI agent, who held her throat and breathed in a pained, high pitched wheeze. Max was a cool one, he said nothing. Tako looked like a little boy who had been tricked out of his lunch money by the older boys.

"Tako, you step over here beside Bradley. Both of you back away from the sofa. That's good, right there."

Lindsey slid her briefcase from under the sofa, opened it and exchanged Flakita's pistol for her own nickel-plated 9mm Beretta. She picked up Jack's pistol, dropped it into the briefcase and zipped it.

"Now, Mr. Bradley, you were already a hero once this

week. Don't push your luck. I want you men to walk through that door in single file. You first Bradley. I will shoot Tako anytime I don't see your hands, is that understood?"

"Yes," Jack said, speaking clearly for the microphone. "You will shoot Mr. Nakamura if you can't see my hands."

"Very professional, Mr. Bradley. Now, lead the way. Step lively, but don't run. We're taking that helicopter for a little ride."

They walked out the front door into bright sunlight. The maintenance men were nowhere in sight. Marko Rivers sat on the steps to his flying machine while he poured himself a cup of coffee from his thermos.

"Lindsey," Tako said in a trembling voice, his dark eyes wide. "What are you doing? What is this?"

She tapped the back of his head with her pistol barrel.

"You know everything you need to know, Tako."

Lindsey walked sideways, so she could cover herself front and back. When they were a dozen steps from the chopper, she said, "Jack, tell the pilot to prepare for takeoff."

"Marko, we're taking off, now!"

The pilot spilled his coffee when he caught sight of Lindsey's gun pointed at Nakamura's head. Without a word, he scrambled aboard and strapped himself in.

Jack started to mount the steps, but Lindsey stopped him.

"Hold it," she said. "You wait here. Tako, you first."

When Tako was buckled into his seat, Lindsey stepped aboard, and then turned to face Jack. "Too bad it couldn't be different. You're a smart one, cool as ice. I like that. But this was none of your business and you've made yourself a royal pain in the ass. You won't do that ever again."

She raised the muzzle inches from his face. Jack's eyes were tightly focused on the white knuckle of her slender index finger as it squeezed the trigger.

Forty-Four

Jack Bradley experienced that famed time warp that was supposed to occur at the brink of death. As time stopped, his eyes moved from the enormous muzzle trained on his face, past the slender finger that tightened on the trigger and he focused on the gold flecks in Lindsey Redding's blue eyes. Gold flecks like his own. Those eyes that captured his fancy just hours ago rendered him unable to move, to speak, to save himself.

Something dusted the hair on his head. It slammed into Lindsey Redding's left eye and sprayed Tako Nakamura with blood. Time started up again for Jack when the bullet punched a hole in the helicopter fuselage and Lindsey's body sprawled backwards atop the horrified Nakamura. Her left leg and arm vibrated momentarily, her heel rasping on the deck. Then she was still.

Jack instinctively snatched up Lindsey's pistol and brief-case. He stood trembling as he watched Marko shut down the turbine while Tako Nakamura struggled to get out from under his lover's bloody corpse.

Nakamura repeated something over and over in Japanese and scrambled past Jack to run into the middle of the fresh cut lawn. Nakamura stripped off his gore-spattered jacket, his tie and his shirt. He dropped to his knees on the fresh cut grass and used his shirt to wipe madly at the blood and tissue on his face and hands.

Jack looked past Nakamura to the slender figure lying prone on Von Bueller's doorstep. As another chopper circled for a landing, Jack trotted back to Von Bueller's house and knelt beside Lolanne Flakita, who lay face down, breathing with a high, strangled wheeze. One hand was at her throat and the other still gripped her back-up pistol.

"Hang on, Lolanne, help is here," he said.

Jack turned her onto her back and cradled her head in a position that let her breathe a little easier.

Flakita mouthed a one-word question: "Computer?"

"Got it right here," he said and unzipped the case with his free hand just to make sure. He couldn't help a sigh of relief. "Yeah," he said, "it's here."

Jack pulled the minimike from his lapel and spoke into it, trying to keep his voice clear and calm.

"Able team reporting officer down, conscious, difficulty breathing due to blunt trauma to the throat."

Jack looked up to see Max and his housekeeper standing in the entryway to the home's massive kitchen.

"Get some ice," Jack snapped. "Wrap it in a towel. We've got to keep her airway from swelling shut."

The housekeeper disappeared and Max barked orders in German at his two maintenance men, who stood behind a garden wall with their weapons drawn. The two men approached Tako with caution and escorted the half-naked tycoon up to the house. Baker team's chopper set down behind the Bell and two suits jumped out, Uzis at the ready.

Jack turned his attention back to Lolanne, who had calmed her breathing, which was coming now in a shrill squeak. "That was a helluva shot, Flakita. I owe you a dinner and a movie for that one."

Flakita's eyes were closed, but she smiled. The housekeeper came out with a bowl of ice and a stack of towels. Jack scooped a handful of ice into a dishtowel and put it into Flakita's hand.

"Here," he said. "You hold it. I don't want to take a chance on pressing too hard."

Lolanne took the towel and arranged the ice over the front and sides of her swollen throat. When their hands touched, for just a moment, she grasped his fingers and gave him a tight squeeze of thanks.

"You'll make it, Lolanne," he promised and prayed that he was right. "Damn! That was a hell of a shot!"

Baker team secured the scene and the evidence. They flew Flakita to the trauma center in Spokane with Jack at her side the entire way. By the time they rolled her into surgery, her lips had gone from pale to blue and her brown, unfocused eyes drifted back and forth under half closed lids.

"You come back, Lolanne," Jack whispered in her ear. "We have a date for dinner and a movie."

Jack had been pacing the waiting room floor for over an hour when Bob Perkins joined him.

"We hit the jackpot on those warrants," Bob said. "You were right about the Fed Ex package. She had a safety deposit box, too and we found another disk in there. The techno geeks are checking out that computer. Apparently, it's designed to keep track of every attempt to copy or transmit from it."

"What about Nakamura and Von Bueller?"

"Looks like Nakamura didn't know anything," Perkins said. "Lindsey was freelancing with Stricklin. The boys don't know yet whether she had time to set up a deal with a third party. Nakamura is shook. He's humiliated because he didn't do anything to help under fire and Von Bueller wants to talk with you when you get back."

"Oh, yeah?" Jack said. "Do I get to clean out my desk already?"

Bob laughed. "Not quite, boss. He said he's willing to entertain that offer you made him and to help you make it work."

Jack stopped pacing. "What offer?"

Bob shrugged. "Beats me," he said. "Something about a joint venture."

Jack's heart took a rush at his chest wall. "Really? Damn! Too bad I made it all up."

"Jack!" a familiar voice rasped behind him. "Jack, are you alright, boy?"

Jack turned and found himself wrapped in a bear hug with his U.S. Senator. The scent of Jack Daniel's hovered in the still air of the waiting room.

"I'm fine, Senator, thanks. There's no word yet about Agent Flakita though."

"Yes, there is," Carl said. "We just passed her in the hallway when they were wheeling her down to the recovery room. She's still out, but she's okay."

"Thank God. She saved my life."

"Well," Carl said, "the sawbones say she'll have to have some more work on her voice box, but she's breathing fine. He says the guy who wrapped her in ice was the one who got her here alive, so it looks like you're even, boy. "Say," he leaned over and delivered a conspiratorial stage whisper, "the media madness is just down the hall and headed your way. What say we let some of our boys at the public trough run interference for us?"

Jack was exhausted and the idea of having reporters

shove microphones and cameras into his face didn't appeal at all. "I'd like to be here when Lolanne—Special Agent Flakita—wakes up," Jack said. "I owe her that much."

Carl Wilder took Jack by the elbow and began leading him out of the room.

"Take my word for it," the Senator said, "she'd prefer to see you after she's had a chance to clean up a little. It's bad enough that she's down and out. You read me?"

"Yeah, you're probably right."

"0f course I'm right," Wilder rasped, "I'm a sitting United States Senator! Now, let's slip out of here and find ourselves a quiet little drink. I've got an offer that just might be of interest you."

Wilder placed one arm around Jack's shoulders and gestured to a handful of agents with the other. "Take care of those hounds down the hall for us, will you? We're going up on the roof for some fresh air."

Waiting for them on the rooftop was Baker team's chopper. Within minutes they were chasing the long afternoon shadows eastward, to The Coeur d'Alene Resort.

Forty-Five

Jack Bradley settled into the driver's seat of his Porsche and headed to the resort's golf course. The Senator wanted one more round on the gold medal links before flying back East and Jack had to admit he looked forward to some fresh air and fun himself. The resort had completed its busiest weekend in history and most of the guests would be checking out or were already on their flights home.

Jack was glad that he had taken Bob Perkins advice the night before and accepted a mystery pill from Dr. Mathes, no nightmares, no trembling hands, just a very good night's sleep for the first time in days.

The first thing Jack did after his morning shower was to call the hospital in Spokane to check on Lolanne Flakita. He was disappointed and then hurt, to find out that she had checked out without saying goodbye. Then, as he drove the familiar road along the lakeshore he realized she was stable and the FBI probably wanted her on home turf for debriefing and recuperation. He was just glad she was well enough to travel and resolved to get a contact number for her.

When he pulled up to the clubhouse, Jack saw that *Double Eagle* had already arrived with the Senator. He checked his watch to confirm he was on time. He was.

I hope Mike was here to let him in, Jack thought.

Jack stood for a moment, looking out over the lake, enjoying the *slap-slap* of waves against the shore and the scent of freshly mowed grass. He took a deep breath and walked to the clubhouse to join the Senator.

What he saw when he opened the door stopped him cold. Lolanne Flakita faced him in a wheelchair, her neck stiff with bandages and her teeth white behind a wide smile. At her side stood a very smug looking Carl Wilder.

"Hello, Jack," Lolanne whispered.

Her voice sounded like a flat tire on gravel, but it was pure opera to Jack.

"Lolanne," he said. "I thought you'd gone. I tried to call . . ."

Then the others came out of the woodwork. The Hansons, Veronica Whitcomb and Clint Diamond, shouting "Surprise! Surprise!" The Hansons pulled a rope and a large banner unfurled from the ceiling that read:

"RESORT ASSOCIATES
JACK BRADLEY PRESIDENT"

Veronica Whitcomb's bodyguards wheeled out a breakfast buffet from behind the racks of golf clothing.

"What . . . what is this?" Jack stammered.

"It's a hotdamn *party*, boy," Wilder said, slapping him on the shoulder. "Haven't you ever seen a party before?"

"Well, I . . ."

"While you were sawing logs, we were a busy bunch of beavers," Carl said. "We formed that joint venture you were talking about, that is, if you still want to do it. We're still a little short, but Max agreed to work a deal with us and Tako Nakamura turned over the money in his local account to you as a token of his esteem. He's backing out of the deal." The Senator handed Jack a receipt for Tako's two million dollar contribution to Hospitality Associates. Jack looked at it numbly, unable to speak.

"Of course, you'll have to go down and sign the papers later today," Wilder said. "That is . . . if you're agreeable."

Jack felt his whole body buzz. He looked at all of the smiling faces around him—even Veronica Whitcomb looked happy—and he quickly came back to Lolanne. She reached up and took his hand, then gave it a good squeeze.

"It's true," she whispered. "They did it for you."

"I want to talk to you about optioning your story," Clint Diamond said. "This young woman and I think that we've got a winner, here. Miss Whitcomb's willing to produce the film and invest the profits in Hospitality Associates. But don't get any ideas, I get to play you in the film."

Veronica Whitcomb stepped forward and, for once, her nose wasn't stuck in the air, "I think this will be fun, Jack, being a partner in the resort." She tossed her head in a familiar Whitcomb gesture. "All I ask is that my suite be ready for me anytime I need it."

Jack's head spun, and he tried to stammer something gracious but nothing came out.

Earl and Betty Hanson stepped up and Betty gave Jack a big hug.

"The Wheelers didn't leave any family," she said. "Both of them were loners and there's not much doubt that Mr. Wheeler will spend the rest of his life in prison. Child Protective Services has agreed to let us go ahead with adoption proceedings for little Helen, here. Getting her is even better than winning the lottery. Our investment in the new joint venture will be in her name. You don't have to save us a room, we're buying one of the condos downtown. We couldn't ask for a better town to raise our new daughter in."

The baby looked perfectly happy sleeping in Earl Hanson's huge arms.

The Senator picked up a glass of orange juice and raised it in a toast. Whitcomb's bodyguards served a round to everyone. "Thanks to you, Jack, we all have the chance to participate in something beautiful, something special. We look forward to a long, satisfying relationship with you and The Coeur d'Alene. Do we have your acceptance?"

Jack had a little trouble seeing their smiling faces through the tears of joy welling up in his eyes. He locked gazes with the beautiful brown eyes of Special Agent Flakita, took a deep breath and raised his glass.

"No man could be this lucky," Jack said and clinked his glass with those of his new partners. "God bless every one of you."

Hip-hip-hoorays echoed in the clean mountain air and rippled through the crystal clear lake waters surrounding the resort. Jack smiled through his tears as he thought, *These great people . . . this magnificent resort . . . I'm the luckiest man in the world!*

Epilogue

Mustafa entered the city limits of Fort Wayne and drove straight to his home. He ran from his car and embraced his wife Jasmine and their children.

Immediately after that he went to his backyard and kneeled down toward Mecca and prayed that the world would be safe for all peoples.